PRAISE FOR *THESE HALLOWED BINDS*

"*These Hallowed Binds* pulled me in from the start and didn't let go. A. M. Daylin's story is richly crafted, masterfully written and laced throughout with Christian symbolism. The fantastical world of Alémor is a feast for the imagination, full to the brim of guardian beasts turned hostile after a dark curse mars the land, a secret battle to set the world to rights, well-written, interesting characters on top of a unique and well-developed magic system. With a story of finding one's destiny, a bit of found family and an entertaining love triangle, *These Hallowed Binds* is a wonderfully enjoyable read. A. M. Daylin's talent promises the makings of a spell-binding series and I can't wait to find out what happens next!"

—KELSEY CHAPMAN,
AWARD-WINNING AUTHOR OF *UNMASKED*

"A. M. Daylin does not disappoint with the unique world and lovable characters of *These Hallowed Binds*. With a world on a steady path to collapse, a cast of amazing characters that captured my heart from the beginning, and an explosive ending full of twists, turns, and surprises, *These Hallowed Binds* had me gasping, tearing up, cheering, and everything in between. Daylin has crafted an absolute rollercoaster in the best way possible. This book is a can't-miss if you love fantasy with golden-hearted protagonists, a unique and well-built magic system, and characters you can truly invest in!"

—TOMMIE MICHELE,
AUTHOR OF THE *DRAFTED DUOLOGY*

"A. M. Daylin keeps you on the edge of your seat while you discover the truth behind the disappearance of Norielle's father and the world. The banter and discoveries are expertly woven on the pages. Readers of fantasy will love this *Lord of the Rings* type of adventure."

—CANDICE PEDRAZA YAMNITZ,
AUTHOR OF *UNBETROTHED*

PRAISE FOR A. M. DAYLIN

"I devoured *Where Darkness Cannot Follow* in a matter of days! Beautifully written, this book utterly transported me into a terrifying desert canyon crawling with dangerous netherbeasts and a powerful necromancer. I loved Ezro and Vaeryn, their courage and determination in spite of setbacks and doubts, and the unexpected twists and turns in their adventure have left me anxious to know what happens next!"

—J. J. FISCHER,
AWARD-WINNING AUTHOR OF *THE NIGHTINGALE TRILOGY*

"*Where Darkness Cannot Follow* is a rich tapestry of raw emotion and harrowing adventure, pulsating with the lifeblood of its protagonists. The anticipation for the next chapter in Ezro and Vaeryn's journey is at its peak—I want more of their story!"

—STEPHANIE COTTA,
AWARD-WINNING AUTHOR OF *THE CONJURER'S CURSE*

THESE HALLOWED BINDS

Also by A. M. Daylin

THESE HALLOWED BINDS

THE EMPYREAL GUARDIAN SAGA

BOOK I

A.M. DAYLIN

MOONCREST PUBLISHING

MOONCREST PUBLISHING

To anyone searching for their place to belong.

Hardship often
prepares an
ordinary person
for an
extraordinary

DESTINY.

C.S. LEWIS

NORIELLE

Children are swimming in the lake that murdered my father, but no one else seems to care.

Their laughter and squeals burn my ears. Every second, I wait for the shrill sounds to turn to screams—for the aquatic hands that grabbed my father and tugged him down to return. They never do.

But I know what I saw.

The watery hands dragged my father deep into the murky depths where the lake weed bound him. His screams bubbled to the surface, silent cries for help. Silent cries that I fled from the moment the hands came after me.

I escaped. Papa's body did, too.

After his soul lifted to the Empyrean.

Passing a bristly pine, I force my feet across the rocky lakeshore. One step. Two. Three steps. *Stop.* The water glistens in the sunlight, stretching for thirty miles before it meets land again at the foot of a grassy mountain. In between, the water lies dormant. Serene and silent.

Unsuspecting. Like a murderer hiding his foul deed under a nice coat and a smile.

Another step.

A shriek turns my attention to the children before I register that the noise is joyful. Rainbows streak the vapors where they splash. A girl spits a fountain from her lips, and I taste death on my tongue. But she goes on, laughing and spewing water into her friends' faces. They giggle and spit back. My stomach knots. How could anyone let their children play unattended in this water? Where are their parents, anyway?

"Don't get too close, Norielle. The lake might come alive and get you," a boy sneers from behind me. *A man,* I should say. Landon just turned eighteen, but considering he still acts like he's twelve, he will forever be a boy to me.

I glower at him as he walks by, shaking out his wavy locks. He saunters toward the lake. Undoubtedly, by his lack of a shirt, he means to swim. And for as handsome as he thinks he is, judging by his flashy grin, I find him sickening to look at. His pretty face could never mask how hideous his heart is.

I wait until he's deep in the water before I reroute my steps toward a private section of the lake. Silt clings to my sandals as I near the water—the closest I've been since Papa's drowning. My pulse throbs in my fingertips as I reach my last steps. Just four more. Three. Then I'll be close enough to lay these petals in the water and say I did it. I finally honored Papa—a whole year later.

I take the next step.

Visions of long, yellow weeds coiling around my father's wrists and pulling him down toward the lake bed flood my mind, and grief clutches my lungs.

"I can do this," I assure myself.

I have to.

I can't avoid this lake forever. It's been a year since the water has shown any signs of sentience. Maybe whatever made it kill Papa has moved on?

I force my feet closer until the toes of my sandals are nearly touching the water. The lake doesn't stir, and the tension across my chest eases with a long exhale. I crouch low enough to see my reflection in the water for the first time in four seasons.

With quivering fingers, I untie my sack, unleashing the honeyed fragrance of wild roses into the musky lakeside air. The soft petals brush my skin as I pluck one out and raise it to eye level, wondering how best to begin this, and if I will feel better afterward like Mum promised—or if I'll walk away from here as empty as I came.

"I'm sorry, Papa," I whisper to the petal as if it might drift across the waters and into the Empyrean to deliver my apology. Then I cast it into the lake.

Its pink, curved body lands like a tiny boat, drifting for only a short stretch before going still. I sigh. Then that is how it will be. Just like the petals, the feelings will remain, won't they? I'll be haunted by my failure and his death until I meet my own.

I raise the bag, digging in for a handful this time, but just as I'm clutching the petals, a guttural scream splays my fingers.

The bag drops, petals spilling around my feet as I stand and spin toward the sound. In the depths of the lake, water spews into the air, whipped by the frantic flailing of someone's arms.

No, not someone.

Landon.

In an instant, I forget I hate him. Panic surges through my limbs, and I scream his name. My voice is loud and vibrant as it breaks into the cloud-streaked sky.

"Help!" His head sinks under the water, then resurfaces. "Norielle, help! The lake—"

"Landon!"

It is only once I'm running along the shore that I see him smile. Then, behind me, a roar of laughter resounds from his group of friends.

I turn. The water is settling around him, besides the wavelets his cackling stirs. Heat crawls across my face. *That cold-blooded, arrogant—*

I don't even know a word harsh enough to suit him. He *knows* today is the anniversary of Papa's death. How could anyone be so heartless? Fine, if he doesn't believe me—no one, not even Mum, does—but to make a joke out of the way my papa died?

I twist toward the dirt road, hot tears wobbling in my eyes. I run past Landon's friends, blocking out their laughs and jabs as best as I'm able. Tepid air whisks between my legs, my long skirt fluttering behind me as I accelerate. *I hate this town. I hate it.* The more I think it, the faster I run. If only I could run so fast, my feet lifted into the sky and carried me far away.

What I saw in the lake was real. I know it was. It had to be—

A hallucination, I hear Mum say. That's what she believes and as one of the town educators, her word is truth around here. *Sometimes when we're afraid, our mind plays tricks on us. That's all it was.*

What if she's right? What if the whole town is?

My feet don't slow until I reach the market that always reeks of fish. I lower my head to hide behind my long hair as I weave down the uneven brick road toward my neighborhood. Home feels like the only place that's safe anymore.

At least, it's the only place where I'm believed. Even if it is by children.

I burst through our front door as tears are leaving their wet tracks down my cheeks. My back slams the door closed—a little too hard—and my youngest sibling hollers my name from the depths of the house.

I wipe away my tears only a moment before Milo appears in the sunlit foyer. His thick brows hike up into his unruly curls, but surprise melts into sadness when our eyes meet—the sight of me a reminder of what today is.

The anniversary of the day I failed to save his papa.

At only six, Milo manages to refrain from heaping more shame upon me; instead, he offers a gentle smile unfit for a boy who puts worms in my boots.

"Mum is making potato soup. Can you smell it?" He gives the air an exaggerated sniff as if to demonstrate how a nose works.

When I mimic him, my stopped-up nose catches a hint of bitter smoke.

"You mean *burning* potato soup." I dash for the kitchen.

If Milo noticed my swollen eyes or pinched voice, he plays it off with the ease of a bard, running behind me with a giggle as sweet as the songs Papa once sang. Precious, young Milo. He should have learned to play the lyre by our father's fingers. Instead, his dreams of growing up to play will be nurtured by strangers, if not choked by grief.

A black cloud billows from a bubbling cauldron as I step into the kitchen. Mum's boney figure is nowhere in sight, but the spoon in the drip dish is still wet. I sprint for it, giving the angry soup a quick stir. Dark flecks of scorched potatoes rise from the bottom, and I trade the wooden spoon for a pair of thick towels and use them to jerk the cauldron from the hearth's hooks. The pot *clunks* against the counter.

"By the Empyrean," Mum groans as she rushes in, passing our long, sun-faded table to open the shutters. Afternoon light spills in, highlighting specks of dust churning in the air. "One minute gathering the laundry, and the house is burning down."

She steps up beside me, snatching the wooden spoon so she can sigh at the damage. I study her profile, her splotchy skin and the redness lining her moist eyes. Doing laundry? I doubt it.

She's been crying about Papa.

And every tear is my fault. Just like her loss of appetite and the ever-present darkness that shadows her once glistening green eyes.

I killed her, too, the day I let her husband die in that lake.

"What's that—?" My younger sister, Cassia, stops at the edge of the kitchen, shutting her mouth when she sees the grave looks on both my and Mum's faces. Her hazel gaze drops, but I don't miss how black her eyelashes look. How wet they are.

I twist to hide a frown, forcing air in and out of my lungs. Mum and Cassia share a melancholy exchange over the burnt soup, but my ears numb their words to mere noise.

I should have gone after Papa, even though it would have led me to the same fate.

Maybe I don't deserve for people to believe me.

"Did you do it?"

The words hardly register in my ears. I turn toward Mum, and she tries again.

"Were you able to lay the petals in the lake?"

A heavy cloak of shame drapes over my body as I recall the petals I abandoned by the lakeshore. "I started to, but then Landon . . ."

Mum smiles—something I didn't expect—but behind her pointed shoulder, Cassia glowers like I spoke of Ta'Nathel, the world-curser, himself.

"What did *he* do?" Cas asks, bitterness aging her voice from twelve to twenty.

"He pretended the lake was drowning him, and I was stupid enough to fall for it."

Mum's smile wilts, and I suppose whatever fantasy she has about me falling in love with the steward's son dies with it.

"He made me look like a fool. *Again.*"

Mum is quiet for a while as she scoops burnt bits of potatoes from the soup. "I'm sorry he tricked you, honey," she finally mumbles, but the absence of compassion in her voice flares my nostrils. "But honestly, Norielle, it has been a year, and the lake has done nothing. Isn't it time to let it go? If there was anything *alive* about the lake, don't you think it would have happened again by now? It was just your—"

"It was *not* my imagination." My fists curl. "Things like this happen all over the kingdom. Why is it so hard to believe—"

"Norielle." Her hand stills, the soup churning around the sunken spoon. "This town belongs to El-Alam. No curse of Ta'Nathel's can touch us here."

A hot retort burns my tongue, but I suppress it. We don't need to quarrel about this on the anniversary of Papa's death. Not again. There's nothing new to say. Just the same rehashed argument we have every time.

And yet, her continued disbelief seems to cut between marrow and bone, deeper than it has since the day I raced home, barely able to speak through my wailing.

I glance at Cas, who offers a sympathetic smile. At the table, Milo scowls as he gallops his carved wooden horse across the surface.

Why is it that they believe me, but Mum won't? If anything, it should be the opposite. Mum is aware of the rumors that stretch across those wide waters from the rest of the kingdom. Lake Daleia's attack isn't the only oddity in Alémor. What about the time a whole group of explorers disappeared in the Rimrook Mountains across the lake? They were said to have died by the stony hands of Rimrir, the mountain golem. Or the rumors of a vortex in the North Sea, inhaling entire ships and swallowing them down into the ocean's depths? Or the numerous reports of attacks by the Empyreal creatures who once protected us but have now turned hostile? Cities have had to build walls to defend themselves against those creatures, and still, she can't believe *this*?

What makes her think El-Alam even cares about our little town, anyway? Wouldn't the rest of the kingdom flock here if they knew El-Alam had made a refuge of Behria? Or is she just too afraid—like our steward—to realize we're in just as much danger as everyone else in Alémor?

Is it really that much easier to believe I'm delusional than to face reality?

But to raise those arguments again would just lead to another harsh reprimand for my lack of faith in our Creator. And perhaps that *is* my problem. Yet, it would be easier to believe He protected our town if I hadn't seen the evidence with my own eyes that even El-Alam's followers can be harmed by the curse our usurper Empyreal Guardian has placed over the world.

"This skirt is itchy," I say to excuse myself. "I need to change into something else."

Mum gives me a long stare, but I walk past her, wishing to spare us both the fight still brewing in the silence. But before I reach the hall, her words pull me up short.

"Norielle, I spoke with the steward yesterday."

I halt, afraid to even look at her by the darkness in her tone.

"He said if you don't stop stirring up this nonsense about the lake, he will revoke my Widow's Allowance."

I squeeze my eyes shut, my spirit seeming to shrivel inside my chest. *He'd revoke her Widow's Allowance? Just to silence me?*

Is he *that* afraid of the truth?

"If that happens, Nori, we won't be able to afford the roof over our heads," Mum adds, voice turning stern. "I cannot let you do that to Cas and Milo. Another word about the lake being alive and . . ." She swallows so hard I can hear it, but her words still come out weaker as she finishes. "I'll have to ask you to leave Behria."

I gasp, feeling the blow of her words like a blistery gust in mid-Veratûm.

"Leave?" The word squeaks in my throat, hardly audible, as I turn around.

Mum sniffs, the red stain of regret drawing out the green of her irises. "Please, Norielle. Don't make me do that to you."

I lower my gaze, brutally aware of the cryptic silence that has fallen over our home.

They'd cast me out. They'd rather lose me than face the truth.

Even Mum.

My heel makes an abrupt turn, and I retreat to the privacy of Cas's and my room. My back slides down the length of the door as I shut myself in. I hit the cool ground, hugging my legs to my chest as I finally allow myself the cry I've fought since I stood in front of Lake Daleia.

But the more I cry, the more my anger seems to vaporize my tears, and soon my eyes are dry and burning. How dare the steward do this? How dare he make me choose between silence and exile? And all for what? To make sure I don't peel away the shroud of denial he's so meticulously kept over Behria?

I can't live in silence—watching the water every day. Knowing what it can do. Holding my tongue.

No, there must be some way to convince this town we aren't safe.

Or—my mind struggles to complete the thought—*prove that I'm the one who's wrong so I can go silent in peace.*

It has been a year . . .

Goosebumps prickle my arms as the thought sinks in—deeper until it's shaking my shoulders. Could it be that I did imagine it all? And now my madness is threatening the well-being of my family?

My gaze leaps to the window where a mild breeze carries the lake's ever-present musk into my room, and suddenly, I know what I must do.

I have to go out onto the lake again myself.

And see if it comes alive.

NORIELLE

I dress lightly despite the chill of nightfall. If the lake tries to drown me, the last thing I need is heavy boots and clothes helping it pull me under.

My hands shake as I tuck my straight hair behind my ears, watching myself in the mirror like I'm looking at a soldier who's about to descend into the war in Raevre. The light of a single candle reflects in my trembling hazel eyes. No matter which way this goes, I won't like the answer.

If I am still alive to have an opinion.

Cas shifts in her bed as I snatch my cloak from the back of a chair in the corner. I still, watching her in the dimness until her breathing resettles. Then I fasten my cloak over my collarbone and tug the heavy wool hood over my head. I'll hang it in the trees before boarding a boat, but at least it can shelter me from the breeze along the way.

With my sandals gripped between two fingers, I creep toward the door. Annoying creaks announce my steps, and I cringe. There's still the door, also, which never fails to make a loud *snap* when the knob is twisted.

Maybe I should tell Cas—and Milo. Just in case.

I shake my head. They don't need to know anything unless I come back with something to report.

If I come back.

I tiptoe to the door and grip the cool metal handle. Teeth clenched, I twist it, bidding it to not make a sound, just this once.

Instead, the coils inside pop louder than I've ever heard.

A rustle behind me chills my blood, and I turn to find Cas rising. Her curls fall in every which way, but she makes no attempt to smooth them.

"Nori?" she asks, blinking to see me in the near darkness.

"Just going to the washroom," I lie.

She squints. "With your cloak?"

I look down. *Stupid.* I've never been a good liar, but I dumbly try another. "I just need to go for a walk. I can't sleep."

Cassia swings her legs over the side of her bed, the mattress springs squealing beneath. "You know why I believe you about Papa, don't you?"

I flick my gaze toward the door.

"Because you're terrible at making things up."

My toes curl. "Cas . . ."

"What are you *really* doing? Going back to lay the petals in the water?"

If only I had started with that.

I nod.

Cas rises, rubbing her eyes before looking about the room. Her gaze stops on her pair of boots against the wall, and my lips thin. But before I get a word out, she's striding toward them, announcing, "I'm coming with you."

"No, Cas, it's late. You don't need—"

"What if Landon is out there?" she asks, snatching a pair of stockings from her wardrobe. "You know how he likes to hang out there at night."

"Then I'll go to a different side of the lake."

Cas hobbles along, stretching the stockings to her knees in between steps toward her shoes. "Just let me come. We can go up to the water together and—"

"*No,*" I snap, a bit too harshly, and she stills, a boot hanging from her hand. I swallow and try again, softer. "You need to sleep."

"Don't you?" She tugs on her boot and props herself against the footboard of her bed to lace it. "Just let me come."

"I can't . . ." But my words fail. How can I explain it to her without telling her what I'm really up to?

Her eyes narrow on me, as if the candlelight illuminated my lie.

"You're going into the water," she says.

My jaw falls, and I wonder how she could possibly guess that besides that she knows me so well. "No," I insist, but my conscience subverts another lie. "I'm taking the boat."

Cassia holds her partially tied laces. I wait for her response, for her to cry and beg me not to go in case the lake kills me, too. But she lets the uncomfortable silence linger so long, my mouth grows restless.

"I just want to test the water. I was in it the day it came alive, and nothing has happened since. Maybe it's *me* it was after." I smile with feigned confidence. "But I'll be careful. Any sign of it moving on its own accord, and I'm turning back."

Cas finishes her knot. "And then what?" she asks, reaching for her other boot. "Won't everyone still think you're making it up?"

I frown. "Probably, but at least *I'll* know."

Cas plants both her booted feet firmly on the ground. "Well, now I *have* to come with you."

"No—"

"If I see it too, maybe people will listen." She bounds toward her cloak, swinging it over her small shoulders.

I almost reject her a second time, but I clamp my mouth shut. She's right . . . to a degree. If I know this town, people will write her testimony off, too, since she's my sister. But maybe, *maybe* Mum will listen if both her daughters witness the same thing. If this does nothing more than win Mum's belief, it's worth it.

"Fine," I say. "But you're staying on the shore."

"Maybe you should do this during the day?" Cas says as we stand, shivering, at the dock.

The boats knock against each other, the only noise besides the creaking of branches in the slight breeze.

Cas's suggestion hangs like the fog over the water. A wise thought. However, something inside me doubts Lake Daleia will awaken if it knows many are watching it. It was in the stillness of morning that Papa and I were here last time, accompanied only by the fishermen. But their boats were so far in the distance, they had no hope of seeing what truly happened.

Papa loved his early outings on the lake. He said it was where he went to pray, to meditate, to think. The night before his death, he'd asked me to accompany him. We were to discuss my future, since, as my father, he was lord of it. But Papa was kind, willing to hear my side and factor in my desires, unlike some other men in this town.

I'd spent most of that night crafting my words about my ambitions. I wanted to meet the Wardens, men and women like my grandfather. People entrusted with divine power from the Creator, El-Alam. But the Wardens—or what remains of them after the attempted massacre—live in hiding. Papa once said I could cross the kingdom and never find them. Even King Arlo's best-trained Hunters can't pinpoint their magic-veiled hideout. It's been that way since the corrupt Empyreal Guardian, Ta'Nathel, slayed our world's true Guardian and cursed us. The king saw the Empyreal creatures, the Sentry, turn vile, and assumed the Wardens had also fallen beneath Ta'Nathel's wicked leadership. Such a belief now consumes the hearts of most everyone in the kingdom of Alémor, Mum included.

Papa always quietly assured me these accusations were false and that the Wardens are still good. The Wardens did once report to Toaph Elbara, our original Guardian, but after his defeat, they turned directly to El-Alam himself. And now, in secret, they still patrol the kingdom, trying to protect us.

I never got to hear Papa's gentle discouragement regarding my hopes to find them or to deliver my modest alternative—to follow in Mum's footsteps as an educator. We'd barely made it out of the shallows before the water overturned our boat and grabbed him.

"Norielle?" Cas asks, and I blink my blurry vision into focus.

"We're already here," I say, finally remembering the question she asked. "Besides, if I wait until morning, I might lose my nerve."

Cas's chattering teeth are her only response.

I scan the boats until I find the one with our family name engraved along the stern. *Papa's boat.* It's been tethered here since it found its way back to shore like a horse returning to its stall.

I stare at it like it's my coffin, and all I need to do is climb in and my life will be over. My pulse quickens as I remove my sandals and cloak, but I have to fight this. I *have* to.

I have to know the truth.

The old feeling of wood bobbing beneath my feet stirs a flutter in my chest as I step in. I sit, breath obstructed by the fear and cold.

"No matter what you see, Cas, you stay on land," I order through quaking lips. "Promise me."

Cas's chest fills, but she only nods.

"I'll be right back. Everything is going to be fine."

Her chin lowers; likely, she doesn't believe me any more than I currently believe myself. But when she says nothing in protest, I unlatch the tether and dip my oar into the water.

NORIELLE

Vapors crowd me like the arms of a ghost as my canoe cuts through a thin layer of fog. I swipe at it, desperate to watch the dark water around me. A moonglade skirts the gently rippling surface and highlights the haze in a way I'm not sure whether to call beautiful or unnerving. But the water is calm, even as I reach the deep.

I let my oar rest, turning to check that Cas is still at the dock and not borrowing someone else's boat in pursuit. Her small form stands just taller than the nightly mist, hardly moving. I think to call out a reassurance to her, but I fear my voice will carry too far.

Or awaken the lake.

Except that's what I came out here for.

My white-knuckled grip tightens around the stilled oar, and I look ahead. The lake is so settled that a crane fly lands on its surface and drinks. I watch it like I expect the water to form a hand and grab it.

The satisfied fly flits away, unharmed, and my shoulders sag. Perhaps I *am* wrong. The water hasn't so much as burbled, and I've been here at least ten minutes now. That's longer than Papa and I were on the lake before it attacked.

Or maybe whatever was in here has moved on?

Or it only wanted Papa for some reason?

Or I made it all up, just as Mum said.

My heart throbs in my chest. I didn't really come out here to prove to myself I was wrong. I came out here to prove that I'm not delusional. That there was a good reason why I fled the lake, why I abandoned Papa without trying to save him—

Or is that why I imagined it? To cover up my shame and my cowardice?

A wave of nausea curls my torso. How haven't I considered that before? All this time, I only wanted to believe this nonsense about the lake because it was easier to accept the lake could do such a thing than it was to accept that I could have at least *tried* to save him, but I chose not to out of fear for my own life.

It was all just a freak accident. We somehow tipped the boat ourselves—placing our weight too far in the same direction. Papa's trauma from the shipwreck during the first war in Raevre must have seized him, and the paralysis of shock prevented him from swimming. And everything I thought I saw was fear-induced madness, just as Mum said.

The lake is not alive.

Not any more than Papa is now.

I shift the oar, intending to turn back, but a deep pressure in my lungs buckles me over yet again—a suppressed cry. One I'd be free to let out if Cas hadn't come. I grit my teeth like a sealed prison door, holding captive any show of emotion until it seems I've crushed it inside myself. Then, with a slow inhale, I force myself upright and focus.

I need to return to Cas.

My oar dips into the settled water, but just as I'm paddling to turn, the oar catches as if I've struck something solid. I gasp, attempting to retrieve the oar, but it jerks from my hand. Before I can scream, the water bucks like a startled steed beneath my boat, knocking me to the left. My body smacks the port side of the boat, and I barely catch the gunwale before the water throws me the other way, flipping the canoe over.

I gulp in air a second before I smack into the frigid water, my momentum submerging my entire body several stretches under. My arms wave desperately toward the moonlit surface, a legion of bubbles surging around my frantic motions. The top of my head just crests the sloshing water when a cold hand latches onto my ankle. I release a muffled scream as it tugs me downward, like a three-hundred-pound weight clings to my leg. The powerful grip thwarts my mightiest efforts to kick and writhe and flail. It drags me deeper and deeper still until the light of the surface fades behind the black depths.

And there, in an utter blackness darker than any night my eyes have ever known, more icy fingers snatch me. They hold me by each limb, towing me down with such force that my muscles seize. Then, just as I'm forfeiting the fight, they release me. My back slams against the silty lake bed where slimy plants, swaying in the stirred water, brush my freezing skin.

I jolt, waving my arms to swim upward, but as if activated by my motion, the weeds awaken to snatch my limbs and coil around me like ropes. Their hold is unnaturally strong, and the more I struggle, the tighter they seize me until the circulation in my wrists and ankles is cut off. Terror shoots through my nerves like lightning, surging waves of blackness over my vision.

My eyes fix in the direction of the hidden surface, far, far from my reach.

Cassia, I think as the last of my air bubbles from my lips.

CALDEN

I race between the evergreens, leaping over mangled brush and mossy boulders. On my wrist, an arrow staining my skin points true east, toward Lake Daleia. My heart thuds. *For all the rushing I've done to get here, Empyrean tell me I'm not too late.*

The water's foggy surface slowly comes into view between the feathery tree limbs. I direct my path to a raised edge of the peninsula and run even harder than before. In between steps, I briefly check the compass-like mark on my wrist again to be sure the arrow remains. The sight of it grants only a fleck of relief. It remains, indeed. Though lighter than before. A sign my time is running out.

I waste no more of it, shedding my cloak, breastplate, and armguards as I race up a rocky overhang. My boots skid to a halt at the jagged edge. In the lake below, the girl's boat floats, capsized—just as the Seer had shown me in his vision. But the fog over the water stirs as if the lake has been recently disturbed.

I unlace my boots, removing the rest of my layers until only my white undershirt and belted trousers remain. Then, with a quick dash down the overhang, I dive into the frigid lake.

A symbol ignites on my forearm—a Peace Ward I drew along the way. The magic spreads through the water like dye, dispelling the lake's rage in an instant.

With wide strokes, I propel myself across the long stretch of water to the overturned boat. I grip it just long enough to catch my breath before plunging beneath the surface.

Only a few strokes down, the faint glow of moonlight fades at my back, encompassing me in a deeper darkness than the underground passages I traveled most of the way in. The globelike lantern attached to my belt ignites at a wordless command, illuminating the water like a drop of sunlight carried into the deep. Silver tetras shimmer as they evade me, but the murky water shrouds my view of the lake bed.

Swimming harder, I follow my instincts until the light finally catches on the long, rippling hair of the girl from the Seer's vision. *Norielle.* Adrenaline quickens my strokes. Every stretch closer, the lantern reveals more of her. Her deathly pale skin, billowing sleeves, closed eyes. She floats toward me, freed by my Peace Ward from the lake's bonds, but her body is motionless.

I'm too late.

I swim after her despite my fear and capture her in one arm. Her cold body presses against my own, but it's not stiff—promising there's still hope for her. If I hurry.

I propel us toward the faraway surface with all the might I have in my free arm and legs. Pressure builds in my lungs for lack of air, tingles running through my limbs to my fingertips and toes.

But I didn't travel this far to see her die. Not when there is hope.

Not when El-Alam has so much in store for her.

After what feels like an age, I burst through the surface of the water with a loud gasp. I want to hear Norielle's breath join me, but she hangs limp, with only her weak heartbeat against my chest to signal she is still alive.

I search for the boat, thinking I might flip it and attempt climbing aboard, but the thickening fog hides the craft. With my strength failing, I can't waste energy searching for it. I focus my efforts on the closest land I can spy through the fog, a low foothill beside the overhang I leapt from.

I swim until fatigue laces my every muscle and, still, I swim. By the time I reach land, I only have enough strength to plop Norielle's unconscious body partially onto the shore. I collapse beside her, lungs heaving. I ran a long way before I reached the lake, and now I've swum at least a mile retrieving her.

But when she still doesn't stir for several long moments, I urge my fatigued body upright and lean over her. Her wet face gleams in the bluish moonlight, dotted with freckles like a lily's petals. I clear a clump of her long hair away from her mouth, then roll her onto her side. After a few seconds, a cough finally jolts her. I lurch back as that single cough turns into a series of desperate attempts to clear the liquid from her lungs. The convulsing keeps her eyes squeezed shut so tightly that she doesn't notice me.

I rub a scar on my neck. Hopefully, she won't react like the last female I was sent after.

I wait, cold drops of water trickling from my hair and onto my clinging, wet shirt. Eventually, Norielle's intense coughing settles to a few quiet sputters, and she sits up. She turns toward the water, and her legs curl inward, as if the lake might pull her back. Her head snaps my way next, a sharp gasp tearing from her throat as she recoils.

A note chirps in my throat, but her voice rasps before I can offer any reassurances.

"Did you see it? Did you see what happened?"

I hold my mouth shut a moment longer than I normally would. I *did* see it, but not with my eyes. Seer Josiah imparted the vision into my mind of Norielle paddling out to the lake. I saw the water stir all on its own, flipping the boat, and her plummeting into it only to be snatched by hands formed from the water itself and pulled to the bottom where weeds ensnared her.

Thirteen days, Calden, Seer Josiah had said. *That's all you have. Be swift.*

I'd left immediately, not even pausing to gather the Bind.

"Yes," I answer, deciding to spare her an explanation of *how.* "The lake pulled you under. Tried to drown you."

Her hand curls against her collarbone, brows creasing. "You—"

"*Nori!*"

The shrill voice slices through her words, and I leap to my feet. A young girl emerges from between the bushy pines, tears shining on her round cheeks.

The array of symbols marking my partially exposed arms seem to burn at the thought of a witness—no matter how young she appears. I tug at my clinging sleeves, but the thin, white fabric does little to hide the wards. In my haste to rescue Norielle, I didn't have time to concern myself with precautions to hide my identity, and the Seer's imparted vision failed to show that she wouldn't be alone.

No matter now. I can't stay to tell Norielle what brought me here—not with another pair of ears to listen.

Norielle rises to catch the girl in her arms, and in this brief moment, while emotion still blinds the younger girl, I flee into the night.

NORIELLE

"Where did he go?" Cassia's question jerks my eyes toward where the man once stood, and my stomach flutters.

He's gone.

But he saw it!

"Wait!" I holler, my ragged voice ringing across the water.

I sweep my gaze across the shore but find no trace of him. I held Cas for so long . . .

Empyrean. He could be anywhere by now.

"He saw it, Cas," I say, jogging toward a patch of trees. "He saw the lake come alive."

I realize she must have, too, which is probably half the reason she's still trembling. But this man—grown and with no reason to lie—*he's* the witness I need. *His* testimony beside mine might be enough to convince Mum—and the steward, at that.

I have so many questions. Where did he come from? How did he rescue me without being pulled down himself? Why would he attempt such a thing?

"Come back!" I yell, scanning the bristly branches as though he might have ascended into the trees.

Why did he run?

"He came from up there," Cas says, pointing toward an overhang.

I squint at the cliff-like form hemmed in moonlight.

"He jumped off it."

My forehead wrinkles. Then he truly must have witnessed it all. But what kind of madman jumps into a lake that seems to have a mind of its own and is bent on murder?

My gaze scales the height, deeming it too great to climb, and I race to circumvent it. My body, though worn from the struggle in the lake and stinging in the places where I was bound, complies on adrenaline alone.

But when my bare feet hike to the top, I find nothing but a chilly breeze that reminds me I'm still drenched. I shiver, folding my arms against my chest.

He's left. My best chance at convincing Mum and the steward is gone.

Cas's sniffle draws my attention back to her.

"I'm so sorry." I said it to her several times while I held her, but I can't keep from saying it again. "You shouldn't have had to see that . . ."

Cas wipes away a tear before looking at me with a boldness better suited for someone twice her age. "I wanted to know, too."

So, even Cas has doubted me before this night.

After scanning the surroundings once more from above, I turn to the foggy lake. From here, it looks like how the sky might appear from above the clouds. The water is almost completely shrouded but the few gaps in the fog reflect the inky darkness above.

My insides twist, the stillness finally inviting me to register reality for what it is. I didn't make up what happened that day with Papa. The lake is alive.

And, apparently, *I'm* who it wakes for.

Cas and I sleep curled together in her bed. Or rather, she somehow sleeps while I stare into the darkness, reliving the horror of the lake.

I should have burst into Mum's room when we got home, shook her awake, showed her the cuts on my wrists and ankles from the weeds, and told her the story. Instead, Cas and I crept in, and I slunk into the washroom to rinse the mildewy stench from my hair and clean the small slits on my skin from the bonds.

How is it that I am brave enough to risk my life in the lake but too cowardly to face my mother?

Tomorrow, I assure myself.

I roll onto my back to stare at the shadow-doused ceiling. Cassia shifts but her eyelids remain sealed. My head swirls with words, attempting to weave the right way to tell Mum about what happened so she'll believe it. But the threads of my tale seem to snag in the same place, no matter how I try to phrase it.

The man disappeared.

He'll be just as much of a legend to Mum as the sentience of the lake.

If only he hadn't run off.

I press my memory for details of his appearance, but everything feels blurred, like a wet painting that's been smeared. Now all I can recollect is his sturdy form, and that his damp hair reached his jawline. But I know, distinctly—despite my failing memory—that he was a stranger.

What was he doing here at night?

The thought badgers me until sunlight halos our thin curtain, and then with hardly a forethought, I swivel my legs off the side of Cassia's bed and gently slide out. The mattress gives a soft whine, but Cas remains asleep.

Good. The man only ran once she arrived, so maybe he'll still be out there somewhere and will be willing to talk with me alone.

I tiptoe to our wardrobe and pick out a pair of fitted trousers and a fog-gray blouse long enough to cover the burns on my wrist. Once dressed, I lace my boots to my knees and sneak into the hall, my shoulders slackening when the door handle's annoying *pop* doesn't wake Cas this time.

I check Mum and Milo's doors. Both are shut, but if I know Mum, she's already awake, dressing for the day.

I rush out the front door and breathe in the invigorating morning air. The complex perfume of mid-Diatûm wildflowers and damp evergreens tickles my senses. Through the abating fog, dots of color line the walkway toward the lake—an array of bluebonnets and buttercups. When I was younger, I used to love picking them in the cool of dawn and taking them home to dry out and press. But today, my legs move briskly by them, carrying me across the market where sellers prepare their shops and booths for the day, and to the lakeshore.

A handful of people already wander the edge, none of whom share my rescuer's strong stature. I evade their attention and set my sights on the cliff-like overhang looming above the misty waters at least a mile out. He jumped from there—maybe he's around there somewhere.

I hurry along the perimeter, boots crunching over shed pine needles and twigs. A lark flits to a nearby tree, its bright song joining in the chorus to usher in the day. Such a peaceful morning by such deceitfully tame waters.

My chest flutters every time I look at the lake. Fishermen are already out there, unaware that I almost died in those depths just hours ago. Would they have been the ones to find me and bring my corpse to the shore?

Would Mum have believed me then? When it was too late?

I walk until I reach the shadow of the rocky overhang. Indents mar the pale sand where my rescuer dragged me ashore, but otherwise, there is no sign he was ever here or of where he went.

My posture sags. Of course, I finally found another witness, only for him to vanish.

I search the area anyway, checking the evergreen branches and around every boulder, then I hike up the overhang. Nothing. Nothing. Nothing.

An urge to scream into the hazy sky nearly prevails, but I settle for a groan and a swift kick to a rock. The stone launches into the lake with a soft *plunk* and sinks. The sight shortens my breath, awakening the memories of last night.

I peel my gaze from the malevolent waters and look toward Auberfall, the nearest town east of here. Despite the lack of trees in the wide valley between us, the town is barely visible in the distance—a mere splotch in a vast plain of overgrown grass and free-spirited wildflowers.

Is that where he came from? Auberfall?

It seems a fair enough guess. I reach into my pocket, jangling my coin purse. There may be enough in there to pay for a carriage to take me, then I could walk through the town, ask around, and—

"I hoped you would come back."

I jump at the low rumble of a voice below me. It takes several sweeps of my gaze to spot a cloaked and armored figure standing between a pair of fir trees. The man retracts his hood, and a breeze waves his blond hair away from his smile before it resettles against his jawline.

That's him, I realize with a flurry of nerves.

"May I come up to you?" he asks.

I swallow, the dryness of my throat alerting me to my prolonged silence. Yet, the best I can muster is a nod.

My heart thuds as he rounds the overhang and approaches. The sun-glare on his steel armor winks as he passes through the trees' shadows. I scan his waist and back for weapons, but spy nothing more than a hand knife. Though I have no doubt he could make do with that if he wished to harm me. But I sense no threat, not from a man who'd risk his life to pull me from the bottom of a murderous lake.

He stops several steps away, and my gaze meets the purest shade of blue I've ever seen in someone's eyes—as if it were from those irises that the color got its name. Dark lashes frame them, a stark contrast to his lighter skin and hair. A flush spreads across my cheeks—somehow, I'd not noticed last night that he looks only a few years older than myself or how handsome his features are.

"I must admit I am surprised to see you," he goes on before I manage to say anything. "Most people would avoid the place of their near-dying for a day or so, at least." His accent softens the edges of every consonant and rolls the vowels like a warm breeze. "Are you injured?"

"Barely," I say, showing him one of my wrists and disregarding the cranky bruise on my left side from my collision with the gunwale.

The genuine relief that settles on his features would fool me into believing we'd been friends all our lives if I didn't know better.

"Thank you for saving me," I say, finally remembering my manners.

He angles himself toward the lake, giving it a contemplative glare before he returns his gaze to me with a weaker smile than before. "I'd hardly think thanks are in order. I was, after all, *late*."

"Late?"

He rubs the side of his neck. "Well, you were at the bottom of the lake. One would probably prefer to be retrieved before then or spared altogether from the event."

My lips twitch, wanting to smile. "I don't think *one* should be picky about how or when they are rescued. Though"—I almost lose my focus for the way his face brightens—"one might like to know how that was possible."

"Is that what brings you here, so close to the lake again mere hours later?" he asks.

"It's one of the reasons."

"Why else?" he probes, curiosity squinting one of his eyes.

"You saw it. What it can do." I wave an arm toward the lake. "No one else ever has."

A crease forms between his brows. "You knew it could do that?"

"It's happened once before," I say, clutching a strand of my hair. *Please don't ask for more detail than that.*

"And you . . . still went out there?"

I shuffle my feet, not wishing to admit aloud that he risked his life for someone who endangered theirs on purpose. "I wanted to see if it would do it again."

He laughs—a reaction I did not expect. "I'd say it did."

"But you knew that already. How?"

"I've seen a few things like it myself." He looks across the treetops, eyes seeming to gleam with history and knowledge beyond his youth. I want to probe about what else he's seen, but another question gets out first.

"Where did you come from? I've never seen you before."

And yet you showed up right when I needed you.

"Those mountains." He points toward the Rimrook Mountains across the lake, and I flinch.

"Where Rimrir the stone golem is?"

"Where Rimrir *was*." His gaze slides back to me. "Several years ago. Before the Wardens slayed him."

My pulse leaps. *Wardens came here?*

"You've heard of them?" he asks.

My jaw falls, but no sound creeps from my throat.

"Yes?" he guesses. "Bad things, I take it?"

"Of course." I lower my voice. "But I can't say I believe the bad things I've been taught. Do you?"

"Believe them? Oh, I defy them, actually." He pushes back his cloak, revealing a small stylus attached to his belt. The glass shaft seems to shine within its leather casing, as if filled with moonlit water.

I gasp, retreating a full step.

A warding pen?

But that would mean—

"You're one of them?" My hand flies to my mouth. "That's how you saved me."

A cloud sneaks over the early sun, dousing the glimmers from his armor. He gives a subtle bow in confirmation, and my chest swells with excitement.

A Warden? Here? That's who saved me?

"What—what are you doing out here? Were you taking care of whatever was in the lake? Is it gone?"

He nods toward a bench-like rocky ridge, gesturing for me to sit. I accept the suggestion, and he plants himself beside me—not near enough to touch unless we reached out to each other, but still, I feel his presence as if the magic he's been blessed with is emanating off him.

"I temporarily neutralized it," he says. "The effects are not long-lasting. Unfortunately, there are things even Wardens cannot rid the world of, not directly."

"Because of Ta'Nathel's curse?" I ask.

"Yes."

"So, the Warden leaders sent you to neutralize the lake?" I watch my fiddling hands to keep from gawking at him.

"Actually, no. That was just a necessary step to fulfilling my true task." He waits until I entrust him with my gaze. "They've sent me to retrieve you. El-Alam has called you to join the Wardens, Norielle."

My wringing hands still, but my heart triples its pulse. A note breaks in my throat, and I cover my mouth. I want to deny the possibility of his words, but the echo of my name from his lips stops me. How could he know my name?

"I'm sure that is alarming to hear," the Warden says. His words barely reach me through the sudden ringing in my ears.

My hand finally lowers from my mouth. "But . . . why? Why me?"

"You'll have to ask El-Alam that," he says.

I stare through him. All my life I've wondered about the Wardens—wanted to meet them—but I never imagined I'd be called to *be* one.

But wouldn't I have to leave here? Forever?

Isn't that what awaits me anyway? Especially now that I know?

He shifts his position, checking our surroundings again. "I hate to rush your decision, but Hunters have been tracking me for some time. It would not be wise to linger here much longer. Perhaps a day more at most. We wouldn't want them to see you leaving with me, should you decide to come."

The trees around us seem to spin.

"Or I could try to lead them away and return in a week," he offers. "But I, um . . ." Now his hands wring each other. "I can't delay much more than that. I must return home soon. I'm needed there."

I squeeze my eyes shut, hoping that when I look up, the forest will stop swirling behind him. But I have no such luck. "Would I ever get to return home?"

"Only in secret and at great risk to those you wish to see."

A sharp pang shoots through my chest at the thought of never seeing my family again, or worse, endangering them by coming back.

"What if I decline?"

He turns, poorly hiding a slight frown. "The call on you will be revoked, and El-Alam will select another for the role which he's chosen you to fulfill."

"The role?"

His nose scrunches. "Ah. I shouldn't have said that."

"What role?" I press.

He pulls his hood back over his head, dimming the light in his eyes. "I don't know specific details."

"But you know something." I lean toward him. "You can't expect me to run away from my home and family without telling me what for."

He leans back to stare at the gently rolling clouds. His jaw dimples beneath his blond stubble, like he's chewing on a response.

"*Please.*"

His head lowers.

"All I can tell you is this." The resolve has faded from his gaze when he looks back to me. "My name is Calden Arao. I am the Sovereign Prince of the Wardens, and I've been tasked with bringing you to the citadel because El-Alam has chosen you to help me with something."

A prince? Help him how?

He stands, leaving me no chance to question him. "I will wait here for you tomorrow morning. Please at least come to tell me your decision, or if you need more time to consider."

He reaches a hand toward me, and slowly, I take it, feeling the warmth of his grip wrapping around my cold hand. He pulls me to my feet, and our eyes lock in a trancelike stare that leaves my fingertips tingling.

"Will you come back tomorrow?" he asks.

"I will."

He shifts away, only to retract the first step he takes.

"Norielle," he says, his kind smile returning. "I do hope you'll decide to accept."

With that, he tugs his hood lower and dashes away.

NORIELLE

I can hardly breathe when I close the front door behind me. I'd run home, being careful to evade Mum's notice when I spotted her thin frame already in the market. She'd lose her mind if I told her who I was just speaking to and why . . . and especially if I mentioned that I'm genuinely considering leaving with him tomorrow morning.

I tiptoe through the house, adrenaline buzzing through my body like bees from a fallen hive. The urgency to decide pulls at me from both sides, seeming to tear a rift in my very soul. To be forced to leave my life and family behind?

Yet, the timing is uncanny. Just yesterday, Mum delivered the steward's threat to exile me, and today? A future direction arrived. It's nothing short of divine.

Save the cost.

I creep into my and Cas's room with a prayer that she's still asleep, but I find her sitting on the edge of the bed. My body petrifies, any clever tale I could offer about where I've been as unreachable as the stars.

Our gazes lock, and just like that, my will to leave shatters.

"Did you tell Mum yet?" Cas asks.

"No," I say, shutting the door in case Milo comes peeping. "I haven't told her yet. I was looking for the man who rescued me."

Cas scans me, seeming to note my boots and cloak. "Did you find him?"

I shake my head, and her brows bunch.

"Mum should be back from the market soon," I say to redirect her. "Let's tell her together."

Cas watches me remove my cloak and hang it up, then she rises from her bed. "I hope she believes us."

"Me too."

Then maybe I won't have to run.

By the time Mum comes through the door, bearing fresh produce for breakfast, I've started Milo on his morning lessons. She calls for Cas and me to come help her cook, and I leave Milo on his bedroom floor with a pile of smooth pebbles to practice his counting with.

Cas and I intersect in the hall, sharing a nervous glance. But I spoke with a Warden Prince this morning and nearly drowned in Lake Daleia last night.

I can muster the strength to tell Mum what we did.

"Brisk morning," Mum comments as she lays her basket on the kitchen table, but as she's pulling out the bread, her hands still, eyes set on us. "What's the matter?"

I step forward, clutching the tuft of my long sleeve. "Mum, it . . . it happened again."

Mum's hands curl and retract from the basket. "What happened?"

"The lake."

"And I saw it, too," Cas leaps in.

The color drains from Mum's face, and my breathing shallows.

"I—I had to test it," I say, my voice wavering. "I took the boat, and it happened again. I was pulled under by the water. The lake weed held me to the bottom." I rush forward, tugging my sleeve away to show her the red marks. "I almost died, but a man rescued me. It's true, Mum."

Her pupils constrict, moving from me to Cas.

"I saw it," Cas says again. "It was alive, Mum."

We fall silent, waiting for her reaction, but all she does is stare between us. Then, suddenly, her palm slaps the tabletop.

"*Enough* with this!" she yells.

Cas and I both startle and step back.

"Norielle, the lake is *not* alive." She rounds the table, snatching up my arm to hold my wrist closer, though she hardly looks at it. "And whatever you did to yourself to create these—this is madness. Madness!"

She throws my wrist down, and I fold it toward my chest, hugging it with my other arm.

"If the steward saw this—heard this—" She shuts her mouth, sucking in air as if trying to quell her temper. Her next words come out quieter but no less furious. "Why can't you let this go?"

"Because it's *real*," I say, wishing I could tell her everything Calden said, or better, bring him here to say it. "This town can't keep pretending we're safe. The curse is coming for us, too, and we should be aware and ready. It's already here." I gesture toward the lake well beyond our walls. "It could happen again, and yet people go out there every day. Children. Milo's friends—"

"You're going to cost us everything if you don't stop." Mum turns her back on me. "Haven't you cost us enough already?"

I stagger back, a numbness washing over my body.

She does blame me.

For Papa.

My mouth seals shut, eyes burning with tears. I stare at the back of her head, longing for her to take the words back, to listen to my story and believe me. She didn't even bother asking who rescued me or if he could testify as a witness. Does she trust me so little that she won't even *consider* I'm not making this up?

Or is she that afraid that I'm telling the truth?

"Norielle, this is the last time I will hear of this," Mum says, her reddened eyes returning to me. "One more mention, and you're asking to leave this house—this town. Do you understand me?"

I attempt to swallow but can't. "I understand."

I turn away, a cold, hard decision locking into place in my heart. If this is how it's going to be, then she doesn't need to worry about me causing her problems anymore.

Because I'm leaving with Calden tomorrow morning.

NORIELLE

I wake before the sun the next morning, slipping silently through the room as I gather my belongings into Papa's old backpack. He wore it during our first war with Raevre, and he'd be wearing it there now in the second if he were still alive. It's the one item I claimed after his death. Cas took his favorite coat, which she wears even though it's three times her size. Milo took Papa's lyre from his early years as a bard, before he exchanged his strings for swords.

But I chose this—his survival pack. Because deep down I knew I'd need it for the day I went to search for the Wardens.

Though, I never expected things to go like this.

I set the bag on the floor and fling open the flap, too harshly. The buckles *clink* against the floorboards. Immediately, Cas stirs.

I freeze, praying she'll turn over and fall asleep again—not that I've had much luck with that recently. But this time, her eyes remain shut.

I sigh, looking into Papa's backpack. His supplies are still neatly tucked into the pockets—everything I could need from a flint and knife to a first aid kit. Papa always feared another war would start with Raevre and wanted to be ready. He wasn't wrong. Not that he lived to find out.

I gather two spare sets of clothes and fasten a rolled blanket to the top of Papa's backpack, cringing at the way the buckles jangle. Cas doesn't shift, and I stand, facing the door. There's another item I need. But I'll have to get past Mum to reach it.

I pick up the bag, only for a flask to fall to the ground. The loud noise jolts Cas. I crush the strap in my hand, wanting both to run while I have the chance and stay right where I am.

I delay too long, and her eyes open.

She shoots upright, mouth falling ajar as she sees the backpack in my hand.

"Are you . . . leaving?" she whispers.

"I . . . I have to, Cas. You heard Mum yesterday," I say, unable to hold her gaze. "I can't keep quiet. Not now. I'll ruin everything if I stay."

"But Nori—" Her voice cracks. "Where? Where are you going to go?"

My mouth hangs open without giving an answer, and the silence seems to pierce through her shock, releasing her sorrow. Her head lowers into her hands, a sob shaking her small frame.

The sight dissolves my apprehensions, and the bag drops from my hand. I rush to her bedside, swallowing her in my arms. She slowly relaxes in my embrace, and my tears stain her nightgown sleeve. My little sister. The closest companion I've had since my late childhood, but especially over this past year after losing Papa.

How can I leave without telling her? After all she's done, doesn't she deserve to know?

"Cas, something happened," I say before I can stop myself. "That man who saved me. He's a Warden, like Grandfather was."

"What?" Cas jerks back.

"That's how he was able to save me, but he . . ." My conscience attempts to snatch away the words before it's too late, but they evade its hold. "He said I've been called to join them. I'm to meet him this morning so we can leave. He's taking me to wherever they've been hiding."

"*What?*" Cas repeats in a soft shriek.

"Please, you can't tell anyone. *Anyone.* Not even Mum."

"Why?"

My back straightens. "Because you know Mum doesn't trust them any more than anyone else around here does, and who knows what the Hunters would do to her if they found out her daughter ran off to join the Wardens."

"No." Cas shakes her head. "*Why* have you been called?"

My gaze lowers to the small space between us. "I have no idea. The man said he's their prince, and I'm supposed to help him with something, but I have no idea what or why. He wouldn't say."

Cas's head tilts, the slightest of smiles finding its way onto her lips despite the tears streaking her face. "You were saved by a *prince?*"

Hearing her say it makes it sound even more ridiculous. "At least that's what he claimed to be."

Her smile spreads—such a beautiful sight to savor before this is over. "How romantic."

I scowl, despite knowing I'd think the same if this were happening to anyone else. Except it's not. It's *me,* and somehow, I highly doubt there's anything romantic to his motives. He needs me for something. *El-Alam* does. This isn't one of the fairy tales Mum used to read to us—it's a call into a life of danger, that just so happens to include a prince.

"Was he handsome?"

I start at her question. *Of all the things to be concerned about right now—*

"He was kind," I say, though my cheeks too easily recall the way I flushed once truly seeing his face.

The pale light slowly creeping in from around the curtain reminds me I need to leave soon.

"I'm sorry. I—I need to get a few more of Papa's things out of Mum's room." I pry myself from her hold. "I have to hurry. Before she wakes up."

Cas flinches, her smile falling.

"I'll pack you some food," she says as she wipes away a tear.

I feel a twinge in my heart. *Of course you will. You'll help me leave. You'd help me do anything.*

I haul the bag toward the door, leaving it there for easy snatching, then I sneak past Milo's closed door toward Mum's room. With the utmost delicacy, I push the partially cracked door open and peer in. Mum sleeps with her back turned toward me and the items I need.

I hold my breath and tiptoe toward the wall where Papa's sword hangs on display. A gentle touch proves it's still sharp, but my fearful expression reflecting in the steel suggests I'm unfit to wield it. It has been over a year since I've handled one, and while Papa considered me skilled *for a girl*—as he loved to tease when he trained me—I've never dueled anyone besides him. And I know he went easy on me.

I slink toward Papa's old wardrobe to find the sheath. The hinges whine as I pull the door open, but Mum remains still. Inside, Papa's clothes hang neatly across the wooden rod, as if he might come back to pick something out someday. A bulge forms in my throat as I dig past the garments, remembering too easily what they looked like on him, how it felt to hug him and feel his warmth through their fabrics. Now all they hold is air and memories.

I stumble across Papa's armor box before spying the sheath propped in the back right corner. I pry it all out, figuring it can't hurt to use whatever armor will fit me. Calden looked nearly ready for war. Perhaps I should, too.

After a few moments of anxious fussing, I find myself strapped in armguards with an unshapely cuirass fastened as tightly as I can manage across my torso. I secure the sheath to my belt, and the sword hisses into place.

I swivel on my heel toward the door, but stop, catching my reflection in Mum's dressing mirror. The cuirass looks ridiculous and blocky, hiding any trace of a feminine physique. The armguards are crooked, and my waist-long hair desperately needs a binding, but my palms are already sweating at how long I've taken.

I need to get out of here before Mum wakes. She'll want to know where I am going, and I definitely can't tell her. She's the one the Hunters would interrogate if they ever got suspicious.

All she needs to know is that I decided leaving was the best of the options she gave me. And that information, I can trust Cas to deliver better than I can.

I gently close her door behind me, bidding her a silent goodbye. I hope she will understand someday why I had to do this—why I couldn't stay and live in silence.

Cas shoves a sack of food at me as soon as I enter the kitchen. I force my shaking hands to take it and stuff it into the backpack, having to discard two polifruits and a wedge of bread to close it.

"You're never coming back, are you?" Cas asks as I'm securing the final buckle.

My hands freeze.

"Someday," I say. Not quite a lie, but a hope.

Cas sniffles, and I pull her into a tight embrace.

"What should I tell Mum? She's going to wonder where you went," she whispers against my shoulder.

"I—I don't know." I pull back, and she averts her eyes to stare at the floor. Mum is going to feel so guilty after this—like she ran me off.

She did.

I shrug off the thought. I probably would have chosen this anyway—with or without her pushing. The curiosity would have haunted me for the rest of my life if I didn't.

Cas suddenly perks up. "I'll tell her you went looking for Kieran."

"*Kieran?*" I almost laugh.

"You used to talk about looking for him. I'll just tell her you decided to finally do it," Cas says, smiling in a way that takes me back six years to when my friend Kieran still lived here. Even at her young age, Cas teased me about him, which was probably Papa's fault. While Mum has always favored Landon, Papa fancied the idea of me marrying Kieran. I far preferred Papa's vision over Mum's.

But Kieran was only twelve when his mother died of a crypt crawler sting, leaving him an orphan since his father had died in the first war with Raevre. His grandparents on the Western Isles took him in, and I never heard from him again. Chances are he's in Raevre right now, fighting in the new war.

"Sure. Go with that," I say, trying to sound lighthearted. The topic makes Cas smile again, even at my expense. I want to see her smile before I never see it again. "At least that will seem like I have some kind of plan."

A shuffle down the hall turns both our heads, and I grit my teeth. I should bolt, right now, while I have the chance. But my feet remain planted once I register who it is. Milo. How can I resist seeing him one last time?

Milo's feet trudge wearily down the hall, and he steps out, curls tangled like he slept with his head inside a tornado. He startles at the sight of me and Cas, his owl-eyed stare clinging to the sword at my hip, then slowly working up past the leather cuirass to my face.

"She's going to find Kieran," Cas says. "Remember me telling you about him?"

Milo scratches his head, dull-faced.

He has no idea. Which makes sense. He never met Kieran, and half the time, I forget about him myself after all these years.

"He's the boy Papa wanted me to marry," I say, and just hearing it out loud makes my stomach twist. *How embarrassing. Why is this our best excuse? Me running away to find some lost friend in the hope he'll want to marry me?*

"Oh," Milo says, then he smiles and says it again, drawing out the vowel. "*Ooh.*"

I shrug.

"So, you're gonna stab him?" he asks, eyeing the sword.

I laugh, though my eyes burn with the threat of tears again. *Milo. Empyrean, how I don't want to miss watching you grow up.* I clutch the straps of the bag, fighting a desperate urge to forsake this wild idea of running away.

"No, I'm just bringing this for protection. He lives pretty far from here. I'm . . ." My voice cracks as I move closer to kneel in front of him. "I'm going to be away for a while."

"How long?"

I run my fingertips across his freckled forehead, brushing away a curl. "Just a while."

His smile wavers.

"It's what Papa wanted," Cas says, amazing me with her ability to stay calm, even at her age. Maybe she's not as upset that I'm leaving as I think she should be. "She's gotta run though, Milo. Mum won't like it, since she has her heart set on Nori marrying Landon, so . . ."

Milo squints, and then he gives a wide grin—his mischievous face. Cas's ploy is perfect. Make it sound rebellious and fun, instead of like I'm abandoning my family.

Which is exactly what I'm doing.

Maybe I shouldn't go.

"Mum will wake up soon, Nori," Cas says.

Part of me wishes Mum would step from her room right now, see how ridiculous I look, and talk me down. But then what? I stay here, either to hold my tongue when I know there's danger or cost Mum the allowance that sustains the family? I'd only spend the rest of my life staring at that cliff the Warden leapt from, wondering what El-Alam wanted *me* for.

I can't.

"I love you, Milo," I say, drawing him into my arms. "I'll be back someday."

"With Kieran," Cas adds, "so I can make sure he's not an idiot like Landon."

Who's the big sister here? I want to chide, but I chuckle instead. She almost has *me* convinced that's what I'm up to. But it's the furthest thing from the truth.

I pat Milo's fluffy hair and kiss him on the hairline, then I steal one last hug from Cas and race outside.

I keep away from the market, not wanting to be seen dressed like this. Though, every step away from home feels like the deepest betrayal. I can't even say good-bye—to my mother. And this is after I left her husband for dead.

I clutch the bag draped over my shoulder as I wind between the evergreens and toward the lake. Perspiration builds on my nape despite the brisk morning, and I curl my cloak around my arms. The deeper I get into the woods, the more questions form about what awaits me. How far is the citadel? Will we be hunted all the way there? What will people think of me, an outsider showing up with their prince?

What if Calden doesn't even meet me?

"Norielle!"

I barely register a voice calling my name. He repeats it, and my nostrils flare.

"Headed off to Raevre?" Landon asks to my back.

I keep walking with my lips sealed.

His steps trail behind, a rude chuckle assuring me he'll follow me straight to Calden if I don't find some way to rid myself of him first.

"I'm leaving," I say, stopping without turning around.

He catches up, a grin sprawled across his overly perfect face as he steps in front of me. "So, you're finally running away."

My eyelids droop. "Is that what you've been waiting for?"

He rests a hand against the tree beside me, blocking my path with his arm. I fight an urge to unsheathe Papa's sword and test my skills on him.

I duck instead, but before I can slip past him, he grips my arm and jerks me against a tree. His forearm crosses my collarbone, pressing me against the rough trunk. I reach for the sword—

"I saw you last night," Landon whispers.

Panic pierces my lungs and deflates every ounce of courage I possess. My fingers slip off the sword's grip. *How much did he see? The lake? Calden?*

"You were out there with some stranger." His lips teeter between a sneer and scowl. "I saw him run off when your little sister showed up."

I flick my gaze to the side with a fool's hope that this *stranger* will appear just in time to help me, but as far as I can see, we're alone.

"Who is he?" Landon presses.

"What do you care?"

He pauses, and for a freckle of time, fear shines in his eyes. "I care because this is soon to be *my* town, and you know Behria has a policy against outsiders. Trade business only."

"That's a stupid policy, for one." I grip his arm, dumbly thinking I might be strong enough to push him away. "And second, why were you spying on me?"

"The policy is there to keep us safe." His forearm presses harder against me. "El-Alam protects *us,* not anybody who decides to show up. Outsiders could mean a breach in our protections, and maybe that's why your papa went down into the lake."

"Then you *do* believe me."

"Hardly." His tone is casual. "Just taking precautions."

I clutch the sword but wait to draw it. He could have me arrested for doing so, and no one around here would believe my word over his. "Well, as I said, I'm leaving. So, if you're worried about me bringing in strangers, worry no more. I won't be causing you any more problems."

His arm doesn't move. "You never explained who he is."

"It doesn't matter. He won't be back here."

He leans even closer, until I can see his pores. "Is that where you're going? With him?"

My brows scrunch. Why does he care so much? He couldn't be . . . jealous, could he?

"Yes, actually," I say. "I'm leaving with him."

He stares and stares, then suddenly he snorts, releasing me so he can laugh until he buckles over. I seize the opportunity to hurry along my way, though I'd like to ask what's so funny.

His laughter fades behind me, and to my relief, he wanders back toward the town. Though now, I know there's another witness in Behria—and likely the worst possible person. At least he didn't seem to see what happened in the lake or notice that my rescuer wasn't just some Auberfall boy I've taken a liking to, but a Warden.

Except Cas is telling Mum I'm running away to find Kieran.

I wince. This lie is going to a fall apart at my heels, isn't it?

I hasten toward the overhang where Calden and I agreed to meet again. Paranoia keeps me checking my back for Landon or his friends. But no one follows me besides a honeybee intent on buzzing by my ear. I listen to its hum harmonizing with the ringing in my head—the sound of frayed emotions, emotions I can't seem to feel anymore. It's all too surreal, happening far too fast to comprehend.

But I know myself. It'll be in the quiet hours of the night when I fully realize what I've done. That will be when the hollow inside turns into a life-sucking vortex of loneliness, grief, and guilt. Even so, I *have* to do this. For Papa. If for no other reason than to help the Wardens stop what happened to Papa from happening to someone else—in whatever small way I've been called to do so.

When I arrive, Calden rises from the shadow of the overhang, his hood covering his blond hair and patching his face in shadows. He notices my bag and armor with a solemn smile that makes me wonder what he's thinking. Is he glad I've obviously decided to come? Or is he wishing

I'd passed on the offer so El-Alam would have to pick someone else?

He picks up his bag, hefting it on his back. "You're coming."

"Yes," I answer with half my voice.

He inhales, his broad chest swelling as if taking me from this place is as hard for him as it is for me to leave. "You should know that safety will be hard to come by. It's a long way to the citadel, and every route has its dangers. So, turn back now if you wish not to endure such things."

I look back toward home, though it's lost in the trees. "I'm not going back. I want to know why El-Alam called me."

"Very well then." He steps closer to me, leaning to catch my fleeing gaze. "I will defend you with my very life. May it be enough."

He turns toward the Rimrook Mountains, and I take my first step away from home.

NORIELLE

Lake Daleia's musty smell drifts to us on the breeze. The expanse of water stretches nearly to the mountain range up ahead. I've never seen the lake from this side, but it looks like a sea between here and Behria in the glimpses I catch through the evergreens.

Around us, the world is quiet besides the hum of wildlife, inviting my questions to fester. I hold them in until we are far enough from the lake that even its scent has left the air.

But when I finally speak, my voice is as small as a child's. "Can I ask you something?"

Calden slows, but he scans the premises and checks something on his wrist before turning to me. "Perhaps quietly."

I shift closer to him as we cross a bald patch between the pines and firs. "People go into the lake all the time, so why did it strike when I was out there? Is it because I've been called?"

My chest tingles at his hesitation. I'm sure I already know the answer, and yet I'm afraid to hear it.

"I'd suppose so," he says, keeping his voice low. "Ta'Nathel despises Wardens, despite what people believe about us serving him. His curse would surely target the Called as much as the already inducted. Not to say that the curse is usually so choosy. It could be mere coincidence, albeit a significant one."

My shoulders slouch, the weight of guilt falling on them. Then it probably was my fault that the lake took Papa. It must have been after me that morning.

Or was *he* called before me?

My steps drag as I consider it. The lake went after him first, not me. Was he meant to join the Wardens? Did he reject the call or simply not have a chance to respond to it? Could whatever role I've been called to fulfill have originally been meant for him, and I've now inherited it?

I glance at Calden again to find him watching me with a concerned stare, surely having noticed my slowed pace. The temptation to ask him about Papa tickles the tip of my tongue, yet the words remain trapped inside my rib cage. If I told him what happened, I'd have to confess how little I did to save Papa. And then what would he think of me? He'd call me a coward and send me home.

Then I'd never get to find out what I've been called for. And as selfish as it feels to stifle the truth, I can't go back to Behria now. Not with the steward's threats.

"You needn't be afraid," Calden says, drawing me from the deep chasms of my mind. "Be only aware of the dangers. As I said, I will protect you no matter what opposes us as we travel. I only cautioned you before, so you'd know that you may witness some frights along the way. And, thereafter, you'll be equipped to face them yourself."

"And you're certain of this? That *I've* been called?"

"I'd have not been sent otherwise."

"But you're not mistaking me for someone else?"

A wry expression crosses his face. "Is it a normal thing for girls in Behria to spend time at the bottom of the lake? Because that's where I saw you in the vision."

"The vision?" I echo.

"The Seer imparted a vision of you to me, so I'd know exactly who I was looking for. There is no mistaking you, Norielle." He gestures toward me. "Not to mention your hair. I've never seen so much of it. Unless that, too, is common of girls from Behria."

"No," I say, suddenly feeling my hair's length as if it were dragging across the ground. "Everyone else keeps it . . . a reasonable length."

"See, then. No mistaking you." He smiles, and I wonder if he thinks my hair is obnoxious. He must, because of the way he said it.

I squash the foolish worry. Of all the concerns I should have right now, what this *prince* thinks of my hair shouldn't be one of them.

I'm turning into Cas.

My thoughts cycle back to the idea of this man seeing me in his mind before ever laying eyes on me. Papa told me once that some Wardens have gifts of foresight, but he never mentioned those Wardens could share their visions. How do they do that? What exactly did Calden see?

And why did they send *him*, anyway?

"Shouldn't they have sent someone else to get me?" I ask, before considering how rude it might sound.

"Someone faster, you mean?" he asks, with an amused sparkle in his eyes.

"No, I mean that you sound important. Don't you have people you could send to run errands like this for you?"

He laughs, and while it's quiet, the deep resonance seems to fill the thinning woods as he starts us walking again. "I'd not consider this an errand. Retrieving you is among the most important tasks I've ever been handed. I wouldn't have trusted it to anyone else, and besides, sending someone in my stead would contradict with the principles of our Order."

My face twists at his answer, but I fail to decide on the right question to ask next before he continues.

"As I said, I was sent specifically because you are to help me with something. Our destinies are entwined, you see."

I almost trip. *Our destinies are entwined? What is that supposed to mean?*

My mouth opens to ask, but he suddenly checks his wrist again and the levity leaves his face.

"We should keep quiet, friend. This area isn't safe for talking anymore."

I squint, trying to see what he looked at that indicated so, but he hides his wrist from sight, and we fall silent again.

"Are you sure Rimrir is dead?" I ask as Calden leads us toward a tunnel entrance glowing in the dusk.

The tunnels were allegedly carved by the stone golem, Rimrir, as a gift to mankind— shortcuts through the Rimrook Mountains. But Rimrir, like the other Sentries who once protected us, turned violent when Ta'Nathel slayed our original Empyreal Guardian and hexed the lands. The curse corrupted the Sentries' souls, earning them their new title of *the Accursed*.

Rimrir, given his proximity to Behria, is the one I've heard the most about.

"I am positive," Calden says. "I was there the day he fell."

I flinch. "Did you slay him?"

"With help," he says, but we reach the tunnel entrance before I can ask how. He steps inside first. The ceiling stands a full arm's stretch higher than his head, gleaming with clusters of luminescent teal and turquoise crystals. The cool light emanating from them ripples along the stony walls in a way that reminds me of the lake, as if the walls weren't stone at all, but water.

Calden walks a half dozen paces before seeming to sense that I've yet to take my first step. He turns, the ethereal light reflecting in his eyes in a way that makes them look inhuman. Like blue stars in the Empyrean.

"Having second thoughts?" he asks.

I resist another urge to look behind me. "No. I've just never seen the tunnels for myself."

He smiles, beckoning me in. "They're prettier inside."

I urge my feet forward until the cool light spills over me in a lacelike pattern. I lift my hand, admiring the splotchy coloration on my palm. What a shame that fear has kept all of us in Behria from beholding such beauty when it was so close. Cassia especially would have loved to see this.

Damp air courses through the tunnels, tickling my ears as Calden leads me from one winding passage to another. Questions brew under my skin, but I keep quiet. He promised more explanations once we were well into the mountain passages, far from civilian eavesdroppers. Though, after walking all day to get here and for still another full hour once inside, I'm starting to wonder how different our definitions of *far* are.

"We're nearly to the Great Hall of Rimrir," he says, his deep voice reverberating off the stone walls and surrounding me. "That would be an ideal place to camp."

Camp. The idea shouldn't alarm me—of course we'd have to camp along the way—and yet, at his mention, my insides crawl. How am I supposed to sleep isolated in the mountains with a stranger nearby?

"I would ask that you try not to wander far once we settle in," he continues. "Rimrir may no longer be a threat in these passages, but there are others who pass through every now and again—others that would be quite pleased to steal you away."

My breath shakes as I inhale. "Who? The king's Hunters?"

"Ah, not in here." He stills at a fork, contemplating the path a moment before taking the left tunnel. "Like you, the Hunters believe Rimrir is still alive. It's Warden defectors I worry about. Blood Wardens."

"Blood Wardens?"

"A topic for another time," he says. "Just stay close, is all."

A few moments of fretting later, we walk into a vast space where the rocky ceiling opens to the moonlit sky, letting in a fresh breeze. Calden scopes out the glistening surroundings before crossing the puddle-splotched floor and stopping on the other side of an ashpit. He must have camped here before.

He pushes back his hood, letting loose his now frizzy hair.

"Now that we have some semblance of privacy . . . I'm sure you have many more questions," he says, tugging off his backpack. It plunks against the ground, and he kneels beside it. "Perhaps we should address only your most pressing ones first, and save the others for after we've rested? It may be . . . much to process."

I stand there, making no effort to drop my own bag. All my questions feel equally pressing. Why me? What does he mean that my destiny is entwined with his, and how could *my* destiny have anything to do with a Warden prince?

My thumbnail scratches the strap of my bag, indecision paralyzing my tongue.

"Or you could always save them all for later," he says, pulling an apple from his pack. He holds it out to me as if to ask if I want it. I shake my head, and he shrugs, chomping into it as he settles on the ground.

His chewing fills the silence until I finally decide on the right question to start with.

"You said that if I rejected this calling, someone else would be chosen to fill my role. I'm assuming that means if I'd died, the same would happen. So, why'd you come all this way to save me if someone else would have been called to replace me?"

"And let you die?" he asks, lowering the apple.

I nod. "You don't know me."

His gaze wanders to the crystal-coated walls. "And wouldn't it have been a shame to never get the chance to."

My bag slides from my weakened grip, and I swing it down like I meant to lower it.

"Sure, El-Alam could choose another," he carries on, "but I wonder, why were you his first choice above all others?"

I crouch beside my bag, keeping myself moving despite the goosebumps on my arms. *First choice.* So, Papa wasn't called—at least, not for this specific role.

"But his first choice for what?" I press.

"I don't know any more about your role than what I have already told you. And even that, I wasn't supposed to say. El-Alam hasn't revealed it."

My lips twist. "That seems a bit unfair."

"The life of a Warden is often unfair."

I cross my arms, taking him in from his aloof expression to his intricate armor. "You're really a prince?"

"The *Sovereign* Prince, yes."

"What does that mean?"

"It means I'm the next in line to inherit leadership over the Wardens." He pauses to rip off another chunk of his apple and chew it. "But if you are trying to discern your destiny based on my role as the Sovereign Prince, I assure you that is an infinite number of possibilities."

I finally sit, having to scoop my hair over a shoulder to keep it out of the dirt. "Do you have any theories?"

"I'm working on them."

I sit taller. "Tell me."

"I'd rather not."

"Can you at least tell me what it means that our destinies are entwined?"

He lets my question linger so long, my own theory emerges from the depths of my mind.

Marriage.

My heart skips. That's what it is, isn't it? He's about the right age, and that would explain why he was so determined to rescue me—El-Alam's first choice for his wife. No wonder he doesn't want to tell me his theories—

"There's several of us, actually," he says just as I'm feeling lightheaded. "A team of people bound to the same purpose. It's called a Bind. I just happen to be the leader, so I'm the one who retrieves those who are called."

"Oh," I say, expelling all my air in the word.

"Don't worry," Calden says. "You'll only have to travel with me alone for a few days before we meet with another member of the Bind—a young woman, a bit older than you seem. Her name is Alani. I thought she'd make a nice companion for you, but given the urgency of the vision, I didn't have the time to wait for her."

"How many are in our . . . Bind?" I ask.

"As of now, three. You'll be our fourth." He tosses the apple core over his shoulder, and it rolls into the shadows. "The Seer said the Bind would be complete when there are five members."

"So, me, you, and this woman, Alani. Who's the other?"

"My younger sister."

Then it must be some sort of council. But why would an outsider be called to join the Wardens' council?

"And the fifth member. Do you know who that is?" I ask.

"Ah, not yet. I hope to have a word about them upon returning with you. And hopefully, insight about our purpose." He pulls on his hood. "Though, I have a feeling El-Alam will wait to reveal that until after the fifth member is amongst us."

My eyes narrow. "So, even when we get there, I might still have to wait to find out what exactly I've been called for."

He smiles. "Impatient, are we?"

"Do you blame me?"

His smile spreads, but he returns to my original question. "It depends on where the final Bind member is sourced from. So far, you're the only member that's been brought in from outside the Wardens. Which is, admittedly, odd. But welcome, of course." He fidgets like he thinks I might be insulted by what he said, yet I'm thinking the very same thing. "It seems to me that if El-Alam has turned to sourcing people from outside the Wardens, then our final member, too, would be an outsider. Which, yes, would delay the hearing of our purpose."

"For how long?"

"A potentially very short or very long time, and none could know until then. *Now*"—he slaps his hands against his lap—"that's quite enough for this night, I'd wager. As I've said, it's against our customs for me to be telling you any of this. And you wouldn't want me to get in trouble with my mother, now would you?"

The smile he flashes holds the hint of a wink and causes an unexpected flutter in my chest. But I quickly remember who I am talking to—the leader of this Bind and the Sovereign Prince of the Wardens.

"If you don't mind, I'd like to get some rest. I've not slept for two nights," he says, rising. "The Seer said I had thirteen days before you were to drown, and everything in the kingdom seemed to want to keep me from making it in time. I'd like to recover before setting out again. And I don't imagine you've slept much yourself. We can discuss more tomorrow."

I tuck my chin. The future leader of the Wardens stayed up two nights so he could rescue *me*?

And here I've been pestering him . . .

"Of course," I say, my voice small. "Thank you again for everything."

He gives me a slight smile before picking up his bag and carrying it to the far side of the chamber. I remain for a while, listening to the wind whistle through the fissure overhead. It carries in a waft of evergreens that smell of home—something I sense will become foreign quite soon, should I carry on with Calden.

My mind rolls over my conversation with him, the long walk to the mountains, and back to Behria. What is Mum doing now? Did Cas sell the story? Was Mum convinced? Is she lying awake, grieving me like she does Papa and wishing she hadn't been so harsh, or are her eyes lit with the false hope that I'll come back with my childhood friend and plans to marry?

Weariness dulls my thoughts, and finally, I rise to scope out a private nook to hide in. I tuck myself behind a wall, not even letting my feet slip out far enough for Calden to see me. I spread my blanket and arrange my things, then I lie with Papa's sword clutched in my hand—lest Calden be less noble than he seems—and force my eyes to close.

CALDEN

A warm tingle against my skin jolts me from my light sleep. My eyes open to blue-tinged tendrils of energy wrapped over my left wrist. *A Snare Ward,* I recall. One I placed there myself to hold me down, lest my curse awaken in my sleep and cause harm to the newest member of my Bind.

I dismiss the ward with a silent command and the energy dissipates, its soft whir fading. In its place, the faint chatter of birds slips through the aperture overhead. The sun piercing through the stone ceiling glares into my eyes, and by the tightness of my skin when I blink, it's surely burned me already.

I shift out from under its assault and lift my opposite wrist to check my Omen Mark—an array of black arrows encircling one that will turn red if an enemy comes within range. It shows no sign of any threat. For the moment.

I rise and softly tread across the chamber to the wall my new Bind member hides behind. I peer around it, sighing when I see her still there. She hasn't run off yet, which is promising, though by the sword gripped in her hands, her trust is yet to be gained. I slowly back away, struggling to peel my eyes from her tense expression. As if even sleep couldn't bring to rest whatever haunts her in the corners of her mind.

She flinches, and I dash behind the wall before her eyes can open and find me there. Not a great way to earn trust, standing over someone while they sleep.

I return to my supplies, expecting Norielle to wake any moment, but by the time I hear another sound from her, I've already eaten, taken a short stroll to scout out the next passage, and shaved the stubble off my jaw.

"Sleep well?" I ask from the rock I perch on once she shows herself.

She delivers a blank look that is both tired and confused. Disoriented.

"Well, you slept long at least," I say. "We need to get moving. Our next campsite is quite the walk away."

"In the mountains?" Norielle asks in a scratchy voice.

"Yes. It will take a couple of days to make it there, through."

She nods and carries her bag into the sunlight, sorting through her food. Rationing, I realize. I watch her, wondering where she learned to do that. Does she travel? And what did she do back in Behria, anyway? She bears the sword of an Alémor soldier, yet the matching armor doesn't fit her form. Was it someone else's? A brother's, perhaps? Does she know how to use that blade?

She glances at me, and I realize I'm staring.

"I believe it's your turn to answer a question," I say to cover up the awkwardness.

She pushes a clump of chestnut hair behind her ear. "You mean your Seer didn't tell you everything about me already?"

"All he shared was your name and where to find you."

She bundles her rations into a linen sack. "What would you like to know?"

"Your armor and sword. Where did they come from?"

She stands, holding a strip of dried meat. "My father."

"Ah. So, he's a soldier?"

"Was," she says, quickly turning to bite off a piece of the jerky.

My mouth seals as I apprehend her meaning. Her father must have died in battle. Those items were likely shipped back to her family, having been emptied of the body they belonged to.

How long ago, I wonder?

I spare her the question, sensing by her turned posture that this isn't a subject she'd like to linger on.

"Have you any training with the sword?" I ask instead.

Her fingertips brush the sword's gold pommel. "Some . . . though I doubt you'd be impressed."

"Well, from what I've seen, it's the ones who don't think they're any good that you have to watch out for."

Her slight smile skews her befuddled expression.

"It's not that their skill is low; it's that their standards are high," I add. "They try twice as hard as anyone else."

She sucks her bottom lip, as if to hide her spreading grin. "Or they really are terrible and are brutally aware of it."

I chuckle. "We'll see. Hopefully, at the citadel, and no sooner." I rise to retrieve my bag. "Shall we continue?"

She hesitates, working her fingers through a knot in her hair. Her gaze shifts back the way we came, and I wonder if she'll ask me to take her home instead. A part of me wishes she would—whatever she's been specifically called to join us for, any chance of her having a normal life is void should she continue with me.

"Lead on," she finally answers.

I'm sorry, I think, but I smile as if delighted and start us along our way.

"Is it true the people of Behria believe they are immune to Ta'Nathel's curse?" I ask once Norielle seems more awake.

She hustles to walk beside me in the spacious tunnel. The blue-green light glides across her gentle features—a lovely sight that I have no place indulging in, so I fix my eyes ahead.

"Unfortunately, yes," she says.

"Why is that?"

She adjusts a lock of her hair, seeming to consider her words carefully. "They think El-Alam blessed our town because we didn't bow to Ta'Nathel like others when he claimed Silvirdia. It's said El-Alam put some kind of protection around the town that shields it from the curse."

"Fascinating." I check my Omen Mark for threats but find it still dark. "And this has seemed true until the lake?"

"The lake is the first oddity I've seen in Behria in all my life."

I study her features for a moment. "Which is how many years, exactly?"

"Eighteen."

"Ah." I delay to see if she'll ask what she's obviously wondering by the way she inspects me, but when she doesn't, I offer it freely. "I've a good seven years on you. My sister teases that I must have harbored the curse because I was born about the same time as it started."

I shut my mouth before accidently delving into the other reason Odessa teases me about this—*my* curse, which is not much less destructive than the one upon the world.

"So, you haven't seen the world before the curse then, either?" Norielle asks, rubbing the ends of her hair between a finger and thumb.

"No. Though I think I'm glad of that." I watch my steps over a stretch littered with rocks. "It seems worse to know what the world was before and have that taken away, than to merely imagine what it was like."

"Is there anything the Wardens can do?"

I inhale, the air feeling weighty in my lungs. "We're already doing all that we can. Ta'Nathel himself is subdued behind a barrier in Northspire. Wardens work constantly to enforce it, lest he escape and do worse to this world than he's already done. But even with that, I will admit, the situation as it stands looks rather hopeless. The curse is unrelenting and worsening by the year."

Norielle's hand brushes the bumpy wall as she walks, slower every step.

"Again, the Wardens are constantly at work to undo the effects and control the damage, but in all honesty, friend, it won't be enough. The world cannot linger as it is. Sooner or later, this curse will cause it to destroy itself."

Norielle gasps, her next response taking far longer than her last. "But why? Why would Ta'Nathel want to destroy the world? Why is he even here?"

"His motivations are hard to discern. With our limited knowledge, we can't make much sense of it either," I admit. "From what we can gather, a Guardian's soul is tied to whatever world they are given to protect—or in this case, have claimed by slaying the former owner. This means that once they've been assigned to or have claimed a world for themselves, they cannot leave it. Ta'Nathel killed Toaph Elbara to take this world and surely to lead it into submission to him rather than El-Alam. Which is, of course, blasphemy. The Wardens trapped Ta'Nathel to prevent him from asserting himself as God over Silvirdia. However, from behind our barrier, he still managed to curse the world in response. We believe he wishes now to destroy the world so he can leave it, seeing as the Wardens have thwarted his original plan." I scratch my head. "Still, this hardly makes sense to me. There are other theories, but no solid answers. We lack information."

"But the Wardens . . ." She turns to me with a trembling gaze. "They can't destroy him?"

"No number of Wardens could hope to defeat an Empyreal Guardian. And even if we could, killing him ourselves would result in immediate death to the world, since his soul is bound to it." I reassure her with a smile that defies my own fears. "There is always hope, though, that El-Alam will send another Empyreal Guardian to us. Another Guardian may be able to defeat Ta'Nathel and thus inherit the world, liberating us from the curse and such a fate."

She looks down, her long locks crowding her face. "But it's been over two decades since Toaph Elbara was slain. Why hasn't El-Alam sent another already?"

"That is another mystery we'd all like answered. But El-Alam is never late, nor is he premature in his responses or revelations. Just as I received notice of your potential drowning in just the right amount of time to rescue you, I would assume the next Guardian will be presented in just the right time to save this world before it's lost. I just hope that he comes quickly because—"

A pinch on my wrist silences me. I jerk my Omen Mark into view—a deep red arrow blazes at the center with its tip pointed right behind us.

"We need to move on," I whisper. "There are Blood Wardens."

She squints like she doesn't understand.

I grab her arm and tug her onward. "The defectors I mentioned."

"Can we fight them?"

The idea twists my stomach.

"I'd rather not." I check the mark again to see if the point has moved. Still the same. They must be coming down this very passage.

I hurry us on to the next split in the path and veer into the dimmer tunnel. The steady decline threatens the stealth of our footfalls and leads us to a place where the air is still. The crystals along the walls gradually disperse, thinning the light until our path lies in pure shadow. I unhitch my lantern and will the ward inside to ignite. A white light illuminates the tunnel, just bright enough for us to see our next steps. I pass the lantern to Norielle for whatever comfort it may bring her. She lifts it, inspecting it as if searching for a flame, but her curiosity dies quickly, and she focuses ahead.

The light crawls over jagged stones, scaring away beetles and spiders. Soon my pauldrons nearly graze the walls, and I have to send Norielle in front of me to make it through the tight channel. But finally, our tunnel connects with another, and we follow the wider path until I spy a small chamber, whose shadowed entryway is nearly unnoticeable.

I pull Norielle inside, then draw a crossed symbol at the head of the two paths leading out. Then I add one more to the wall, a Shroud Ward, which will prevent their Omen Marks from detecting us in this area.

I pay my Omen Mark a quick glance. It's still red, but barely.

"We should be safe down here," I whisper.

"What are those?" she asks, pointing toward one of the symbols I drew near the entrance.

"Snare Wards. They're traps. If someone steps on them, a vine of energy will wrap around their foot and hold them there until I tell it to let go."

"And what about that?" She points to my wrist. "Some kind of tracker?"

"An Omen Mark, and yes, basically." I reach for my pen again. "Would you like me to draw one on you? So you can keep an eye on them, too?"

Her gaze wanders to each of the passages. "I guess that would be smart."

She stretches her arm toward me, and I hold it steady. The pen's dim luminance glistens on her fair skin as I etch the ward above the red lines that the lake weed left on her. The arrow in the center of the mark turns a dull red as I withdraw my hands.

"Will I be able to do all this one day?" she asks, pivoting to watch how the arrow rotates to remain pointed toward the Blood Wardens.

"Yes, once you're formally inducted," I say. "But for now, we'll just have to cheat a little."

She looks back at the mark on her wrist, then holds it closer to the lantern. "What does it mean if it's getting brighter?"

I grimace, checking mine to see that she's right.

"That we need to be quiet," I whisper, dousing the light in her hand until it's fainter than a single flame—just enough to see the Omen Marks when held close.

I draw another ward on my palm that I hope I won't have to use, and step closer to Norielle. It wouldn't take long for them to realize she is powerless, and them only killing her would be a merciful act considering their reputations, should I fail to defeat them.

But I won't, I assure myself, though the assertion feels flimsy considering my habit of freezing in such encounters. The defectors aren't like Hunters and the Accursed.

I knew some of them before.

The red of the Omen Mark turns as bright as fresh blood. Close—very close. But to move now would only draw attention.

A woman hollers, and my muscles tense. But at her second shout, I realize her voice is unfamiliar. Another defector answers—words I can't discern—then two more respond. *Four. Not so bad.*

All sound unfamiliar.

But then I hear others. Two more? Maybe three? Frustration sharpens their tones. Their voices carry like they are near the divide, just before this chamber. Will they go the other way or am I about to find out just how many there are?

I turn to Norielle, who's glaring at the mark on her wrist. When she glances up, I force myself to smile as if to promise her that I have this completely under control.

The defectors' footsteps start again, and their voices grow louder. Closer.

My lungs expand. They're coming this way.

NORIELLE

The light goes out. All I can hope is that Calden did it and not the defectors.

I grip Papa's sword, though I doubt it will help me much, and ease the blade from its sheath. The footsteps draw closer, voices murmuring back and forth. From the little I can discern, it seems they are arguing about which direction to go.

Not here, I pray.

Calden stands in front of me, though in the blackness, I see nothing of his form. I struggle to keep my breaths as silent as his. *I will defend you with my very life. May it be enough,* he said.

I wish I could tell him not to bother. If it comes to it, who is really more important here? The girl who can be replaced or the future Sovereign of the Wardens?

"This way!" a woman shouts from afar; her voice echoes along the stony shaft.

The footsteps halt, someone grunts, then they head toward the voice. I inhale, the acrid scent of rock so strong I can taste its bitterness at the back of my throat. I breathe it back out in a slow sigh. The noises dissipate into the distance, leaving us in a quiet so deep I notice my own heartbeat.

The lantern in my hand illuminates, and Calden's face appears out of the shadows. He checks the symbol on his wrist against the light before his glistening eyes return to mine. With a raised finger, he indicates we should wait a little longer. I watch the matching symbol on my wrist until the red dims to solid black.

"Will they come back?" I whisper when Calden's shoulders finally relax.

"Doubtful," he says. "They are probably just passing through like us. But let's get out of the area just in case. There's another route out of the mountains. We'll take that one."

Calden waves his hand, and the symbols on the floor vanish.

He leads me along again, relying on a map that looks a hundred years old. We don't speak, and I can hardly keep from checking the mark to see if it's turned red. But as hours pass, the arrow never colors again. My thoughts finally let go of the threat of Blood Wardens, only to return to the information he shared with me before the defectors came near.

Our world is destroying itself.

The *whole* world. Including Behria.

"Calden," I say, drawing his concerned gaze to me. "What if El-Alam doesn't send another Guardian? How much time does the world have left?"

Will Milo even get to grow up?

"I wish I could say," he says toward the serrated ground. "But all we have is guesses based on how much chaos abounds."

"And what's yours? Your guess?"

"I'm not sure you want me to answer that."

I hold my tongue a moment, but then abandon my reasoning. "Please."

His boots crunch for several steps before he answers. "As it stands, the curse seems to be wreaking more devastation every year. What began as an increase in disastrous weather has, of late, turned into sweeping catastrophes. Deserts have frozen over. Whole islands have sunk in Schillon. Raevre all but burnt to the ground last month in a consuming wildfire. And that's not to mention the increasing number of attacks from the Accursed."

He goes quiet again, leaving my frustration to fester at the confirmation of these events. We heard about much of this in Behria, yet many still chose to believe they were no more than rumors—as if denial would alter reality.

"I'd say we're maybe a quarter through the destruction," Calden says, drawing me back to my question. "But I dare not imagine what the world may be like another twenty-five years from now, unless we receive a significant increase of Wardens to help abate the curse. However, thanks to King Arlo and his Hunters, it doesn't seem that will be happening any time soon."

I try to swallow his heavy words, but they form a lump in my throat. "Doesn't he know the Wardens are trying to help?"

His laugh has a bitter edge. "No. He'd rather blame us, since the curse started when we trapped Ta'Nathel. He fails to recognize that mortal death is not the worst thing that can happen to a person. It is better for the whole world to perish while upholding its faith in El-Alam than to turn against our Creator in worship of Ta'Nathel. For one death is temporary, and the other, everlasting."

Silence stretches between us until light finally sweeps through the darkness. My shoulders relax as a hint of fresh air slips into my lungs. I follow Calden's accelerated footsteps out of the smothering tunnel and into an atrium of sorts. Rays of sunlight cascade over the crystals that project from the open ceiling like teeth and reflect shards of orange and purple down the rocky walls.

Calden kneels in a clump of grass by a tall column and dips his flask into a pool of water. I swing mine off to copy him, but just before I can dunk it, Calden holds out a hand to stop me.

"Let me see that first," he says, securing the wooden stopper onto his filled flask. He loops the long strap across his torso, and as the flask resettles near his hip, I notice a symbol that resembles a two-leafed sprout glowing on the leather casing.

"It's a Purification Ward," he explains, taking my flask. He pulls his pen from his belt and etches the same mark onto mine, then he dips it into the water for me. When he hands it back, the mouth of my flask shines as if he's sprinkled stardust inside it.

"Don't drink it right away," he says. "It takes a couple of minutes. When it stops glowing, you know it's safe."

A smirk cracks on my face, but I manage to stifle the laugh that tries to come with it. The idea of water that once glowed being safe seems suspicious, but when the wards fade and I see Calden drink his without any immediate consequences, I allow myself to try it. The water tastes like someone dropped a bead of tree sap into it, and I find myself gulping it down and going back for more.

Calden laughs as he stands. "If you have any minor illnesses, they are gone now."

"It heals?" I ask, the dripping flask stilling in my hand.

"Not really, just cleanses the body. Rids us of infections, too. Works great for cleaning cuts," he says. "And you'll never need soap again. Just treat the water with a Purification Ward and jump in."

"Incredible," I say, taking one more sip.

I close my flask and look around the atrium. After the dank places we just walked through, I'd believe it if someone told me we'd stumbled into the Empyrean. The shimmering crystals and freckles of color they refract are mesmerizing, and to be able to smell the mountain air slipping in with the tepid breeze . . . I've never seen a place so tranquil.

Besides the threat of Blood Wardens returning.

I check the Omen Mark again. Still black.

"The Blood Wardens," I prompt, and Calden swivels from his intense stare at the sky to face me. "Can you tell me more about them? How powerful are they?"

"They are as powerful as Wardens, if not more so, due to their ability to discard certain rules regarding the use of power," he says, leaning against the rocky pillar. "Some have joined the Wardens only to turn away, but they take with them the knowledge of wards. In the days before the curse, a Warden who left the Order would simply lose their power, rendering their wards useless. But in recent years these defectors have discovered an alternative means to making wards work even without El-Alam's endowing—*blood*." His gaze turns distant. "They drain the blood of the Accursed and use it to write wards. But the consequence of using such tainted magic is eternal—eventually resulting in a permanent corruption of their souls, a fate from which they can never return."

I fold my arms, my questions multiplying. "They can't be helped?"

"At first, yes," he says. "We have a sort of rehabilitation process at the citadel. An early defector still has hope of redemption, but those that have continually used Blood Wards are too far gone to restore. Their whole beings become tainted by the darkness, and their humanity is all but lost. They become mere vessels of destruction."

"And if they had found us . . .?" Fear clips my question, but I must know.

"I would have done whatever it required of me to bring them down and protect you," he says. "But you must understand why I would avoid doing so. As Sovereign Prince, I recognize some of their faces."

The realization dawns on me with a heavy downward pull, and I sit on a large rock.

"I don't know them all," he says, claiming a boulder near me as his own chair. "Even those who were not called into the Wardens can join the Blood Wardens these days. But the chance of seeing a lost friend and having to . . ." He clasps his hands, shaking his head. "I just would prefer to avoid it."

"Are there many of them? Friends of yours that have defected?"

His chin lifts, but he doesn't look my way. "There are a handful of acquaintances, but of close friends, only two. I brought one back, hoping we could help him, but he was too far gone."

"What happened to him?"

His knuckles whiten. "My mother killed him. She had no other choice."

I sit with the weight of his answer a moment before mustering the courage to speak again. "What about the other?"

"She's out there somewhere. Far more lost now than he ever was."

The tension riddling his face compels me into silence, though I want to ask more about her. She was a close friend? How close? If he saw her again, would he be able to kill her if he had to? Or would that cross the line of doing "whatever it takes"?

"I'm so sorry," I finally say, hoping he'll sense I'm relieving him of further discussions on the subject.

His smile returns, though it doesn't warm his eyes. "Thank you, Norielle."

Calden shifts his attention to the food in his bag, reminding me I ought to do the same before we set out again. But as I chew another strip of deer jerky and a piece of hardening bread, my tongue feels numb to the taste. How many enemies do the Wardens really have—do *I* now have? Blood Wardens. Hunters. The Accursed.

The world.

But when I look back to Calden with the intent of bringing it up again, his pallid countenance and the un-eaten pear in his hand stops me.

Of course, the moment he senses my gaze lingering his way he straightens, bites into his pear, and stands to pace around the chamber, admiring the sunlit crystals on the walls.

Typical of a leader, to be distressed and act like he's fine. Papa was the same.

But what did it? Talking of the world's state or the mention of his lost defector friend?

I watch him without meaning to. The sunset-hued refractions glitter across his armor and fair features as he saunters around the midsized atrium, as if we haven't already been walking enough. He pays me no notice until the pear is eaten, and then he chucks it away like the apple core. But the only reaction I get from my staring is a one-note chuckle before he wanders to his bag to throw a fistful of almonds into his mouth.

Then, he turns toward me, sliding his pen from his belt.

"Norielle, let me see your other wrist."

I hold my arm up to him without question, and he takes it, his gentle grip supporting my hand. Cool ink slides across my skin, forming a symbol that I realize matches one on his own wrist—a circle with three rings surrounding it and an arrow piercing through the center. His arrow points to me, and mine to him. But there are two small arrows on his that he doesn't add to mine.

"What's that?" I ask as he's lifting the pen.

He looks up, warm light gleaming in his rich blue irises like dawn over the ocean. His grip lingers on my hand. "It's a Bind Mark. That way, should we somehow get separated, we'll be able to find each other again." He glances at his hand and lets go, forcing a wide space between us, though I feel as if strings were attached to our marked wrists. "As the leader, I'm able to track all of you that way, but yours will only ever lead you back to me."

I stare at the dark arrow and back to the man it points to, fighting a sudden lightness in my head. This is unreal. All of it. What am I doing here with the Sovereign Prince of the Wardens, with my destiny tied to his, and a dying world to somehow help sustain?

"Make sure to keep those hidden whenever we are out in the open," Calden says, picking up his bag to lead us on. "Hunters know to look for such marks."

11

NORIELLE

After another day and night in the tunnels, our steps incline toward the morning sunlight spilling in from the exit. My heart palpitates at the sight—we've finally made it to the other side of the mountains. And now I'm one step closer to pledging my life to the Wardens and whatever specific role El-Alam has called me to do.

I pick up my pace, eager to see the sky again through more than just holes in the ceiling. I want to see it touch both sides of the horizon and feel the uninhibited air caressing my face.

I step out after Calden scans the premises. The sun hits my skin, and my lungs fill with air that carries a pungent scent. Grass. A whole field of it stretching from here to the infamous towering walls of Aldrian far ahead of us. My eyes lid until they adjust to the alarming amount of light, overwhelming after three days in the dim tunnels, but finally they start to take in the details. The spires projecting from the top of Aldrian's walls. The spruce trees scattered around the base of the Rimrook Mountains, only to give way to an open valley speckled with white flowers. In the distance, a flock of birds rise from another forest that dips into the notoriously dangerous Dûnori Ravine. Just being this close to it makes my skin tingle at the thought of the ferocious beasts inside.

"This isn't your first time leaving Behria, is it?" Calden asks.

I glance back as if, somehow, Behria would still be within sight. "It is."

He pulls up his cloak, tugging the hood so it shadows his eyes. "Welcome to the world, then. That's Aldrian over there."

I resist the urge to tell him I'm not an idiot, since anyone with a freckle of education should recognize the famous city. Its size is second only to the capital, Atalia, and it's the only city in the kingdom with two walls around its perimeter.

"That's where we're headed." Calden starts into the field, going only a few steps before he reaches toward the ground. Before I can see what he snatched, he spins toward me. "Here, hold this."

I open my hand without thinking, and he drops one of the white flowers into my palm. My head jerks back. Why did he give me a flower?

But then I catch the hues shifting in the slender petals. They turn from white to a deep purple with a dash of gold at the tips. I lift the flower closer, inhaling the buttery scent. The corners of my lips rise as the shades deepen. We definitely didn't have these in Behria.

"Hmm," Calden says, plucking another to hold in his own hand. His remains white in the center, but the edges dye a bold blue. "They're soulcasts. The color is said to reflect our souls," he says in a flippant tone. "Or so says the superstitious."

I hold mine up, pondering what my colors could mean, but Calden tosses his over his shoulder.

"Probably nonsense."

"Then why'd you pick them?"

He smiles, but his strides lengthen, as if to promise he won't answer my question. I drop the flower and rush after him.

"Gold," he says. "The color of refining and endurance—just as gold withstands even the hottest flames, so can she who bears it."

"I thought you just called it nonsense."

"And purple, the color of virtue and authority, often worn by royalty and priests." His steps slow as he meets my eyes. "Perhaps it isn't nonsense after all."

I glance back for my flower to hide my blushing cheeks, but find both flowers have faded to white behind us.

"What does yours mean?" I ask.

He focuses on the valley. "White, the color of purity and wisdom. My mother would get a good laugh from that. And blue, healing and restoration, for which I suppose an argument could be made. But, eh, maybe the flowers only work for girls."

"Yours is more convincing than mine."

He laughs as he starts walking again. "You think me wise, Norielle?"

"You are a prince, aren't you?" I move to follow him.

"My mother would more quickly entitle me a *menace*."

I raise a brow.

"And a *disruption to the Order of the Wardens*." He says this in a higher tone as if to impersonate her, and I can't help but laugh.

I watch my steps to evade the soulcasts. "Why do I feel like you are making this up?"

"Oh, you can ask her when we get there. I'm a bad influence on younger Wardens, she'd say, and I have a knack for bending rules and causing the Wardens problems."

I fail to see it. In the three days I've spent with him, he's proven himself almost too innocent and polite to be real. Maybe I *should* believe him and chalk the rest up to a ruse.

Either way, his light words feel like warm tea against a sore throat. I spent all day yesterday imagining a future where El-Alam *doesn't* send a new Empyreal Guardian and the Wardens fail to be enough.

I need this conversation. This field. The warm breeze stroking through my hair like loving fingers.

But just as I'm starting to settle into this feeling of calm, a shrill scream shatters my peace. I twist around, just in time to dodge the sharp talons of a massive bird. I draw my sword as the bird shrieks again, fanning out its blue-and-black wings. Its beady white eyes fix on me as it dives after me again.

I steady my sword to defend myself, only for an arrow to shoot through the sky and directly pierce the bird's squawking beak. The bird plummets to the ground, a limp wing flopping over my boots.

My brows cave at the arrow sticking out from it. *Where did that—?*

Another arrow hisses by me, taking out another bird with an equally fatal aim. I spin in search of the archer, only to find a bow in Calden's hands.

"When did you get that?" I ask.

He only laughs before he sends another arrow flying at what appears to be nothing until another bird materializes from the air itself—just in time to be skewered.

Calden readies another arrow, squinting at the sky. I clutch my sword hilt, wanting to put it to some use just to show him I can, but after several moments, Calden lowers his bow. Then, in a blink, the bow vaporizes in his grasp.

I jolt, stirring another smile from him. But to ask how he did it would be stupid. *Wards.* That's always the answer. And so many of them, I don't know how I'll ever learn them all.

He kneels before the nearest bird and, with a pinch, dissolves the arrow and bird into dust. I gasp as the breeze flicks the remains into the grass.

Could he do that to anything? Anyone?

Me?

"Those were windcriers," Calden says, leaving me no space for questions. "Spies for the Hunters, which means they'll be close behind."

"Do we fight them?"

"Not if we can avoid it," he says, pivoting toward Aldrian. "We need to make for the city."

I look across the field. There's at least two miles separating us from the city and nothing to obstruct their sight along the way. "Won't they see us?"

"Not up close, if we hurry." He disintegrates the other two birds. "I have a friend there. She will hide us until they've passed through the city."

"But can't you—"

"Argue with me when we're safe," he interjects, nodding toward the city. "For now, we run."

NORIELLE

My lungs are heaving by the time we cross Aldrian's shadow. The great walls make me feel like a small child as I near them, and the metal spikes that line the top are nearly as tall as I am. Our feet skid onto the packed dirt road behind a caravan in almost perfect unison. Calden and I look up at each other, but before I ask what we're supposed to say to get in, the caravan rolls forward, and the guardswoman's attention moves to us.

"What's the hurry?" she asks.

"We were racing," Calden says. "Could you tell who won?"

The guardswoman's eyes narrow, then briefly glance over to me. "The girl."

I lift my head, as if bolstered, hoping that will help support Calden's guise.

"Felt like a tie," Calden grunts before laying on a polite tone. "We're here to visit my grandmother."

I glance down the road to see if the Hunters are out there, and vaguely, I catch sight of a pack of travelers on horseback off in the distance. *Is that them?*

"Didn't you just visit her, Cade?" the guardswoman asks.

Cade?

"Oh, is there a limit to how many times I can visit my grandmother now?" he says.

I feel the guardswoman's eyes settle on the back of my head. "And who is she?"

Calden stalls with a low hum. "Rielle from Atalia."

I hide my scowl. How obvious is *Rielle?* And Atalia? Like anyone would believe I'm from the capital in this oversized armor. Why did he have to go with that?

"She's a friend," Calden adds when the guard doesn't budge.

The woman stares at him, her expression souring the longer she looks. "Thought you told my daughter you didn't have time for *friends.*"

The way she says it tells me she means something far more than friends. *For Empyrean's sake, we don't have time for this.*

I glance at the riders. They are so close now that their faces are coming into view.

"Not in Aldrian," Calden says plainly.

The guardswoman's eyes lift to the coming riders. "Well, get in here."

We step through the first gate, and the guardswoman shuts it behind us. Then, before us, a second gate is opened to a city that looks nothing like it did from the outside.

Along the smooth road sit cobblestone buildings with shingles that look like they were carved from the mauve bark of the alela willows dispersed throughout the city. Children run through yards of verdant grass tossing disks and laughing, like they have no idea how dangerous the world is just outside these walls. In the center of it all stands a fountain that towers as high as the treetops with tiers shaped like birds in flight—one of Aldrian's other trademark features. Papa told me about how he used to sit on its edge, playing his lyre. It was one of his favorite places to perform before he joined the military.

"I saw the Hunters," I whisper once we are away from the crowd. "There were five. They're headed this way."

Calden turns us down a lane flanked by white houses. "Not a worry for my grandma."

I lean closer to him to keep my voice low. "Is that really who she is?"

"Might as well be," he answers. "Did I mention to you that I'm adopted?"

I flinch. "No. I thought you were the Lady Sovereign's son?"

"By adoption. She found me discarded by a lake and took me in herself. Her mistake." He winks at me then stops, gesturing with a hand toward a yard gnarled by weeds and overgrown bushes. "Here we are. Grandma's house. Always open for us to stay in, but may I warn you, she does charge a fair price."

My breath catches. "I . . . I haven't brought much money . . ."

"Oh no, friend, not money." He starts into the yard, having to push away the poking bush branches just to get through the walkway. "Stories. That's her fee."

"Make-believe or real?"

"Either will do. And I'm sure she's good and sick of mine, so I'm counting on you."

I offer him something between a smile and a wince, then his knuckles rap against the door. "Grandma! It's Cade!"

A few moments later, the door is flung open, revealing a stout woman with white locks flowing down her back. She smiles wide, a grin that convincingly passes her off as Calden's grandmother, despite him denying she's a true relation. She hugs him, eyes bulging as she notices me around his broad shoulder.

"Ah, there she is!" she says.

"Yes, the latest in my Bind."

The woman gives him an odd squint before beckoning us forward. "Come in, come in."

We enter a warm home full of sunlight and little trinkets. Every space is filled with something: a book, a statue, a fancy cup. Even her couch is covered with different patterned pillows and quilts. The woman locks the door two different ways, then turns to me with a spark in her eye that contends even with Milo's youth.

"Oh, my dear, what a relief to see you," she says with a hand over her heart, then she twists to face Calden. "You made it in time. I was so worried."

"Hardly." Calden tosses his gaze toward the woman's knickknacks. "She was already at the bottom of the lake when I got there. I wouldn't consider that *in time*."

She lays a hand on my shoulder. "Oh, you poor darling."

I almost tell her it was my fault, but she continues before I can make a sound.

"Norielle, isn't it?"

"That's me."

"Ila Halbrook," she returns, motioning for us to follow her deeper into her home. "Can I get you anything to eat?"

"Actually, Ila, we may have brought with us a problem," Calden interjects. "There's a Hunter unit headed into town."

Her hands stop just before the pantry door. "Oh, you have a way, don't you?"

"This is only the second time."

"How far?" Ila asks.

He looks at his Omen Mark. "In the market, by my guess."

"Oh, well, we still have some time then." She opens the pantry anyway and retrieves a wrapped loaf of bread, then shoves it into his arms. "Take this, and I'll get some soup started. Maybe it will be ready by the time they're finished snooping around, so I can get a proper meal in you two before nightfall."

I feel some of my tension slip away. This must be normal, if she's so calm. Or else she's pretending she's not afraid. Is she also a Warden? Wouldn't she be in danger, too?

Ila hums as she hobbles around her kitchen, laying out carrots and potatoes across the countertop. Calden grabs a pitcher of water and pours it into a pan, then hangs it over a burning hearth in the corner.

"How has your journey been, Norielle, dear?" Ila asks as she sinks a knife into one of the potatoes.

I try to think of a single word that could capture the experience, but the best I can think of is, "Eye-opening."

She chuckles. "Yes, I imagine so. Are you taking to everything all right?"

"She hasn't tried to kill me yet, if that says anything," Calden chimes in.

Ila casts him a look that I can't see through the screen of her hair. "And if she did, I'd hardly blame her."

"Funny." Calden scowls, tearing off a piece of bread from the loaf. He tosses it to me with hardly any warning, and I catch it on instinct alone. He rips another piece off and turns his back to us, wandering into the living room.

Ila laughs, then looks over to me. "So, besides that, how are you taking to everything?"

"All right, I guess," I say. "It still feels surreal."

Ila's head bobs as she starts chopping the carrots. "Yes, and don't expect that to change for a while. Where are you from again? I can't remember what Calden said on his way through. Auberfall?"

"Behria."

"Oh, Behria," she says, and I can't tell whether she doesn't recognize the name or if she's familiar with my hometown's reputation for thinking we're one of

El-Alam's favored towns. "Does your family know anything of where you are?"

I glance at Calden, realizing I haven't told him that Cassia knows yet. But no sense in lying.

"My sister does, but she's clever. We came up with a cover story and—"

"They're approaching the neighborhood," Calden interrupts, holding the Omen Mark up.

"Quick this time, aren't they?" Ila looks at her unfinished work. "Well, you know where to go. Take the bread with you, at least."

"Thank you, Ila," Calden says, taking back the remaining loaf. "Follow me, Norielle."

He leads me through a short hall and into a bedroom that is as cluttered as the rest of the house. Calden stoops down, drawing something on the center of the wood floor. A large ring of light pierces the boards, and as it fades, I see metal and hinges appearing. A trapdoor? I gawk at it as he pulls it open, revealing a ladder leading into a dark basement. He pulls his lantern from his belt, ignites it, and holds it out to me.

"You'll have to go first so I can seal it," he says.

I take the lantern and descend the ladder into an empty space that stretches about the length of Ila's house. Once my boots scrape the dirt, Calden tosses the bread to me, then steps onto the ladder. The door thumps shut, then he lays his hand against it and all trace of it vanishes. I hold the light up to look around the space. There is nothing down here except another ladder propped against one of the dirt walls. Just when I was getting comfortable with the idea of seeing real walls again . . .

"I take it the Hunters are coming inside the house?" I say as Calden reaches the bottom.

"They didn't do that in Behria?" he asks.

"Not that I remember."

"It happens quite often here, but Ila is a master at dealing with them. She wasn't made a safehouse keeper for nothing." He sits down, and I throw the bread back to him, having little interest in it now. He catches it, then pats the ground like I'm supposed to sit next to him. I don't. He looks away, tearing at the bread again. "So, you told your sister."

"I couldn't help it."

Calden's lips form a line. In his silence, the muted *thump* of Ila's knife continues like nothing is wrong.

"I know I shouldn't have," I add. "I couldn't just leave without telling her the truth. Telling *someone*."

Calden pats the ground again, and finally it registers why. We need to keep our voices down, and I'm not helping from where I am. I sit about an arm's length away.

"How much did you tell her?" he asks.

"Hardly anything. She'd seen you that night, so I told her what you were and why you came, and that I had to leave with you. That was it."

Air billows from his nose, but his tone is measured. "Would she have told anyone else?"

"No. No one else—"

A muffled pounding interrupts me—someone banging at the door. We both still, turning our noses toward the ceiling. Footsteps follow, and I can just make out the conversation overhead.

"You see any new faces recently?" a Hunter asks.

"Oi, with these eyes?" Ila jests. "Not lately. But what's the face you're looking for?"

"A young woman from Behria traveling with a man." My heart stops.

"The girl has long, brown hair. Skin's fair and freckled. Hazel eyes. Eighteen. Not much to go on for the male, besides that he was last seen by Lake Daleia with the female. He has a sturdy build and light, jaw-length hair."

Calden and I hold each other's gazes, and I try to apologize with my eyes. Why would Cas tell them? What did they do to make her speak?

"And what's the trouble?" Ila's tone is as casual as before.

"We received a report from the steward of Behria. His son witnessed some odd behavior from a resident just before she ran away, armed."

I exhale but my fists clench tightly enough to shake. *Landon.* I'd almost forgotten about my interaction with him just before leaving town.

I should have known.

"The Behrian girl is suspected to be consorting with a Warden that we've been trailing for some time."

"Aye, I see," Ila answers. "Well, I'm sorry. I don't get out much, as my nasty yard might suggest. I haven't seen them, but I do hope you find them quickly."

Heavy footsteps clomp over our heads. They pace through the room above us, and the wardrobe's hinges whimper. A rustle from the clothes. Then footsteps again. "Clear," a different voice says. Someone else repeats it, then the footsteps head back down the hall.

"No need to worry, ma'am," a woman says. "We've got units headed everywhere we know to look. We will find them."

"Bless you," Ila says, and I wonder if it makes her stomach turn to say it.

Their voices become too muffled for me to distinguish through the floor, and eventually there is silence again.

"Let's give it a bit longer before we go up. Until they're farther away," Calden says, eyeing his Omen Mark.

"Do you think they talked to my family?" I whisper.

"No way to know for sure, but it sounds like the steward's son gave them what they needed. The Hunters must have traced me to Behria and interrogated the steward." He looks at me, seeming to read my anxiety by my grimace. "As long as your sister knew what to say to plead ignorance and no one else knew anything, I'm sure they are just fine."

"Cas is the smoothest liar in the world—besides Ila, maybe," I say, partially to reassure myself. "And I know she wouldn't tell Mum or Milo."

"Milo," Calden repeats, and I realize I've never told him my brother's name. Whatever he thinks of it, he returns to the topic at hand. "I trust they are well, then. There would be no need to press them for information if the steward's son readily gave it."

My eyes burn. "I'm sure he loved that."

"An enemy?"

"You could say that."

Calden ponders this a moment before leaning his head against the dirt wall. "The real trouble now is going to be getting out of the city."

"You must be afraid of them."

"No," he says, almost too quickly. "I can fight them if I must, but that's the problem. The more we fight the Hunters, the more we prove them right about us. That we're hostile. Violent. Untrustworthy. Servants of Ta'Nathel. The less we fight, the less aggressive we seem."

"Does it even matter at this point? They're going to hunt you either way."

His mouth opens, but then shuts like he's genuinely considering my question.

"Wouldn't it be better to try and intimidate them?"

He gives a small huff. "No. Fear never leads to trust." He stands, looking up the ladder. "Come on. It should be safe now."

CALDEN

Steam hisses around the steel lid of Ila's pot, filling the room with a savory aroma that promises a fully satisfied stomach. Over the soft bubble of simmering soup, Ila's voice carries from the spare room as she invites Norielle to wear any of the clothes in the guest wardrobe. One of Ila's favorite things, having a new person to dress in clothes she's sewn herself.

Norielle's responses are too quiet to make out, but a moment later, Ila's voice rings from the doorway. "The washroom is behind the middle door here, dear. Please, use anything and everything you like. It's all in there for you."

I smile. Ila's always so nice to new people. It's the ones she gets used to that need to watch out for her fierce side. But even then, she's as loving as a grandmother should be—even her rebukes smack like a kiss on the forehead.

"She's a darling," Ila comments as she shuffles into the kitchen.

I lower my gaze to my hands folded on the alela wood tabletop. She isn't wrong, but she knows better than to initiate such conversations with me, especially about a member of my Bind.

Steel clangs as Ila gives the soup a quick stir before returning the lid and settling in the chair beside me. Her warm hand lies against my arm, nudging me to meet her gaze.

"Any trouble with the curse?" she asks under her breath.

I shake my head. "Thankfully not. I've been holding myself down with a Snare Ward every night, just to be safe. I don't want to relive what happened with Alani."

Ila's chin tucks, like she's swallowing my answer. "That's wise."

"It's been months," I say, turning to look at the covered window. "I'm beginning to wonder if it's finally over, or if I'm just overdue for another episode."

"Does she know about it?"

Norielle . . .

My body sinks against the chair. "I haven't told her yet, and I plan not to. Not until we have Alani with us." *If then, even.* I meet her concerned gaze. "I just don't want to frighten her away from her destiny. But I'm being careful. As careful as I can."

Ila frowns, the rare expression smoothing her laugh lines. "Maybe you should rest here for a few days. It may help to wait out the Hunters, anyway."

My impatience crawls along my skin like ants. There's no waiting them out, but Empyrean knows I am exhausted. The flight to retrieve Norielle was enough, but having to explain everything and be twice as on guard with the worry that my curse will awaken in front of her . . .

"Truly, I wish you could stay a week or two," Ila says, her tone lifting with her smile. "I'd like to make her a dress for her induction ceremony."

"Oh, you know my mother is probably already working on one herself," I say. "She's always delighted when a girl is brought in."

"Well, maybe I'll start something anyway. Perhaps there will be another occasion to dress her up for. She's so lovely, isn't she?"

My fingertips drum across the table. Why must she do this? And right on the tail of our discussion about my curse?

"Sure, the next induction ceremony. There's sure to be another soon. The Bind has one more member to gain after her."

Ila's humor drains a fraction, like she fully hoped I'd jump in to say how very lovely indeed my new Bind member is, and how lucky I am to get to know her.

As if I have any place having such thoughts.

She sighs. "Yes, there's an idea. I'll ask her if she'll let me take her measurements tomorrow."

The washroom door opens, and Norielle steps out with her damp locks dripping onto her fresh blouse and a long skirt fluttering with her strides. I jerk my gaze away, not wishing to stare, but Ila nearly knocks over her chair as she stands to admire her artistry displayed on Norielle.

"You'd think I'd made them just for you," Ila says.

Norielle indulges her with a girlish swirl that seems to reel my focus back to her, like it or not.

Lovely, Ila called her.

She's beyond it.

Ila's satisfied hum warms the atmosphere. "I hope you're feeling better. You look so."

"I am. Thank you," Norielle answers. A rosy stain coats her cheeks when her attention shifts to me.

I give her a quick smile before pretending an itch on my hand distracts me.

"The soup is about ready," Ila says, gathering three bowls from the cupboard. The ceramic dishes clank against her countertop, and I rise to do the serving for her, so I have something to do besides thinking about dragging this girl—who seems far more innocent without her armor and sword—into a life of constant danger.

"I hope Calden told you the charge for staying here," Ila says, setting the table.

"I have," I say before Norielle can answer. "In fact, she's agreed to pay the cost."

"Ah-ah-ah, my boy," Ila chides. "Two rooms means two stories. One each. Don't think you're getting out of this."

"You've heard all of mine." I carry two steaming bowls to the table by my fingertips. "What more do I have to tell?"

"Surely there's a story in you worth repeating—one Norielle hasn't heard."

Norielle smiles at me, a curiosity twinkling in her eyes that couldn't be denied even if telling a story would end me.

Besides, it's hopeless to argue with Ila. She's as stubborn as she is kind.

"Fine, fine," I give in.

I set the final bowl down, and we all join together at the table like a small family. The late sunlight dances on the fluttering curtains beside the table, a mild breeze wafting the steam over our bowls. For a while, Ila presses us no further, letting us enjoy nearly searing our tastebuds on her soup. But eventually, her expectant gaze finds its way to me and stays there.

I lay down my spoon. "I suppose I could tell you more of how I came to be adopted by the Lady Sovereign."

Norielle and Ila both nod.

I tap the side of my bowl. "Well, before the Sovereign passed away in battle, my mother and he longed to have a child. But for several years, my mother was barren. They worried there wouldn't be an heir to replace them someday, so every night, they and the Warden Elders gathered to pray that El-Alam would provide."

Norielle's spoon stills as she listens, so intent I almost lose my place.

"Then, one day," I say, as I recall where I was. "She went for a walk in the woods up north, where a lake lay, secluded. It was her favorite place to roam whenever she needed a break from the citadel."

"And she found you," Norielle says while I sneak a spoonful of soup.

I nod. "I was swaddled up, lying in a basket. Not a single trace of anyone to explain how I'd gotten there. My mother believed El-Alam had put me there himself, an answer to her heart's desire to have a child. She adopted me and declared me the divinely supplied heir before all the Wardens. Ironically, a few months later, she conceived my sister. And the girl has hated me ever since." I chuckle at my partial joke, then jab my spoon in Norielle's direction while she's still staring at me like I've told a fairy tale. "Your turn, friend."

Norielle stirs her soup awhile, and every whisk seems to deepen my curiosity. Over the last few days, she's done much asking and little speaking otherwise. I've hardly had the chance to learn about her unless I prodded her for information, and I didn't want to seem overly invested. But at least here, Ila's to blame.

"I'm not sure my stories could really compare to the ones you hear," Norielle says to Ila. "This is my first real adventure."

"Not so," I say, suddenly remembering a detail she slipped to me in an early conversation. "The lake. Didn't you say it came alive once before? You never did share more about that."

Norielle's spoon slips from her fingers, color draining from her face.

My lips curl inward, sensing that was entirely the wrong question to pose.

"That's not a good story." Her vocal cords sound clipped.

I strangle my curiosity, only for Ila's to betray her.

"Did it hurt someone you love, dear?" Ila's tone is compassionate at least, but I still shoot her a frustrated look. She misses it.

Norielle seems to shrivel in her chair. "My father."

I inhale, drawing both their eyes to me. So that's what happened to him. Not the war at all.

Ila's eyes question me, and I give her the subtlest nod to affirm what she's guessing—Norielle's father was more than hurt by the lake.

It killed him.

"Oh, my dear, I'm so sorry," Ila says, stroking Norielle's hand.

Norielle shakes her head. "It's fine. It's . . . I just don't like talking about it."

I push my soup away. Though a bit remains, I'm too sickened by what I've done to this otherwise calm moment.

She said she'd seen it come alive, so she must have witnessed it—watched her own father die.

And yet she was brave enough to challenge the lake again? Just to know?

No wonder El-Alam chose her to join the Wardens.

I fill my lungs with the intent to release my air into an apology, but Ila steals my chance.

"Well, dear, you must be so exhausted. That's quite enough of my chattering. I think I'll go wash up myself and leave you two to get settled."

We both thank her as she gathers our dishes. She discards them in the washbasin. Then she turns, giving me a look that feels like an unspoken order, before bidding

Norielle goodnight and disappearing behind her bed-room door.

But what does she want? Me to keep pressing Norielle over what she obviously doesn't wish to discuss? Or is Ila expecting me to somehow make her feel better after the pain I've stirred in her?

I turn to Norielle. She sits twisting a clump of her nearly dried hair. She glances at me, an unreadable emotion in her eyes. But it seems to request I ask her no more questions.

"My apologies," I say. "I didn't realize."

"You don't have to apologize," she says, letting the lock of hair fall back with the others. "At least you believe me about what happened."

"No one else did?"

Her lips twitch. "Cas and Milo did . . . or at least, mostly did. But no one else. Not even my mother. She thought I hallucinated."

"Hallucinated?" I echo, feeling a pang in my chest. "Are they that set on believing the curse can't reach them?"

"That afraid."

The smallness of her voice sends a hot wave through my body. What a wretched thing, to witness such a horror and not even be believed about it.

Where was she when it happened? I want to ask, but I dare not push her any deeper into the waters I pulled her from.

"You are incredibly brave, Norielle. You know that?" I say instead.

Her gaze turns glossy, the opposite of what I'd anticipated. "I'm not. That was desperation."

"To be believed?"

Her lungs fill and deflate before she lifts her eyes to me. "Even if only by myself."

"I wish I'd been faster," I say. "I could have reassured you."

She falls silent a moment before meeting my gaze with a tiny smile. "You shouldn't be so hard on yourself. You traveled thirteen days, spent two nights awake, and swam to the bottom of a living lake to save a stranger. And you *did*. That's incredible. I should have died, but you prevented that." She looks at her wrists, where the marks from the lake's weeds have finally healed. "Now I have a chance to do more than prove to people that I'm right. I can actually help them."

My brows draw together. "And how is that not brave?"

She opens her mouth like she might refute me, but nothing comes of it besides a deep look into my eyes. Every thread of responsibility in me urges me to turn away, to stop being so friendly with her, and yet, I can't seem to help it. There's something settling about her, especially here, that makes me feel more comfortable than I should.

That in itself is enough of a danger, and yet—

"I'm sorry," Norielle says, shuddering. "I really am exhausted. I should go to sleep."

"Yes," I say too hastily, and she flinches. An awkward laugh jitters out, just to make it worse. "You should. I was just thinking, I ought to do the same."

The sunset through the window illuminates the red flush on her cheeks, and my heart pinches. What am I doing to this poor girl? Dragging her to the Wardens? Stealing her from her family? I should just leave her here and send another to take her home. I could claim El-Alam revoked the call. That he decided to spare her this difficult life. Why shouldn't I? Someone else will be called, anyway. Someone who might seem less . . . innocent.

I blink the temptation away, realizing we've yet to stand, and she's still waiting for me to move. And of course she is. I'm the leader.

I rise, walking to douse the candles amid Ila's overly decorated shelves. I pinch the final flame before looking at her again, and she's still watching me. But her gaze darts away.

"You'll be safe here," I promise. "I'm just in the room over if you need me, and Ila knows a thing or two about wards herself. You still have that Omen Mark, yes?"

She checks her wrist, holding it toward the fading light from the window. "Yes."

"As long as it doesn't brighten, you have no cause to worry." I pivot toward the hall. "I'll see you in the morning."

"See you then," she returns, but as I step away, I wonder if she will.

Or if my heart will have persuaded me to leave her behind.

NORIELLE

When I wake, the Omen Mark is dark red and pointing toward the market. Just as it was last night. I sit up, pushing the heavy quilt onto my lap, and look about my temporary room as I reorient myself to how I got here. Everything still feels like an odd dream, from the moment I paddled onto Lake Daleia to the moment I laid my head against Ila's feather pillow.

I shift so my feet dangle over the bed and check the Bind Mark to see if Calden has emerged from his room yet. The thin arrow points outside the house.

No. Not just outside. Toward the market.

I hold both my wrists up, comparing the angle of each point of the two tracking marks.

They're a perfect match.

I gasp, my bare feet hitting the cool floor. *The Hunters. They've taken him.*

"Where's Ila?" I whisper to myself as I dash across the small room. I swing my door open, finding both her and Calden's doors already flung wide. My heart stutters. *Empyrean, have they taken her, too?*

I jog toward the kitchen, praying I'll find Ila there, but when I round the wall, my feet slide to a stop.

A man sits at the table, haloed in light from the window.

I blink, straining to see him through the sun's glare. The tips of his wavy dark hair hang just over his strong brows, and an olive doublet covers his tawny skin—not a fleck of armor on him.

He gives me a blank stare as he sips his tea, but a slight smirk rises to his lips when he lowers the cup, revealing his neatly trimmed beard.

I reach for my sword, but of course, it's not there. My hands ball into fists, ready to defend myself against someone I can only assume is a Hunter who's already captured Calden and Ila but rendered me a small enough threat to get comfortable.

Except now I notice Ila in her living room, straightening a new trinket on her shelf—a small stone statue of a pine tree. She smiles as she turns around. "Oh, I hope you'll keep it."

It takes me several long seconds to realize what she means. My nightgown. *Oh.*

My face warms. I'm standing *in a nightgown* in front of a strange man.

And he's still smirking at me.

"Where's Calden?" I ask Ila, resisting the urge to flee.

"In the market," she says. "Would you like some tea? There's still hot water left."

"Why is he in the market? I thought he—" I stop because I don't know what I can and can't say in front of this man. Who is he, anyway?

"He's shopping," the man says, with a voice that's somehow both smooth and hoarse at once. "Isn't that what people do in the market?"

I shoot him a sharp look, but a shiver in my spine when our eyes lock keeps me from speaking.

"People think he's merely my grandson, dear," Ila says. "They've known him a long time. No one would suspect him of anything."

I lift my wrist with the Omen Mark. "But the Hunters are out there."

"You're not supposed to have that," the man interjects, stroking his beard.

"Calden drew it on me."

"Wasn't supposed to. And the Hunters aren't in the market." He lifts his own Omen Mark. "They're outside the gates."

My brows dip.

"He'll be back soon," Ila says, passing me to reach for the kettle. She carries it to the man at the table and refills his cup. He smiles at her, and for a moment, he looks familiar, but I'm not sure why.

"This is Elias," Ila says, but the name doesn't summon any memories. "He's one of our scouts. He's here to see Calden."

I nod at him.

"And Elias, this is Norielle. As you know, another member in Calden's Bind."

"He's always been spoiled," he says, a wisp of steam streaking over one of his dark eyes. "Nice nightgown. Did Ila make it?"

I'm still too alarmed by his presence to think of anything snappy to say back, so I decide to be curt instead. "She did."

We exchange a silent stare before I become too uncomfortable and turn into the hall, regretting that I came out without dressing myself in something proper. Inside my room, I find a pair of pants and a dusky blouse that fits decently when tucked in, then I strap on my sword so I feel less vulnerable with this *scout* in the house.

How did he get by the Hunters? Or was he already waiting for Calden somewhere else in town?

I pick the knots from my hair and tame it with a comb, then I drag myself back to the kitchen. The man, Elias, still sits at the table, now accompanied by Ila. Their conversation quiets as they notice me, and Elias's brows lift. But he keeps whatever he's thinking to himself.

"Keep all of that too, dear," Ila says to me, motioning toward my clothes. "I'll give you an extra bag if you need one."

"Thanks," I say, but my eyes are on her front door, partially because I'm still not convinced Calden is safe, but also because even if he is, I'm not sure I like being here without him here to act as a buffer between me and these strangers. Especially when the newest one doesn't seem to know when to stop staring at someone. *What's his problem?*

"Heard from the Hunters you were stirring up trouble in Behria before you ran off," he says from behind his cup. "What were you up to?"

My gaze darts to Ila, but she's looking at the table.

"That's none of your business," I say.

"Everything is my business," he says. "I'll just go back and ask the Hunters instead if you won't fess up yourself."

"Why would you talk to them?" I ask.

"To know *their* business so I can help people like you stay safe."

I swallow. Why can't Calden be here right now?

"What'd you do?" Elias asks again, this time without his smirk.

I take a deep breath, and the air rattles from my nose. "I wasn't trying to cause trouble. The lake there, Lake Daleia, it's alive. I was only trying to warn people."

I don't know how I expected him to react, but the continued blank look on his face isn't it. "Did they believe you?"

"Not particularly."

"So, you jumped in to prove them wrong."

Ila's attention moves to me now. Her gray eyes seem to tremble.

"To prove to myself I hadn't lost my mind," I correct him, even if he is partially right.

Elias runs his finger down the handle of his cup. "How long were you under before Calden fished you out?"

"I don't know. I was unconscious when he reached me."

"You lucked out," Elias says, in a slightly friendlier tone. "I was there at the citadel when he received the vision. Didn't tell anybody what he saw then, but he left within the hour. Guess he knew where you were headed." He scratches his chin, then looks back to me. "You know, he wasn't supposed to tell you that you're a member of his Bind."

"Why not?"

He scoots his chair back. "Because it's supposed to be a surprise, Nori."

Nori? How dare he—

"I don't like surprises." I layer my tone with darkness, so he knows I'm including him in that.

He chuckles. "Maybe you should learn to."

My face warms as he turns his back, muttering, "Gotta trim those bushes," then he's out the door. I whirl back to Ila, looking for something from her, but I don't know what.

"That boy, always likes to stir a bit of trouble," she grumbles, before looking to me with a sympathetic grin. "Calden will be back anytime now, dear. How about I fix us a nice treat while we wait?"

I peel my eyes away from the door again and push my smile back on for Ila's sake. "Sure, that sounds nice," I say, but as I turn around, something registers. Something that my sheer shock dumbed me to. Ila said Elias is a scout and that he's here to see Calden. But why? What news has he brought with him that couldn't wait for us to reach the citadel?

CALDEN

I stroll along the road toward Ila's neighborhood, pleased that for the first time in over two weeks, I don't have to hurry. It's the perfect day not to. The sky is lightly veiled by clouds, diffusing the sunlight so it scatters across the white buildings. A slight chill breathes through the trees, carrying a mixed aroma of soulcast flowers and distant rain. A storyteller's tale dances over from below the fountain, tempting me to turn back and revel in it for a while.

But I turn the corner, waving to an old man in his yard. We've never spoken, but he always waves. So, I always return it and try not to wonder what it would be like to grow old in a nice place like Aldrian, enjoying beautiful days like this without anything better to do than wave at people passing by. It's foolish for me to think of it, considering who I am.

I reach Ila's lane, and all my thoughts shatter at the sight of a figure in her yard. He crouches by the bushes, something sharp gleaming in his hand. A Hunter?

I rush a few strides closer, squinting.

Wait. I know that dark tousle of hair. What is *he* doing here?

When he doesn't seem to notice me, I creep the rest of the way to Ila's yard and sneak up behind him.

"*Lias*," I blurt, hoping to startle him, but he doesn't even flinch.

He finishes trimming the branch before standing, a sly look on his face. "Calden," he says, resting the hedge clippers against his shoulder. "Figures you'd bring the Hunters here."

I glance around, double-checking that we are alone. "Wasn't part of the plan."

"Met your new Bind member. She seemed pretty worried about you. Maybe you should've kissed her goodbye."

A hot breath fills my lungs. "You know how inappropriate that would be."

"Tell the girl that." Mischief sparks in his eyes. "Then tell her to come talk to me."

I scowl at him, though I doubt he means it. He's never slowed down for anyone, even with all the girls from the cities to the citadel clamoring for his attention. He's just trying to irritate me, and lucky for him, it's working. "Why are you here? Besides to be a pain."

He looks around, his expression turning serious. "I have a word from Seer Josiah."

"Let's hear it."

"He had a vision about her." He gestures toward the house.

"Norielle?"

He nods. "He saw her fall into the hands of the Blood Wardens."

I flinch. "What? Where?"

"He couldn't tell, besides that it was within the passages. Said you weren't around."

My knees lock at the thought of Blood Wardens dragging Norielle away into some foreign darkness to be used as a ritual sacrifice or, worse, converted into one of them. Her soul would be tainted forever, never to see the Empyrean.

"No." My back straightens so I stand a half-foot taller than him. "I would never let that happen."

"Looks like there's a chance your best intentions aren't going to be enough," he says. "Might be smart to think about enlisting someone's help."

His smirk tells me he means himself.

My jaw clenches at the thought, though normally, I'd readily bring him along. "I'm not looking for your help this time."

"No one ever is, yet they always thank me later."

"I have Alani. She's meeting us in the havens."

"I'm going that way anyway, after I run up to Boldor to warn them about the extra Hunters you've lured in," he says, gesturing toward the upper city. "Just give me a day. Besides, you know you should take extra precautions. Especially considering your *little problem*." His brows lift, as if to be sure I don't miss what he's referring to. *My curse.*

A sour taste coats my tongue. That would be *exactly* how such a fate could come to pass. If my unconscious hands didn't kill her first. "Let me think about it."

He raises a brow. "What's there to think about?"

"Whether or not I can put up with you."

He snorts, surely noticing my unusual degree of apprehension, but I wave him off before he can say anything else and head for the door. His clippers snap another branch behind me, promising at least a few minutes to think before he expects my answer. I walk inside to the savory scent of cheese-battered biscuits wafting from the table. Norielle sits in the living room, threading a ribbon from her blouse through her fingers. She drops it, her shoulders falling when she sees me.

"You're back," she says, almost rising before she pulls herself back into her seat.

An unwanted sense of delight at her relief bucks against my need to feel no more about her than anyone else in my Bind.

"Of course," I say, as though I hadn't considered abandoning her here last night. "I was just replenishing my supplies."

Her thumb rubs the Bind Mark. "I thought the Hunters had you."

"Empyrean, no. I apologize for the fright. I intended to be back before you woke." I fling my bag onto the table next to the biscuits. "I take it you met Elias?"

"I did."

I wait, expecting her to say something more about him, and hoping despite myself that it isn't good. But she says nothing else.

"He's a scout," I add to fill the silence.

"Ila told me."

I saunter to the living room and sink into the worn cushions of the chair across from her.

Norielle shifts toward me, the subtle glow from the covered window brightening one side of her face. "She also said he had a message for you. Is something wrong?"

My gaze escapes to my folded hands, and I debate if I should share or not. But it seems the fair thing to do. "The Seer had a vision. He's seen a potential outcome of us somehow becoming separated along the way to the citadel, and you falling into the hands of Blood Wardens."

"*What?*"

I force neutrality into my tone as I surrender to the course of action I know is best. "But Elias has offered to come with us to help avoid that potential future."

Her lips fasten together.

"He's a skilled fighter and has helped me many times before. I think it would be wise to bring him along, just to be safe."

There's a long pause before she finally speaks. "And that will keep it from happening?"

"It might. Even the foreseen future can be avoided, so long as one alters what they are doing in the present. What Seer Josiah sees is usually the outcome of continuing to do things the same as we are now. Not to say that the future is always changed by a shift in the present, but we can try, at the least." I smile, hoping to bring the color back to her face. "Dare I say it, if anyone is well suited to help keep Blood Wardens away from you, it would be Elias. He knows the passages better than even myself."

Every breath seems to enter and leave her with effort, but before she can respond, the front door bursts open. Elias's worn boots clomp into the common room, a vexing smirk fixed on his face as he glances toward Norielle and back to me.

"I need to head out if I'm gonna make it to Boldor today. Tell me how fast I need to be," he says.

A dismissal rises in my throat, but I swallow it. I need him. Like it or not. "Be back by tomorrow night. We'll leave the next morning."

For once, his smirk evolves into a genuine smile. "Good decision." He looks about the room. "Where's Ila?"

"Taking a nap," Norielle says, nodding toward the basket on the table. "She wore herself out making biscuits."

He swipes one from the plate, chomping it as he retrieves a small satchel—his lyre—from the corner of the room. "Someone tell her I said bye, and her yard is clear."

"I'll tell her," I say.

He adds another bag to his back. "Oh, and Cal," he says, flicking his gaze toward Norielle. "You ruined her surprise." The door shuts behind him before I can question what he means.

I look to Norielle for an answer.

"He said you weren't supposed to tell me that I'm in your Bind."

Great. And he'll be sure to tell on me to Mother, too.

I rise to lock the door behind Elias.

"How can he talk to the Hunters without being discovered?" Norielle asks.

I grab a biscuit on my way back to the common room but turn toward the window instead of my chair. Through the old glass, I see Elias striding along the lane in a near gallop. "He's an unsuspecting bard, or that's what everyone along his route believes."

"A bard? Where is he from?"

"Bridgewood, I think." I let the curtain fall. "Honestly, I can't quite remember. It's hard to keep track of so many people. Why?"

Norielle shrugs. "He just seems familiar."

"I believe his route leads him toward Behria. Perhaps he's made an appearance there?"

She hums thoughtfully, but our conversation collapses back into silence. I let it linger awhile, until the anxiety of Seer Josiah's declaration creeps over me like a cold tide. I shake myself before I get lost in the undertow and straighten.

"Since we're stuck here, what do you say I teach you a ward or two?"

She perks up. "I thought I can't use them until I've been inducted?"

"Doesn't hurt to start memorizing them, does it?"

Her smile spreads as she rises, a youthfulness filling her voice. "I'd love to!"

The darkness in my spirit seems to recede behind her enthusiasm. "Have a seat," I say, motioning toward the table. "I'll gather some parchments."

16

NORIELLE

"Not quite," Calden says for what must be the fourth time. His politeness and patience with my inability to draw a *leaf* with the proper form and angle is astonishing.

I set the pen to the page again. Its pungent ink fills my nose as I take a deep inhale and try another leaf. Calden's watchful gaze makes my hand tremble. Why is that so intimidating? It's not like I've never been hovered over while taking a test. Mum was horrible about that—

"Perhaps you should try tracing mine a couple more times," Calden says, and I cringe.

I thought this one was going *well*.

I cross it out, cheeks burning. All my life, I've been called a quick learner, and here I am, fumbling like I've never held a pen before.

"I'm sorry," I say, laying down the pen. "I've never been good at drawing."

"It's more about muscle memory than art." He takes the pen to draw another Purification Ward. The two-leafed sprout matches the first as if it were a stamp, not an illustration. He sets the pen before me again, giving an encouraging nod toward the paper.

"It has to be exact?" I ask.

"Not necessarily, but it's best to practice with precision, lest you find yourself in a hurry when the time comes to use it."

"It's a *Purification* Ward," I say, giving him a weary look. "If I'm in a hurry to draw this, then I should probably be drawing something else."

He laughs. "That's fair."

"Where did these symbols come from, anyway?" I ask to give my frustration a chance to dwindle before I try again.

"From El-Alam, of course," he says, buying into my distraction with an enthused smile. "They are the written form of the Empyreal language. It's scribed in glyphs rather than letters like ours. So, this"—he taps his perfect illustration at the top of the page—"is the glyph for *purify*."

His explanation tickles my memory. Now that he's said it, I do faintly recall Papa mentioning something about ancient Seers penning the wards as El-Alam revealed them. But he hadn't said they were part of an entire language.

"Can you speak it?" I ask.

Calden tilts his head.

"The Empyreal language?" I clarify.

He turns toward his shoulder, hiding a bashful smile. "I'm not very good at it."

"I wouldn't know the difference." I lean to send him a pleading look with wide eyes and tilted brows, the same look I'd give Papa to earn his favor. "How does 'purify' sound in the Empyreal language?"

His lips remain sealed and gaze averted for a long moment before he looks back to me. *"Katharis-defae."*

The pleasant sound of his accent caressing the strange phrase tickles my ears, and the corners of my mouth tease upward.

"Su es perskélro," he adds, the words rolling off his tongue with only the slightest hiccup to denote his discomfort in using them.

"What does that mean?" I ask.

"It means, *you are persistent.*" He chuckles, then he gestures toward the pen. "Now, let's put that persistence back to work."

A temptation to ask what else he knows how to say swells in my chest, but I take up the pen again. I set it to the page, only for Ila's bedroom door to suddenly open. Calden jumps, swiping the paper from underneath my pen and stuffing it beneath the empty parchments. Before I can ask what's wrong, he snatches the pen from my hand and shoots me a cautious look.

Ila lumbers into the kitchen.

"Have a nice nap, Miss Ila?" he asks.

"Oi . . . I slept a bit longer than I meant to." She turns toward her kettle, and I question Calden with my eyes.

His strained smile reminds me of Milo, when my brother was up to something.

Was he not supposed to be teaching me wards?

"Where'd my boy go?" Ila asks, looking about her home.

"He had to deliver the news about the Hunters to Boldor," Calden says.

A frown twists Ila's lips, and I can't help but wonder why she'd be disappointed. If anything, I expected her to be relieved that Elias left.

"He asked me to tell you goodbye, and that he finished trimming the bushes for you," Calden adds. "He'll be back tomorrow evening."

"Good." Ila fills her kettle and sets it over the hearth. She stokes the flames, then turns with a fist bunched against her hip. "I haven't seen him in an age—if my yard wasn't enough proof. He does plan to stay the night?"

"Yes, but he'll be leaving with us the following morning," Calden says. "Or rather, with Norielle."

Ila and I both jolt.

"I'm going to go up ahead of you," Calden directs his next statement to me. "I don't think it's wise for us to be seen in the town together again, not by the Hunters. And besides, I'd like to scope out the ravine before we head into it."

"The ravine?" I echo. *Why is everything he's saying right now a surprise?* "The Dûnori Ravine?"

"Yes. That's where the nearest entrance is to the Wardens' secret passages. The way to the citadel."

"In the *Dûnori Ravine?*" I emphasize. "Where the *fel-lions* are*?*"

"It's quite a good place for an entrance—a place most people would avoid."

My body turns rigid. The lionlike Accursed beasts inside the ravine are the reason Aldrian has two walls lined with sharp spikes. The fellions' roars are said to throw a man through the air, and their claws are sharper than swords.

"They won't be out," Calden reassures me just as my vision starts to blur. "They only hunt at dawn and dusk. If you arrive there by late morning, they'll have just gone back to sleep. And Empyrean forbid they come after you, Elias will keep you safe."

My temples throb. *We're running from Hunters into fellion territory to reach passages where Blood Wardens want to capture me?*

He warned me it would be dangerous all the way to the citadel. Maybe I should have taken him at his word.

"I thought I had to stay with you," I counter. "You mentioned us getting separated . . ."

"That's before Elias was factored in," Calden says, though I don't miss his hesitation. "It won't be for long. I'll be in the ravine waiting for you two to arrive. There's no chance with all the Hunters about that the Blood Wardens would be around, anyway. They don't dare travel into towns the way we do."

I turn to Ila, as if in all her age and wisdom, she might dispute Calden's plan. She pours her tea, nodding all the while.

My insides squirm. I have to travel *alone* with that scout?

"And you really trust Elias?" I ask. "He'll get me past the Hunters and to the ravine safely?"

Calden's gaze dodges me. *Is that a no?*

"With my life." His tone is convincing despite his reaction. "As I said, he's a skilled fighter, and he knows the routes well. I've pulled him off task for aid many times. He's reliable, if a bit unpleasant sometimes."

I study him awhile, trying to discern the significance of his hesitation. But when I can't tell, I switch methods.

"Ila said he likes to cause trouble."

"She isn't wrong," Calden starts, but Ila speaks over him.

"Not *real* trouble." She sits beside me with her tea; its peppery scent spurring an itch in my nose. "He's a bit of an instigator, yes, but he's got a good heart."

Instigator. That sounds like someone I know.

Landon's face dissolves from my mind as Ila's soft fingertips brush my wrist.

"You'll be safe with him," she assures me. "And Calden is right. It is best you two aren't seen in town together. It will be much easier for you to pass through the gates with Elias."

My mouth seals in submission, recognizing I'm outnumbered, and I cast my gaze toward the tree figurine on Ila's shelf—a gift Elias brought her, I'm assuming. He's thoughtful, at least. Maybe my embarrassment over the way we met has caused me to judge him too harshly.

Calden and Ila carry on a conversation, discussing various Wardens Ila has seen recently, and my attention turns back home. What is Mum doing now? Did Landon tell her I ran off with a suspected Warden? Did she find out through murmurs in town? Is she praying for my life, thinking I've run off to serve Ta'Nathel, still stubbornly oblivious to the fact that the Wardens serve El-Alam Himself?

Questions—the only thing my mind seems to be filled with lately—surge until finally, the screech of Ila's chair against the floorboards pulls me out of my head. Ila stands, excusing herself to use the washroom, and I remember Calden's eagerness to hide the paper with the wards.

"Is this something else you're not supposed to be doing?" I whisper, indicating the pages with a nod. "Teaching me wards?"

"Mother is against it," he says, rolling the pages together to further hide the evidence. "It's not the *official* order of things. But I think it's a waste of time not to teach you if there's a moment for it. You have to learn, so it might as well be now."

I check the hall. "But Ila would tell."

"She'd tell someone, and that someone would tell my mother."

He must mean Elias.

"And you don't think I would?"

His smile withers.

A laugh catches in my throat. "I won't. But I can't promise she won't find out if she asks me. I'm a terrible liar."

"Poor planning, then, on my part." He chuckles, and for a moment, he holds my gaze with a smile that almost makes me feel like we can be friends, not just a leader and his Bind member.

But then he stands, snatching up the pen and parchment.

"I better put these away before Ila gets curious," he says. "We'll try this again some other time, should we have the chance."

CALDEN

The familiar sensation of cool ink against skin slows my heart rate as I draw a Conjuration Mark upon my palm. The simple symbol takes only a few quick strokes to complete, and in seconds, its swordlike image sinks into my skin like a tattoo, never to wear or smear until fully used up or dismissed by my own willing.

I hold my arms toward the dim candlelight on the table, inspecting the array of wards I've added in preparation for the morrow. Satisfied, I slip my pen into the snug leather loop on my belt and cast an unwitting gaze down the darkened hall. Norielle and Ila turned in over two hours ago, and not a creak has come from their rooms since.

My eyelids are heavy at the thought of rest, and yet, I remain seated on the couch, as if turned to stone by the thought of submitting myself to unconsciousness and all its dangers. I've held up well against the threat of my curse, but somehow, the longer it takes to show itself, the more

I fear it. It surely can't be over. It's luck—or El-Alam's mercy, perhaps—holding it at bay for Norielle's sake.

Though why El-Alam's mercy overlooks *my* sake in allowing this ongoing torment, I may never understand. But that is a weed of a thought—one that must be cut down at first sight, lest it grow to strangle my faith. No future Sovereign has any place for such doubt.

A sudden shuffle outside the front door accelerates my pulse, and I lift my Omen Mark into view. The deep red arrow remains pointed toward the upper city as it has every time I've checked, but by the time a knuckle raps against the door, I've realized who is here.

Elias—back from Boldor to accompany Norielle and me.

What a joy this will be.

I rise, taking my time to reach the door and even more to disarm the locks. The swelling dread in my chest freezes my grip on the door handle. For all the times I've enlisted Elias's help, never have I felt such disdain about it.

What's wrong with me?

My question is foolish. I know exactly what is wrong. There's only one difference between this time and all the others. Norielle. And whether I want to admit it or not, Elias is an unwanted intrusion on the privacy we've enjoyed. Not to mention it was hard to miss the way he looked at her with such intrigue and, dare I say, yearning.

Why should I care about that?

I open the door to find Elias standing back with a heavy-lidded stare.

"You were fast," I say in place of a greeting.

"Said I would be." He steps in, dropping his bag beside Ila's couch without noticing my belongings on the other side. "Is Ila already asleep?"

"They both are."

Undoing his cloak, he tosses it onto a bronze hook on the wall and strides into the kitchen. He adds a few chunks of wood to the dying hearth, prodding it until the flames renew. Embers flitter inside the stone hollow as he whirls to retrieve Ila's kettle.

Of course, no conversation can be had until he's satisfied his obsessive tea habit.

Once the kettle is filled and set over the lapping flames, he swivels toward Ila's living room shelves, adding yet another trinket to the overflowing assortment. The carved dog sits between a wood fisherman and a porcelain vase—another testament to how many times Elias has stayed here, and each one a reminder that I have no right claiming Ila as my grandmother. Not when I've seen her a tenth of the times he has.

"Any Hunters in Boldor?" I ask.

"A few," he says, returning to the kitchen. He pulls a tea tin from the cupboard and adds a mug beside it, finding everything with enough ease for this to be his own home. "Most of them are around here, watching the ravine. Not sure what your plan is to get us past them, but I don't think we're doing it without a fight. You sure we shouldn't wait a few days?"

"They could be here for weeks, and I'm needed back home," I say, nose scrunching at the tea's pungent aroma as he fills a strainer. "Besides, I *do* have a plan, and I expect it to work just fine."

Elias leans against the counter. "Go on."

A brief moment of second-guessing slows my response, but I squash it. "I will head out first on my own, and you will lead her out of the city and meet me in the ravine."

He bites his lip as if to hold down his smile, and my muscles tense.

"The Hunters specifically saw her with me," I continue, forcing my tone to remain unaffected by his reaction. "So, perhaps if we aren't seen together, it will prevent them from noticing us. Just be sure she keeps her head down."

The kettle whistles, and he quickly grabs it. Steam puffs over his cup like rainclouds as he pours. "Sounds a little flimsy, but we'll make it work."

He sets the kettle aside and grabs his cup, meeting my gaze with such spark, I'm almost afraid of my own idea. What is it about Norielle that has him so alight? Or he is just messing with me, as usual, hoping to stir a reaction for his own amusement?

"And if things go south?" he asks.

"You'll keep her safe at any cost."

"You got it." He smirks as he passes me, but his expression becomes serious once he sits at the table. When I don't follow, he knocks the tabletop with his knuckle, giving me an expectant stare. If I were my sister, I would chastise him for his irreverence towards each of our titles. Yet his boldness is one of the reasons I've taken to recruiting him. I don't much care for the excessive sense of propriety most Wardens display toward me. Every bow and formal address feels like another brick being added to the wall between me and others.

How can one be the soon center-of-all-matters and yet feel so very alone?

I take the chair across from Elias and nod for him to speak.

"There was some news from the north I'd brought back to the citadel," he says, "but you left before it reached you."

My shoulders pull back, bracing for more unwelcome insights about the state of our world.

"The storm crystal on Mount Stellmar erupted. The lightning nearly destroyed the two surrounding towns before the Wardens on watch could subdue it." He taps the lip of his cup, a soft tinging filling his pause. "Seems to me like Ta'Nathel's curse is growing stronger than us."

"The people in the towns, are they . . . .?"

"Alive?" he finishes for me. "Most of them. They had time to evacuate. Didn't go home to much."

I lean my head against my hand, rubbing my hairline. "If King Arlo would just recognize we are trying to help, our numbers wouldn't be so suppressed. Then maybe we'd have a chance against this calamity."

"Would we?"

My hand lowers to the table, but my gaze doesn't lift. "It would at least buy us more time while we await a new Empyreal Guardian."

Elias grunts, lifting the strainer from the tea. "If one ever shows." He steps away to discard the leaves and returns with a weightiness in his gaze. "I think you'd be smart to stop counting on that. The world isn't going to survive on your optimism alone, Cal."

I glance at the couch, suddenly longing to be on it, asleep.

"Another Guardian is our world's only lasting hope, Lias." I scoot my chair back. "And I will continue to trust El-Alam to provide one until I see the world crumble before my eyes."

Elias's cup stills before he sips, then he lowers it. "You really don't think there is any other option?"

"We can't slay Ta'Nathel. That would end the world."

His eyes grow dull. "I wasn't suggesting that."

"Then what?"

He stares a long moment before his gaze drops to his tea, and he shakes his head. "Just seems like there should be a way to break his curse."

A sour laugh escapes my lips. "If I am any proof, curses aren't broken. They are managed."

"Sounds like you've given up."

I turn toward the shadow-laden living room. "I've not given up, Lias. I've made peace with reality."

When a sigh seems his only response, I stand, turning on my heel for the washroom as an excuse to escape the conversation. Two steps in silence fool me that it's over before he speaks again.

"I'm not convinced."

I stop, looking partway over my shoulder. "This isn't your burden to trouble yourself with."

"Maybe that's part of the problem," he says, chair popping as he stands.

I face him, my eyes silently requesting an explanation.

"You need to learn how to share." He drops his emptied cup in the washbasin, a grin crawling back onto his exhausted face. "Stop being so greedy. It's the weight of the world—there's plenty to go around."

I almost smile, feeling a prick of guilt that I nearly refused his offer to come. This isn't the first time he's proven himself a surprisingly caring friend. "I need practice with that. Tomorrow will be a good start."

"Trust is what you need," he corrects me, crossing his arms. "And maybe some sleep. You look wretched."

My heavy gaze drifts to the dusty floorboards between us.

He bumps my shoulder as he walks by, then he shuts himself into the washroom I was headed for. I sigh at the closed door and pivot back toward the couch. My body slumps into its flattened cushions, a fresh headache throbbing from the base of my skull to the back of my eyes.

It's the weight of the world, he said.

And I feel it shifting onto my back more with every passing day.

NORIELLE

alden and Elias are already at the table, polishing off their morning beverages, by the time Ila finishes dressing me. Properly fitting leather and steel armor hugs me from my collar bone to my thighs, stiffening my strides as I step out to gather my boots. Ila follows behind me, tugging at my cloak to adjust it. Her hands recoil as Calden and Elias notice us.

Elias's smarmy smirk crawls onto his face. His sticky stare seems to inspect every piece of armor as if Ila has done something wrong, but Calden's once-over lasts as long as a blink.

"Was this your armor, Miss Ila?" Calden asks.

"Yes, indeed." Pride emanates from her voice. "For what little chance I had to wear it, here it is. Practically new."

I find my gaze unwittingly returning to Elias, but he's finally moved on to staring at the base of his teacup. He throws back the final drop as Calden rises, adorned in his full armor just as he was through the Rimrook Mountains.

"You look like a proper Warden," Calden says as he passes me to drop his empty cup into the washbasin. The soapy water sucks it down with a gurgle, and he sweeps up his bag from beside the couch where he slept last night so Elias could take the other guest room.

I made sure to be fast asleep before Elias ever got in.

"I'm going to head out, then," Calden says, shifting toward Elias to issue his next command. "Give it thirty minutes, at least. Then make your departure. I'll be awaiting you in the ravine."

Elias nods. "Don't get caught."

Somehow, even his concern has a barbed edge.

"*You* don't get *her* caught," Calden counters.

He strides toward Ila, giving her a long hug that makes me forget she's not really his grandmother. He steps toward me next, and for a fool's second, I think he'll hug me farewell, too, but instead he stops a whole stretch away.

"Keep your head down in the town. Let Elias talk if you are approached." He pivots as if that's all he has for me, a set of orders, but then he turns back with an undeniable concern in his gaze. "Be safe, Norielle."

He pats my arm and smiles at me in a way that makes me already long for our reunion in the ravine.

With a final piercing glance at Elias, Calden—my one source of security—leaves me behind.

"Better eat while you have the chance," Elias says.

My eyes linger on the front door, and I almost miss what Elias said. The subtle squeak of Ila's pantry spins me around.

"I'll fix you something, dear," she says. "Save your energy."

"Thanks," I say, gathering my boots from beside the front door. I sit on the couch next to Calden's sloppily folded quilt and begin slowly lacing my boots.

"Scared?" Elias asks as I start on my second boot.

I spare myself the glance up. "Would you blame me for it?"

"You don't need to be."

"Sure. Hunters. Fellions. Blood Wardens." *You.* "It's nothing."

Elias's chair whines as he leans against the backrest. "I'm no *Sovereign Prince,* but I'll keep you safe. There's nothing out there that I'm not used to dealing with. I travel in and out of that ravine more than he does."

I drop my tied laces, checking for Ila's reaction, as if a contortion in her expression might reveal Elias's over-confidence. Instead, she's grinning, and her fingers are fluttering as she searches through a set of mason jars.

What's her deal?

"And what's your plan if the Hunters recognize me?" I ask Elias.

He folds his arms. "Make them regret it."

"Which means?"

"Calden's mama orders us not to kill Hunters unless we have to, so don't worry. No one will be dying today unless they are fellions or Blood Wardens."

"And if the Lady Sovereign hadn't made such an order?"

He chuckles, and the cadence stirs that feeling of familiarity again. But I still can't place it except to go with Calden's guess, that I've seen Elias play in town before. I hate to think how I probably enjoyed it, too, for bards are rare in Behria. I'm sure no trace of his unpleasant personality was on display then.

"You really don't trust me at all, do you?" he asks.

"We've just met."

Something cold crosses his face, stealing away—if only for a second—his arrogant air. "Yet something tells me you didn't hesitate to trust Blondie."

Again, I look to Ila, wishing she'd say *something*. She pinches her lips tight as she butters my bread and slaps on a heap of bright red jam.

"Circumstances were different," I say. "He pulled me out of a lake bent on killing me. It was easy to assume he meant no harm when he risked his life to save me."

"What do you think I'm doing, *stranger*?"

My toes curl in my boots. *Risking your life to keep me alive.*

I keep the thought to myself. "Sorry."

He stands, stretching his neck from side to side. His iron armor is nearly hidden beneath his olive cloak and a sword hilt pokes from his hip.

"I get it," he says. "Just try not to make yourself sick. I've got a handle on this. You're gonna be fine."

Half an hour later, just as Calden requested, I'm leaving the safety of Ila's home with my life in Elias's hands. Ila bids us safe travels, giving us each a squeeze as tight and lengthy as the one she shared with Calden. Elias leaves her arms with a promise to return sooner than last time and a kiss to her cheek.

My stomach unwittingly flutters when his attention returns to me with a winsome, if overly confident, smile. "Let's get you outta here."

I swallow a lump of apprehension in my throat and follow him outside.

He leads me through the massive city, throwing on a friendly demeanor as residents recognize him and request he stop for a song in the town center. He repeats the same lines at least three times before we've even crossed the fountain: *Sorry, Sunhearth is waiting for me. I'll be back before Alatûm.* But even after it's clear we're leaving Aldrian, I don't miss the long stares from people—particularly the young women who all seem to turn the same shade of pink if he bothers to glance their way.

I grimace. He's probably not even talented. They just want to look at him longer.

"Head down," he mutters, leaning toward my ear.

Right. I lower my face, and my reply comes out like a grumble. "You're famous here, I take it."

A dry laugh chirps in his throat. "They're all gluttons for entertainment here. Helps them forget the danger beyond the walls."

"Where we're going."

"I've got you, Nori."

My glower scathes the side of his face. He has no right to call me that. But I don't get to chastise him before a guard from the inner gate hollers at us.

"Heading out, Elias?"

He can use his real name?

"I promised Sunhearth another show by the evening," Elias says. "How's the road that way?"

"Eh." The guard exchanges a look with his colleague on the opposite side of the gate, and he lowers his voice. "They just caught one of them Wardens they've been looking for. The male."

The guard's casual words slice though my center.

Calden.

Elias whistles through his teeth, calm as the breeze. "Good. Was worried about that. He off to King Arlo now?"

"Uh . . . no." The guard shifts a bit closer to Elias. "We saw them take him to the ravine."

Elias lets out an amused snort. "What are they going to do, feed him to the fellions?"

I fight an urge to whack him in the arm. Act or not, Calden is in danger. This is no time for him to be making jokes—

"I'd guess the other one must be down there," the guard says. "The girl."

I dip my head a bit lower to hide my face, fiddling with my belt as though it's not on quite right.

"Thanks for the warning," Elias says. "Well, we better get going. See you around, Vic." Elias waves, but we only get one step before the other guard yells to us.

"Wait."

My breathing stills.

"Who's she?"

"My cousin," Elias answers without a pause. "She's in training to be a soldier. I picked her up in Boldor yesterday. She's looking after me on my travels to Sunhearth, considering the circumstances."

Me protecting *him?* I'd laugh if my pounding heart didn't feel like it was going to crack my rib cage.

I turn my hip, pushing my cloak away to show my father's sword so I can silently feed into the ruse.

"Didn't know you had family in Boldor," the guard says, his expression settling.

"Got family all over the kingdom. Part of why I love to travel." For the first time in the whole conversation, he wavers in his lie. But he steps forward, and the guards turn their attention beyond us.

We pass through the second gate without further interrogation, and the moment my feet hit the road on the other side, my strides turn into a trot. But Elias snags my arm.

"Easy," he says under his breath.

I wrench myself from his grip and shoot him a look that I hope communicates everything I can't say. *How can I go easy? Calden's been captured by Hunters!*

He fixes his sights ahead, offering no other response. I force myself to keep his moderate pace, though it physically pains me not to run. Once we're far enough from the ears of Aldrian guards and passing travelers to speak, I whisper, "Can you help him?"

"Should I?" he asks, but when my expression turns vile, he rolls his eyes. "Look, I'm in charge of protecting *you*, not him. And if I know Cal, he'd rather be left for dead than for me to lead you straight to the Hunters."

I stop walking, right in the middle of the road. "You're not going to help him."

"I didn't say that."

"You implied it." I toss a glance toward the ravine, hands shaking. "Elias—"

"I'm just wondering if I should take you back to Ila's first before I go leading you—the one they are looking for—straight to them."

"He's already been down there half an hour," I say, fighting an impulse to dash that way myself. But what good would that do? Hunters are King Arlo's most elite warriors. Papa said their skill exceeds most soldiers', and they're twice as ruthless. They'd have me in bonds before I could even draw my sword. "Who knows what they're doing to him? We can't waste any more time—"

"I don't like it."

I glance each way down the road to be sure no one is listening. "Your Sovereign Prince is in danger. *I* can be replaced. I doubt he can."

"My Sovereign Prince gave me orders to keep you safe at any cost. His life amongst them."

My heart flutters. *Did Calden really say that? For Elias to place my life ahead of his?*

"And don't say you can be replaced," Elias adds, but his strides start again, heading away from Aldrian. "Maybe in a mission. But people aren't replaceable."

My feet hesitate to follow him until I have to jog to catch up. What would make him say that?

"See those trees?" Elias murmurs before I can form a single theory.

I look ahead. The road cuts through the flat field before snaking between an entourage of weeping alela trees. Their long, pale branches sway in the light breeze, creating a leafy veil between the trees and Aldrian. Their numbers lead right down to the ravine.

"Once we get deep enough, we'll turn and make our way to the down ramp," Elias says. "Then I want you to find a nice spot to hide up here and leave retrieving your sweetheart to me."

"Excuse me, he's *not*—"

"If neither of us comes back within the hour, get yourself back to Ila's house while the same guards are at the gate. They just saw you leave, so they're less likely to question you on your way back in. All you have to say is that you forgot something."

"And what would the Hunters do with you both?"

We pass beneath the shadow of the first tree. "Is that really a question?"

He leaves me to assume the worst, but I don't press it any further. Soon, the trees crowd our backs, and he stabs a finger toward the ravine to command me to turn. We bolt, strides snaking between the drooping willows. Elias draws his sword as we approach the drop-off where the ground descends into the Dûnori Ravine. He pushes my shoulder down, a silent order for me to crouch. I hunker low, squinting to see through the brush. Well ahead, several armed figures march alongside the river. One figure is dragging a captive by a rope while others point blades at his back.

Breath hisses through my teeth. That's him.

"Stay hidden," Elias whispers, then he creeps onto the down ramp—a slim path that weaves from where we stand to the base of the ravine. Branches stretch over it, though some lie broken with leaves still ripe as though they were just snapped off.

When Elias's feet hit the ravine floor, he checks for me, then shoos me back with his hand.

A muscle in my jaw twitches, and the moment he's lost in the foliage, an impulse jerks me toward the ramp. I can't just sit up here and wonder what will happen to them. It's *my* fault any of this has happened.

Mine and Landon's.

I sneak along the zigzagging path to the bottom just as Elias did, delicately balancing speed and stealth. When my boots pad onto the soft ravine floor, I peel my sleeves back to check the Omen and Bind Marks on my wrists. They point in the same direction, but the Bind Mark is present, which hopefully means Calden is still alive.

Or else it's pointing toward his dead body.

A knot ties in my throat. If he dies on my behalf—

I clutch my sword, checking my surroundings as I ease onto an unkept pathway. A weathered rope fence separates me from the trickling creek, one that would have once guided people through the ravine before the fellions became hostile. Now apparently the Wardens are the only ones who are brave enough to enter this trench.

Footprints imprinted in the dense soil lead me for at least a quarter mile before a cluster of messy tracks ends the trail. I kneel to inspect them and find them turning distinctly to the left—the same direction my Omen and Bind Marks lead.

I rise, fear tightening my chest. I could still go back. I *should* go back, and yet, the thought of abandoning Calden feels unimaginable after what he's done for me.

I slip into the wispy grass, passing through a fountain of silky willow branches. The shadows dim the color of the mauve tree barks, growing darker the further I follow the marks. The vague murmur of distant voices reaches my ears, shallowing my breaths. But I press on. Just as I did toward the lake. Step after step. Until—

A hand cups around my mouth, trapping my scream.

I attempt to lift my sword, but my captor squeezes my wrist, overpowering my effort. The hand over my mouth pushes me, my back flush against his chest.

"What are you doing?" the man hisses against my ear. *Elias?*

He spins me around, nostrils flaring as he releases me. "It's like you *want* to die."

My gaze skitters away from his dark glower. "I want to help."

"Then go back to where I left you." He points toward the ridge, hidden completely by the willows.

"No." I lower my voice. "This is my fault. I can't just sit back and wait. And you can't prevent me from following you."

Elias stares at me through three heavy pulses of his chest. "Fine," he says, walking past me. "But stay out of their sight."

I nod, though it's no promise, and follow him deeper into the trees.

Once we near the cliffside, Elias beckons me behind a bush with curled branches. He presses me low and points through a small gap in the leaves. I peer through it, finding Calden and the Hunters just barely in view.

Calden stands beside the wall of the cliff with blood dripping from a fresh slash on his cheek. Six steel-armored Hunters crowd him. One holds a rope that knots Calden's hands against his back. Two others stand at a distance, each holding a bow with an arrow nocked and ready to shoot. Another with a hulky frame has a dagger pointed at Calden's throat. The other two watch the perimeter with swords raised to attack.

"Open it," the hulky Hunter orders.

"I'll need my hand if I'm to do that," Calden says.

The man flicks his dagger toward the Hunter holding the rope, a silent order to untie him. She cautiously approaches, and I take note of the sword on her hip as she loosens one of Calden's hands from the bonds. She coils the rope around his torso to resecure his other hand to his back, then yanks it taut until his cloak crinkles from the pressure. He gives her the most irritated smile I've ever seen before pulling his pen from his belt. She rewards him with a harsh tug of the rope toward the cliffside, and finally, I realize what is happening. There must be a door here, like the trapdoor in Ila's house, and they are using him to get inside.

But didn't Calden say this is the passage to the Wardens' secret routes? We can't let them in there!

I nudge Elias, screaming a silent, *Do something!*

He mouths *"wait"* just before light explodes through the forest. My eyes squeeze shut, vision turning red under my eyelids. My eyes flutter open as a series of alarmed shouts burst from the Hunters. Four have loosened their stances, arms shielding their eyes, but the two with swords have whirled toward Calden.

Still, Elias waits.

I'm just shifting to push Elias into action when Calden's ropes disintegrate, raining like sand off his arms and back. He swivels toward the charging swordsmen, holding out his fist. Before the men can reach him, a long weapon materializes in his hold, clanking against the first sword to swing. The Hunter's sword dissolves into a silvery cloud of dust.

Both swordsmen stumble back, only for Calden to slash his newly appeared weapon—a long staff with a blade on each end—at the disarmed Hunter's breastplate. More dust rains from the man's body as the steel protecting his vitals disappears.

My sword almost falls from my grasp. What was I doing thinking he needed *my* help?

Calden turns to the second swordsman as the first retreats, but as they engage, one of the archers returns to their position.

"Cal—" I start, but my yelp is cut short by a bluish orb launching from Elias's hand.

The buzzing sphere collides with the bow, blasting the wood to shards. The archer screams, hands covering his eyes. I catch a hint of red trickling from his nose before the man stumbles away.

Elias leaps onto the scene, obliterating the other bow with another blast. But this time, the splinters barely nick the archer's face, and the man reaches for his sword.

"Enough wards, Lias," Calden says, swirling his swordstaff toward the burly Hunter. The man dodges the attack. "We'll lure the fellions."

Elias draws his sword, taking on the archer-turned-swordsman in a flurry of assaults and parries. But in the middle of the two Wardens' battles, the woman who once held Calden's ropes finally seems to clear her vision, and her gaze hones in on me with the hunger of a lioness.

She charges past the occupied men, steel singing as she frees her sword from its prison. I rise from my crouch, instincts awakening just in time to block the attack.

My sword quivers in my hold as she adjusts her stance, but I tighten my grip. *Papa trained me*, I remind myself. I try to imagine him standing before me instead of this woman, even as she begins striking at me with a violence my father never would have directed toward me—even with a blunt blade.

My blocks barely protect me, and my strength hardly contends with her power. But somehow, I hold my ground, swipe after swipe, jab after jab, until finally, another blade whooshes between us. It clanks against her sword and a puff of gray powder bursts into my face. I jerk away, coughing.

By the time I look back, Calden has the woman pressed to the ground with his boot and the rest of the Hunters have fled.

"Return to King Arlo," Calden growls at the woman. "And tell him your unit was spared by the Sovereign Prince of the Wardens. We are *not* your enemies. We are servants of El-Alam."

He lifts his boot, and she rises, eyeing each of us before running back the way we came. Calden watches her go, then turns to me. A bruise discolors his brow, and the blood from his cheek slips down his neck and under his cloak.

"Are you all right?" he asks.

I nod.

"Good." He turns toward the cliffside. "Come, now. Hurry. We've surely woken the fellions."

19

NORIELLE

Calden stops beside a flat surface in the cliffside, about a mile from where we fought the Hunters. He slips his pen from his belt, etching the same symbol he used to open Ila's basement, and light shines through the rocky wall, forming an arch just higher than our heads. The stone beneath smooths into wood, then metal hinges and a knob manifest from what once appeared like bumps in the rock.

A door. Appearing right here in the cliffside.

Even after everything I've seen, I still find myself gawping.

Calden opens the door, and white light spills out from inside. He checks his Omen Mark, then beckons me to enter first. I step beneath a solid crystal ceiling, glowing as if painted with moonlight. I lower my enamored gaze to realize what I expected to be a barren cave looks more like a home, complete with a rickety table and a couple of sagging chairs. There's even a shelf built into the wall like a countertop, holding an assortment of dishes, and a hearth in the corner ventilated by a small hole in the wall.

Calden seals the door behind us, all trace of the entrance vanishing into the earthen wall.

"Before you say anything," Elias says just as Calden is filling his lungs to speak. "I told her to stay behind. She came right up to the party anyway."

Calden shuts his mouth and focuses on me.

My chin dips toward my chest, but instead of the chiding I expect, he laughs. "Actually, I'd say that went quite according to plan."

I start. "According to plan?"

"You don't think Hunters could catch me that easily, do you?" He smiles, bending the streak of blood on his face. "I let them. Then I told them you were already in our passages so I could lead them out of your way and run them off. I intended to be a bit faster, but . . ."

"Well, doesn't that figure," Elias says, picking at dirt under his fingernails. "They finally catch you, and it's on purpose."

"It got you two here. Worth the tussle." He sniffs, his attention shifting toward a small tunnel. "Do you smell a fire?"

I inhale a whiff of the humid air, catching the sweet scent of flame-eaten wood layered with smoke.

Calden looks at his Bind Mark.

"Alani?" he whispers.

His steps quicken toward the shimmering tunnel, and he waves for me to follow. I glance at Elias, who's still fussing with his fingernails. He lifts a brow and gives a slight smile but doesn't budge. I still, that sense of familiarity tiptoeing through my mind again. I once knew a boy who hated getting dirt stuck under his nails. Watching him pick at them used to make me cringe.

"Careful. Once Alani starts talking, she never stops," Elias says, ripping me from my rumination. He lowers his hand, giving me one of the comelier smiles he's offered so far, but he spoils it the moment he opens his mouth again. "'Less you'd rather hang back with better company."

I scoff at him and turn to find Calden waiting for me. He leads me past several closed doors with keys hung on hooks next to them. The last door on the right is partially ajar, revealing a simple bedroom, and the hook beside it is empty.

The tunnel feeds into a wide space where the ceiling is higher and only a few shards of crystals glow across its surface. A dying fire lightly smokes from the center of the chamber, and in one of the chairs encircling it, a woman slouches against her backrest, fast asleep. Her curly auburn hair is scattered across her face with a clump stuck in her mouth.

Calden clears his throat, and she shudders awake, immediately snatching something from her belt. She pulls back her arm to hurl it—a small knife—but just before it leaves her hand, her alarmed expression dissolves into a sprawling smile.

"Calden!" Her squeal rings through the room as she tucks her knife away.

"Yes, fortunately," he says. "Otherwise, you might be dead. We've been talking down the hall, and here you are asleep."

She tugs her wild hair out of her mouth. "I was *praying*."

"No, you weren't."

"I *was*—last I remember, anyway. Did you save the—" Her head inclines in my direction, and she jumps. "Oh. *My*. Well, there goes my big question." She leaps to her feet, rushing to me with a haste that makes me wonder if she wasn't asleep after all. "My goodness, you're adorable. Isn't that Ila's armor?"

I purse my lips. *Adorable.* Great. Now I really sound like someone cut out to join the Wardens.

"It is," I answer her.

Her smile crinkles her nose. "So nice to have another lass in the Bind. That isn't, well . . ." She glances at Calden, seeming to recalibrate her words like she suddenly remembered Calden and the other young woman are siblings. "Always so busy."

"Her name is Norielle," Calden says. "And don't be deceived, she's handy with that sword."

Heat festers across my face. Don't be deceived? Is he *agreeing* with her?

"I'd hardly call what I did out there being handy," I counter.

"Standing your ground against a Hunter? That's no small feat."

"A Hunter?" Alani interjects, her hair bouncing when she spins toward him. "My goodness, is that what happened to your face? I thought perhaps she'd tried to kill you, too."

"No, some people have enough manners to have a conversation before deciding to throw a knife at someone's throat." The fondness in his tone contrasts oddly with his words and leaves me even more confused. Why would Alani throw a knife at the Sovereign Prince? Wouldn't she recognize him? Or did she attack without looking?

Based on how quickly she almost did so a moment ago, maybe I shouldn't be surprised.

Alani huffs, but her grin only grows. "Sooner or later, I'm sure you'll say something that'll have her at your throat."

"And I'm sure I'll deserve it." His smile turns toward me, and I realize the most disturbing thing about all this. He's so calm. All of them are—as if what happened in the ravine was just part of a typical day.

Will every day of my life be like this?

"So, Hunters?" Alani asks, trotting toward a pile of wood near the wall. "Good thing this is the farthest I got."

I volunteer to revive the fire and leave Calden to fill her in on the details. He covers everything quickly, adding unfamiliar terms and places while I arrange the sticks into a little steeple. Alani follows along with Calden's tale with the occasional hum, and by the time I've rekindled the flames into a crackling fire, they've switched to recounting her travels to reach us, which apparently began on the sea.

After another slew of foreign words are exchanged, Alani suddenly pops up from the seat she took, her ginger coils springing with her, and addresses me. "I need some tea. Would you like some? It's mullenberry leaf."

"N—"

"Yes?" she blurts over me. "All right, then. I'll be right back!"

She flits down the hall, squealing Elias's name in a similar fashion to how she reacted to Calden. Her boisterous laugh echoes down the hall as she says, "I thought you'd already left!" Elias's low response is barely audible, let alone discernible. But whatever he says, she exclaims how happy she is that he's here and offers him tea.

"I should go stitch this," Calden says, dabbing his facial wound again as he rises.

I open my mouth, wanting to offer my help. Papa taught me the basics of first aid, stitching included, but the reality of what I'd have to do, how close I'd have to get, and how nervous I'd surely be stops the offer in my throat.

"Is something wrong?" Calden asks.

I snatch up the first thought to cross my mind. "I was just wondering, what is that ward you've been using? The one that turns things to dust? I never even saw you draw anything."

His eyes light, like this is the perfect excuse for him to put off jabbing a needle through his flesh.

"It's my Master Talent," he says, stepping back toward the fire. He stops behind a chair, resting his battered hands against its tall back. "When someone fully masters all the standard wards, they are granted additional power and access to higher level wards. They also receive their own Master Talent, which is unique to every Warden and doesn't require a ward to use. Disintegration is mine."

The idea seems to shine in my mind. There are ranks to being a Warden? New levels to climb to? How powerful could I learn to be?

"I'm sure you'll earn one someday," Calden adds. "Not a doubt in my mind."

"That's bold, considering how my first attempt to learn one went."

He chuckles. "Someone has to believe in you, Norielle."

At that, he smiles and retires into one of the rooms in the hallway, leaving me sinking into my chair.

CALDEN

A trance blurs my thoughts and all sense of time, long after I finish clipping the ends of my sutures. The sting is sevenfold what it was before the stitches, and my sloppy work is sure to leave an ugly scar for years to come unless we make it home in time for someone to heal it.

I change into fresh clothes and cast the tattered bed a long look. Hideous as it is with its frayed wool blanket and dusty pillow, it seems to beckon me like the pull of land to a long-traveled sailor. But the thought of trying to rest under the brilliant crystal ceilings turns me toward the door instead.

I enter the tunnel, inspecting my shirt buttons to make sure I didn't miss any in my groggy state before stepping into the vacated front room. The scent of firewood and the murmur of voices draws me beyond it, to the back chamber.

Around the roaring campfire, two figures occupy the chairs, both with tea in hand. I delay, realizing neither is

Norielle, despite this being where I last left her. *She must have turned in for the night already.*

"Come now, Elias, I made you tea. Doesn't that earn me at least one song?" teases Alani, oblivious to my presence.

Elias stares into his cup, taking so long to respond I almost think he won't.

"Half of one, maybe." His tone is flat and worn.

"It's *mullenberry*," she says, as if declaring the foulest of all teas is a master key to unlock a whole concert. "That's your favorite, isn't it?"

I take a step back. Perhaps I shouldn't interrupt Alani's moment with him.

Or should I spare Elias this discomfort?

"I've taken more to starroot these days," he says. A lie, I'm sure of it. He was just drinking that sour mullenberry leaf this morning at Ila's table. And the evening prior.

Alani huffs, but a girlish giggle softens any intended blow. Again, I consider entering but curiosity for how this will play out on its own keeps me back.

"Just let me finish my tea, at least," Elias says.

The delight that illuminates Alani's face denotes an absolute disregard for his annoyed tone. But whether such glee is due to her love of music or her innate need to swoon over every man near her age—besides myself, blessedly—I can't tell. Possibly both, but likely the latter. Even my attendant back home wasn't spared her ogling.

Yet Elias has never looked at her in that way once.

I clear my throat, stepping into their sight as though I've freshly approached. Both their gazes sweep to me,

Alani's smile growing while Elias's contains a rare hint of relief.

I resist a laugh. A bit of innocent distress serves him right.

"Has Norielle gone to sleep?" I ask.

"Just a few minutes ago," Alani answers before Elias can finish opening his mouth. "She was so tired. Poor thing. Sounded like you gave her quite a fright."

I settle into the chair nearest Alani.

"You really ought to consider telling people your insane plans before going about them. You'd save us all a mound of troubles." Alani's eyes would deliver a reprimand as strong as Mother's if not for her smile.

"And what would have happened had I told them?" I ask. "They'd have followed sooner, and more trouble would have been had for the lot of us."

I glance at Elias, whose expression holds no opinion.

"Besides, all is well now. We're where we need to be."

Alani sighs, takes a long slurp of her tea, then recovers her chipper demeanor. "So, Elias is joining us on our journey back to the citadel?"

"Yes, on account of a vision from the Seer."

She nods knowingly, concern slowly sapping the vibrance from her eyes. "What do you suppose the defectors would want from her?"

I forbid my imagination to conjure any images as I speak. "Likely to claim her for their ranks before she gets too indoctrinated by truth and reason."

Alani stares at me, face sobering, as she seems to consider something she doesn't share. Yet, it's as apparent as if she'd spoken it aloud. She's questioning if I'll be able to defend Norielle in such a case and considering my precautions in bringing Elias along.

"All I can hope—outside of avoiding it altogether—is that it isn't *her*," I murmur, yet my meaning doesn't escape either of them given the way their stares deepen.

Both of them know well enough who I mean and why. They are two of the few I've told my story to.

"But surely we'll avoid it," I say with feigned confidence.

Only Alani's face settles.

"We'd better," Elias says, paying his Omen Mark a cursory glance.

I copy him.

Alani shifts in her chair, squinting at the hall as if to check for Norielle. When she looks back to me, her lips are twisted sideways. "What do you suppose El-Alam picked her for? An outsider?"

Despite Alani's innocent meaning, a shadow seems to creep from Elias, darkening his presence in my peripheral vision. *Outsider.* He was one of those not terribly long ago, as the Wardens' most recent inductee. But in his handful of years with us, he's certainly made himself at home.

"I'm not sure yet, to be honest," I confess. "She seems to have much potential in her heart, but what for, exactly, I haven't determined yet. It would be easier to guess, perhaps, if El-Alam told us what the Bind is specifically supposed to do."

"You're the future Sovereign, how hard can it be to figure it out?" Elias says. "You know what you're supposed to do. That's why El-Alam hasn't said anything yet."

Yes, stop the curse from destroying the entire world or, at the very least, postpone it through my term as Sovereign. How could anyone forget?

"Sure, but even in that there are unlimited possibilities regarding what El-Alam could want of me and the Bind," I say, quieting my voice lest Norielle hear and grow afraid of her destiny. "I understand the general direction of the mission, but not the specifics. That is what we await."

"Maybe *you're* supposed to figure out the specifics," Elias says.

My brows knit. "It's better to wait for His instructions than to run anxiously in a hundred directions, wasting energy and resources, on my own faulty ideas."

Elias shrugs. "Just a thought."

"Calden . . ." Alani's honest tenor snaps my focus her way. "How have you been?"

The seeming randomness of her question forestalls my immediate reply. The fire crackles and shifts, its murmurs filling the silence as I discern her true meaning.

"No episodes yet," I answer, slumping further into my chair. "It seems El-Alam has shown Norielle mercy by withholding any encounters with my curse."

"Have you told her?" Judgment prickles Elias's question.

My throat clenches. "Not yet."

Elias winces. "You haven't warned her yet?"

My gaze pivots to Alani who, while less judgingly, looks at me with similar disapproval.

"I wanted to wait until we were here," I say. "I thought she might run from me otherwise, thus putting her at risk of being captured by Hunters. Of course . . ." I catch my words fading behind a tide of insecurity and a growing awareness of my weak rationalization. "Now, she may well run into defectors' hands, so . . . perhaps it should wait until the citadel."

"Cal, she *needs* to know." Elias leans forward in his chair, discarding his empty cup on the seat beside him. "You really want to chance what happened to Alani on a newcomer?"

"I've been doing my best to prevent it," I argue. "And it's been so long, it may well be over."

I cringe at myself. Fantastic, now I'm lying to not look like a fool in front of them.

Elias's stare hardens. "Sure, sounds good. Put the innocent girl's life at risk for the sake of your own pride. Great, Cal."

"*Trust*," I say. "For the sake of her trust."

But my hands curl at how idiotic that sounds.

Elias gives me no time to correct myself. "Right, because—if she survived—she'd be sure to trust you after finding out what you've been hiding from her the hard way."

I bow my head in defeat. *I know. I know. I've been selfish.*

Yet I can't propel my lips to confess it.

"You need to tell her, Cal."

I nod. "I will."

"*Soon.*"

A frown squirms onto my lips despite my efforts to resist it. If he weren't here, I might consider telling Alani what really bothers me about it. Though, how could I expect understanding from her when a similar fear kept me from warning her also, and my curse nearly took her life?

"I will," I say again, and without another utterance, I return to my room.

NORIELLE

As my eyes open, a tangle of memories and nightmares retreats to the far corners of my mind. I shift onto my back, air cooling the perspiration on my neck, and stare at the soft, moonlike glow overhead, hoping it will extinguish the remaining images from my head. But they linger like splinters in my imagination—visuals of Papa at the base of the lake but not alone. Cas, Mum, and Milo are bound in lake weeds beside him.

I sit up, pulling my sweat-dampened hair over a shoulder and picking at knots to distract myself from hours of tossing and turning. Even lying on the dirt floor of the Rimrook Mountains brought me better sleep than here beneath these glowing crystals. How does anyone rest under constant light?

Once my hair is somewhat tamed, I remember the marks on my wrist, checking each one. The Omen Mark is dark. The Bind Mark still points to the room across from me.

What hour is it?

I rise to change, determined that at this point, even if it's still the middle of the night, I'd rather stay awake than return to the endless terrors in my mind. My pulse gradually settles as I open a chest at the foot of my worn bed and retrieve fresh garments, handsewn by Ila herself. But as I dress, I catch a faint noise trickling through the wall.

I freeze, holding my breath to listen—

Music. Soft music, drifting from somewhere down the hall.

Elias, I realize with a grimace.

Still, when I register it's not just his harp carrying the melody, but his voice, I can't help but creep toward my door to hear it more clearly. Just as my ear is brushing the old wood, his song finishes. Unwanted disappointment sags my shoulders. Why should I care what he sings like? A pretty voice isn't going to make him any better of a person. If anything, it makes him more annoying.

I lace my boots and open my door with the delicacy I used to sneak from my and Cas's room, intent on detecting which area Elias occupies and going the opposite way. But the moment I step from my room, a new song begins—the chilling minor progression shooting from his lyre and straight into my heart.

I recognize it within two measures.

But it can't be. Papa wrote that.

My feet turn the way I didn't intend—toward the music—and I tiptoe into the hall. Just as he starts to sing, I reach the end where I can press myself against the wall to stay hidden. His quiet voice is like smoke, peppered and dark, yet smooth as it drifts over the intricately played strings.

"I hear her voice across the waters
Like a distant memory
As she sings, I'm carried farther
To a hopeless reverie"

My hands clutch each other, nails digging into my palms. That *is* Papa's song. He wrote it for Mum before they married, when he was deployed to the first war in Raevre.

"But is it so naïve
To wish that we could be
Together once again
And not torn by this sea?"

I can almost hear Papa's voice in Elias's place, a fuller and deeper sound—and my and Cas's young voices joining in for the chorus.

"Two shores, one sea,
Will the tide bring you back to me?
I would swim, I would sail
I would cross the waters deep."

Elias takes the chorus again, then slips into a melodious hum, just as Papa would, and I find myself lured into the front room where he sits, plucking his strings as if lost in another world.

I suck in a breath, compelled by loyalty and love for my father to open my mouth, and let him live through my own voice. Though, it shakes as I sing the final lines with this man who shouldn't know this song.

"But whatever would it matter
If she sings
Not for me."

Elias's forehead crinkles, and his fingers abruptly stop short of playing the outro. The strings ring as our eyes meet.

"My papa wrote that song," I say from across the room.

Elias stares at me—oddly, not smirking, not scanning. Just staring.

I step closer. "How do you—?"

A cold waft down my spine silences my question.

The boy who hated dirt under his fingernails—the one my father wanted me to marry—Papa taught him to play his lyre and every song he knew or wrote.

I gasp, the realization slapping me across the face. *How did I not recognize him sooner?*

But it couldn't be—

"Kieran?" I whisper.

A genuine smile transfigures his face. "About time, Nori."

My eyes widen, still not believing it. How could Kieran be here? What are the odds we'd meet again like this? And he looks so different. Kieran was a small boy, one Landon liked to tease and call a "weakling." And he never liked his hair to get long enough to touch his brows. Or for people to pay him much mind.

And yet—I ease even closer to him—I can see it now. Those eyes, dark as tunnels with just a hint of light at the end. Warm, tawny skin denoting that his family migrated from the Western Isles. A mischievous grin that perpetually suggested trouble, despite him being a loyal follower of the rules.

"I thought I'd give you a chance to figure it out first," he says, propping his arms over the curved mahogany of his lyre. "Didn't think it would take this long."

A weak feeling in my knees sends me into the chair across from him. "I'm so sorry. I knew something about you seemed familiar. I just—I just didn't expect to see you again."

"Too good to be true, right?" he says.

I frown. *That* is the reason I didn't recognize him. The boy I knew wasn't half as arrogant.

"I'm kidding, Nori," he adds with a roll of his eyes. "When did you get so serious?"

"When did you get so conceited?"

He shifts so his thumb can aimlessly pluck at a low A string. "Not conceited. You're just not used to seeing me without my tail between my legs."

I look at the table, the lines in the wood blurring. A memory slips over me of a younger Kieran, always doing what he was told and getting mocked by Landon and his friends. Getting knocked over just for a laugh. Hiding in the pines, throwing rocks into Lake Daleia when he thought I wasn't watching. That same boy lost his papa the year mine returned from the first war in Raevre, and, while the rest of us were still taking studies, he went to work with the fishermen so his mum could afford to eat, since the steward opted against granting them the Widow's Allowance. And in return? Landon made him into a joke, just as he later did to me.

After all that, Kieran's mum was stung by a crypt crawler scorpion, dying the most painful death known in Alémor. Papa helped him get to his grandparents back on the isles. And that was the last we saw of each other.

"When did you become a Warden?" I ask.

His expression flattens. "After the death cycle carried on to my grandparents. I only lived there about two years before they passed, too. Didn't know where to go, so I grabbed a lyre, came back to the mainland, and took to the streets. Few months in, some Warden recruiter found me and said I'd been called to join them."

"Your Bind leader?"

He shakes his head. "I'm not in a Bind. Not everyone is. That's for *special* people. I'm just a scout."

"Why'd you change your name?"

"New life, new name." He shrugs, fidgeting with another string. "Not a lot I want to remember about who I was or what brought me here."

I hug myself. *My poor friend. And all this time, I've been so harsh to him.*

"But it's good to see you, Nori." His smirk sneaks back onto his face, if only slightly. "You and your family were the better part of my childhood."

I smile, only for an immeasurable sorrow to break it. "You should know something."

"You forgot about me," he says with feigned amusement. "I figured that out already."

"I didn't. And that's not it." I wait for his expression to sober before I speak again. "My papa died last year. Lake Daleia . . . it killed him. Just like it tried to kill me."

His mouth parts, and for once, his arrogant air dissolves. "Nori . . ."

"I was there." I discreetly check my Bind Mark to make sure Calden isn't coming down the hall. The point still favors his room. "We were on the boat together when it flipped. It pulled him under, but Kieran—*Elias*—I . . ."

"What?"

Tears swell in my eyes, and though I curse them, I can't stop them from dripping onto my cheeks. Somehow telling *him*—my long-lost friend, who loved Papa nearly as much as I did—rips the wound afresh and the guilt clutches my heart with piercing talons.

"I fled," I croak, and the rest of the story spills out alongside an irrepressible sob. "It pulled him down. I started after him, but then the lake came for me, and I was so scared. I—I just fled. It should have been me that died. Cas and Milo"—I pause, remembering he never met Milo, but I don't find the strength to explain—"they should still have a father, and my mum—"

"Whoa, stop." Elias lifts a splayed hand toward me, but his words and expression are gentle. "Nori, you can't blame yourself for that. Anyone would flee."

"I *abandoned* him."

"And if you hadn't, you'd be dead." Elias's words barely escape his lips before a door opens behind me.

I dab my eyes as footsteps pad down the dirt hall. By their weight and the life sapping from Elias's eyes, I can tell who it is. Calden.

I shoot Elias a look that I hope he understands. *Don't tell him.*

"Oh, you're both awake," Calden says, a tinge of disappointment in his tone.

Was he wanting to be alone? Or did he hope to find only one of us?

Does he know about my past with Elias?

I muster a feeble smile and twist to find Calden standing like he's half-awake. Purple stains splotch the skin beneath his eyes, the color almost as dark as his new bruise. His disheveled hair sticks to his skin, plastered there by sweat. The stitches on his cheek have scabbed like he irritated the cut in his sleep—or lack thereof, by the look of him—and he apparently gave up rolling his second sleeve to match the other, which shows the full array of prepared wards on his forearm.

"You look fit for a grave," Elias comments.

Calden's weary gaze hardly acknowledges him before turning to me. "Are you all right?"

Am *I* all right?

"Are you?" I ask.

My question flies straight past him.

"I thought I heard crying."

My lungs expand and all my words seem to blow away. He can't find out what I did. He can't know how much of a coward I am. He'd never let me stay in his Bind.

"It's the ceilings," Elias says, and I spin to face him with my mouth ajar.

Is he demented? What kind of explanation is—

"Ah, yes. I should have warned you, Norielle."

I twist back to Calden to give him the same bemused look.

"These crystal-coated ceilings are known to cause horrible nightmares." Calden notices his drooping sleeve and rolls it toward his elbow. "They used to do quite the opposite—fending off nightmares—but that, like much else, changed when Ta'Nathel cursed Silvirdia."

"Can they be scraped off or something?" I ask, staring at the deceitfully beautiful ceiling.

"They'll only grow back stronger," Calden says. "We've tried neutralizing them with Peace Wards, but nothing seems to work. Some things in this world are too far gone."

My shoulders tense at the thought. How long before that becomes true of more things? Of everything? Of the whole world?

"I'm sorry your sleep was troubled," he continues, rummaging through a bag on the floating countertop. I notice his sleeve has already started to fall again.

"Yours was too, I take it?"

He winces at his stubborn sleeve before sending a smile my way. "What gave it away?"

A twang from Elias's lyre draws my attention back to him. His half-lidded stare shifts between me and Calden, then he stands.

"Well, I better get suited up," he says. "Got a journey today, don't we?"

Calden nods. And once again, I'm left out of their plans.

"Won't we just be in the passages?" I ask.

"Way's blocked," Elias says before Calden can. "Another fun consequence of living in Ta'Nathel's world. The tunnels are starting to close in on themselves in some areas. This happens to be one of them."

"We'll have to go through the ravine," Calden adds.

"It's about a six-hour hike to the next access point. We'll be clear from there." Elias rests his hand on the back of my chair. "From fellions and Hunters, at least. That's when we really gotta worry about the Blood Wardens."

He walks on at the same moment that Alani steps from her room, ginger hair bound in a crown of braids and clad in agile leather and iron armor.

"Did I miss the music?" she asks as Elias is passing her.

"Next stop, hun," he says. "Hunting time is almost over. Got a window to snag."

Alani chirps a small laugh, only for her face to contort when she sees Calden—our leader, looking the least ready of anyone to leave. He's finally settled on a slice of bread with a heaped slab of alela nut butter, which is now decorating his fingertips and the side of his mouth.

Somehow, even his mess seems intentional.

I suddenly feel Alani's attention on me, and she smiles in a way that reminds me of Cas. Except when Cas gave me that look, it was when she caught me and Kieran alone together.

Elias.

Is he even the same person?

"Would you like some?" Calden asks Alani, looking brighter than before.

"Not before morning tea, considering there seems to still be time for it," Alani says, with a look up and down the length of him. "Shall I make you some?"

"I'll pass on the swamp water." Calden grins and redirects his attention to me, holding up what's left of his bread. "Norielle? Tea? Bread?"

I stand. "Sure, I should eat something while I have the chance."

Calden pats the air, signaling for me to sit. "I've got it. Unless you're afraid of my hands."

I disregard his command. "I'm not, but I do think you have more important things you could be doing." I reach toward the bread knife in his hand. *What business does the Sovereign Prince have serving me?*

He keeps the knife, and the serrated edge saws through the bread. "I find this important," he counters, trading knives to spread the pale mauve butter across the slice in two long sweeps. He holds it out to me. "And quick enough."

I take it, almost forgetting to say thanks for the way my nerves spark when our hands brush against each other.

In the corner of my eye, I catch Alani poorly hiding another smile. I quickly turn my back and focus on filling my stomach, even as it twists. I shouldn't be feeling this way about Calden. He's the *leader.* The future Sovereign.

And the boy my papa wanted me to marry has come back to me.

CALDEN

Shadows crawl over the narrow walls of the ravine just as we reach the midpoint of our travels—dark clouds, heavy with rain. Wind sweeps in the pungent scent of wet earth, stirring up mist from the musty river, and already I sense a flood. Worse than that, a fellion hunt.

Elias leads the party, slinking beside the river through the tight pass. He was pleased when I asked him to head up the line, as if that somehow made him in charge. But the man knows nothing of leading anyone, and how little being a leader has to do with standing ahead of someone else. It's about taking responsibility for other people, serving them. Not feeling important.

But I let him have his moment.

He glances over his shoulder to Norielle, who follows nearly at his heels. His eyes don't bother looking for anyone else to make sure we haven't been dragged off by fellions, and the smirk he tosses her way prompts a twitch in my brow. Whatever conversation these two had this morning must have shifted Norielle's opinion of him from aversion to adoration, and I wish that didn't make my fists clench.

Another breeze skitters through the gaps in my garments, drawing my attention back to the sky. A cluster of even darker clouds skulk beyond the towering wall to our left, but I have a feeling they are only the edge of a vast, oncoming storm. Ahead, Elias looks up and his steps quicken.

I venture to a nearby willow, pushing away its draping branches. With my pen, I etch the same ward I used to temporarily blind the Hunters—the Glory Ward—against the purple bark, but I don't will it to light yet.

I rush to another tree, drawing the same ward there as well. Then I return to the path, trotting to catch up. Alani glances my way, her skin pale as she points to the sky.

"I know," I silently mouth then smile to reassure her. Because, of course, everything is always fine as long as I seem like I have it all figured out.

But the smile falls away as she faces forward again. A couple of decoy wards won't be enough if a pride of fellions decides to come for us once the storm starts. They do love a bonus hunt under the cover of rain, when they are the hardest to hear coming.

Another gust of wind stampedes through the ravine, plucking loose leaves from the trees that tower over the willows. I watch one with a yellow tip as it flutters through the air and falls into the river, where it is carried away by the rolling current.

Now there's an idea.

I spot another leaf as it tumbles down and snatch it. I draw another Glory Ward on it and hold it over the river until the storm exhales again. I release the leaf, and it spirals away, eventually landing in the river to be carried downstream. *Why haven't I done this before?*

I repeat this twice more, then I race toward the group, wind swatting at my cloak.

The clouds roll further across the sky, darkening the ravine. A crackle of thunder echoes off the cliff walls, driving the birds back into the trees for shelter. If only the trees could protect us. But we're four hours from the last haven and still two from the next. There will be no hiding. Only running, and that's if we're lucky.

Within minutes, heavy raindrops splash against the leaves. My steps slow. Should the fellions show, they'll target the slacker. Better they come for me than anyone else.

When the rain picks up, Elias waves to us, then he runs ahead. We bound after him, though I keep my distance. Rain splatters the river and pelts the trees, a commotion loud enough to mask our rattling gear as we run along the flooding path.

After a sprint, Elias raises his hand, slowing us to a brisk walk. I scan behind us, rain spilling from my oilskin hood, but the haze and shadows are nearly impossible to see through. My hand itches to summon my swordstaff, just to feel ready, but doing so will only announce our presence, if we haven't yet been detected. It will have to wait until the very moment it becomes necessary.

Empyrean forbid that it does.

Elias prompts us to run again, and we take off. Our feet splash in the rising water as we traverse a tight curve that leads to lower ground, an even more dangerous place. The deeper into the ravine we go, the closer to the fellions' dens we'll be.

Elias keeps us running longer this time, but once he decelerates, I ignite the first Glory Ward on the tree far behind us. A flash like lightning turns Norielle around. With the sheet of rain, I can hardly see her face when she looks to me, but I give her the same reassuring smile I gave Alani.

The sprint then walk cycle carries on for half an hour, and yet the rain only grows heavier. The now gushing river sloshes excess water onto our path, threatening to fill this place wall to wall. Elias and Norielle are lost to my sight; my only indication of them still being ahead is Alani passing Elias's signals back to me.

She lifts her hand to signal another sprint, but just as my feet lunge forward, a violent wind slaps my back, flattening my cloak against me. My steps falter, and I register the low rumble that accompanies the harsh gust as more than thunder—a roar.

I turn to find the culprit, but another powerful blast booms from the beast's lionlike mouth. The wave crashes into me, and I topple backward, water splashing as the air is punched from my lungs. I raise my hand, summoning my swordstaff with a pre-drawn ward just before the fellion leaps on top of me. I pin the long shaft behind its bloodstained teeth. Its humid breath forces a rancid stench into my nose as it bears down. My elbows shake under its incredible weight, made even heavier by pounds of muscle and thick, reptilian skin. But just before it can rake my face with its lethal claws, I urge a ward etched onto my swordstaff to activate—a Vitality Ward—and a pulse of energy throws the beast back.

I scramble upright, teeth clenched in regret. The more wards I use, the more fellions will come. But it was that or death.

The fellion charges with claws extended, and I swipe at it with my swordstaff, nicking its tough skin. The beast growls, attempting another strike, but with a twist to gain momentum, I stab a blade through its gaping jaws, piercing the back of its throat.

The beast's yowl gurgles to a moan as it collapses, its reddish mane and blue blood staining the water around it.

But as I look up, another fellion pounces across the river. My swordstaff whooshes to protect my front. The beast rears, taller than myself. I slice my blade through the soft skin beneath the creature's front leg, but it recoils only a second before charging again with the wounded leg curled in.

I swing after it, missing, and the fellion slashes toward my legs. I jump back, only to feel a blast from my side, almost tipping me over again.

I ignite another decoy ward as I regain my balance, for what little it may help us now.

The two fellions engage me on either side, and I find myself locked in a defensive position, unable to so much as scratch either of my enemies. The temptation to use wards to fight them swells. I could kill them in seconds—yet even my power may prove insufficient if I lure the rest of the pride to me.

I finally get a solid hit on the previously wounded fellion. A slash right across the eyes, and it stumbles back. I swivel to face the second beast, and as its mouth opens to roar, I maneuver my swordstaff behind its teeth, locking it in. Then, with a twist, I snap its neck. Its limp body falls to my feet, only for the other's paws to slam against my back and push me face-first into the ground the moment I turn. Water surges into my mouth and nose, and my hands are pinned beneath me, gripping my weapon. The beast releases a guttural growl as I struggle to push myself up. Its thick paws move to my shoulders, its teeth surely about to pierce my skull when, suddenly, it lets out a shriek.

Retreating, the beast shifts its attention to someone else, who I spy through the haze as I push myself from the ground.

Alani.

Her rope dart spins at her side, readying to strike with a precision I never doubt. But my relief lasts merely a blink before another surge of air sprays the rain against my back. I spin, squinting to see what's coming.

One. Two. No, *three* more fellions.

I see my decoys are working, I scoff to myself, then I will for them all to activate, hoping the bursts of energy they release will be strong enough to make this three the last of the beasts to attack. I glance at Alani as she's swinging her dart in the direction of the fellion's already damaged eyes, then I search between the trees for Elias and Norielle. But I don't see them.

A claw swipes into my peripheral vision and I react a moment too late. Its nails snag my forearm, piercing my leather armguard and peeling back my skin.

My teeth grit as I go back on the offense. The other two fellions bound toward me, but a knife sinks into one's neck, and it shifts directions toward Alani. The second's eyes stay fixed on me. And unless that was thunder, I hear another coming our way.

El-Alam, I pray, forcing strength back into my body, *grant Elias the sense to get Norielle to the haven without us.*

NORIELLE

Excess water from the heavy rain dribbles through the tree branches, filling the ravine with a choir of drips and plops. The freshly filled river gushes at my right, barely containing the water in its trench. Overhead, the dark clouds thin, but the sun has dipped behind the west wall, draping the ravine in blue shadows.

I shiver in my damp clothes as Elias and I slosh through the floodwater toward the next haven. He refused to go back for Calden and Alani, even after the rain ceased. Yet his assurance that they'd be fine felt brittle, like an unfounded optimism.

It makes the quiet all the more unsettling.

"He knows what he is doing," Elias says when I glance behind us for the hundredth time. "Just like with the Hunters. They'll catch up."

"Can't we at least wait for them?"

Elias's tone drops. "I told you, Calden ordered me to keep you safe. I obey my orders."

I huff, clutching my arms to fight off the chill.

"Nori, he'll be fine. Besides, we're nearly to the next haven."

I lower my face and follow in silence until he leads us off the path and into a stretch of slimy mud. The slick ground slides beneath my feet, off-setting my balance. Elias strides to the cliffside where he draws the ward to make a door appear—a Key Ward, Calden called it. I watch the light cut through rock and dirt with far less amazement than I felt last time. Passing through this doorway feels wrong, like I'm abandoning my Bind to their ill fate—just like I abandoned Papa.

But Calden and Alani aren't Papa, I remind myself. They are Wardens, raised to handle such encounters. What would I be able to do to help them?

Elias holds the door open for me, and we enter a space nearly identical to the last haven. The same nightmare-giving crystal ceilings, the same makeshift kitchen, another timeworn table. The only differences I spot are a dilapidated couch and three tunnels leading out of this space instead of one. A soft golden glow shimmers from the one on my left. The right tunnel turns too sharply to see down, and the middle tunnel has only three doors, followed by a dead end.

I check my Omen Mark but find it black. The Bind Mark still points to the ravine. If Calden died, would it disappear? Or would it point to whatever remained of him?

I cringe at the horrific thought. There wouldn't be a body to point to. Not with fellions.

Then Elias must be right.

I hope.

"I'm going to change," I say.

Elias nods, and I enter the first door in the hall. Once the lock clicks behind me, I plunk my bag onto the bed, left unmade by whoever stayed here last. Calden said there are Warden suppliers that come through to wash the bedding every few weeks. Still, the thought of laying my head against a pillow where some stranger sweated and maybe even drooled makes me miss home.

My bed. Across from Cas.

I shove my thoughts of her away, like always, before they weaken me to the point of tears.

I dig out the other outfit Ila made with the fancy dark blouse and pants. The fabric is slightly damp from the humidity, but it's better than what I'm wearing. I undress, put on the new clothes, and spend a few minutes wrestling a comb through my hair. Even with it partially tied back, the wind tangled the locks into nests.

I should cut it.

But I won't. Papa loved my hair. He said it reminded him of when he met Mum, before she chopped her hair to a more manageable length to keep me from using it as a rope when I was still toddling about.

I yank my comb through the final knot, impatience snapping several strands of hair. But just as I'm tossing the comb back into my bag, I hear a deep, resonant voice outside my room.

My distress falls off me like a heavy coat, and I rush toward my door, feet bare against the cool dirt. I burst out, only for my heels to hit the ground, preventing a near collision with Calden.

I tilt my gaze to meet his, and we both backstep.

"You're okay," I say, unable to restrain the relief in my tone.

His hand stills over his armguard that he was in the middle of unstrapping. "Glad to see Elias got you here safely," he says with an exhausted rasp in his voice. "As planned."

My brows crinkle. "That was planned?"

He teeters his hand. *Partially.*

"I always have a plan, friend. Even if I wish not to execute it." He shifts to step around me. "If you don't mind, I'd like to clean up."

I move out of his way but catch the vibrant red of blood beneath his shredded armguard before he can hide it from sight.

"You're injured," I say.

He stops walking. "Hardly, considering. It's Alani who took the worst of it."

"Is she all right?"

"She is now. I've already healed her."

Healed her?

He enters his room before I can ask more questions.

I peer into the front room but find neither Alani nor Elias. My lips twist, but a sudden shiver reminds me how cold it is, even in here. Too worn out to care what anyone thinks, I return to my room to yank the thick wool blanket off my bed and drape it around my shoulders. It reeks of dirt and a hint of someone else's sweat.

I explore the other two tunnels. The tightly wound one appears endless, whereas the warmly glowing one opens to a chamber with radiant purple and gold crystals glimmering across the walls. *The colors of my soul,* I think, remembering my soulcast flower. The luster is reflected by a pool of water that has collected in a low section of the ground. Beside it, a ring of chairs encircles a budding fire where I find Alani unraveling her braids. A rip in her pants reveals her blood-coated thigh, yet through the slits in the fabric, I see undamaged skin.

He really did heal her.

The awe crumbles quickly behind a question. *Can't anyone heal* him*?*

"We've gotten through the worst of the journey," Alani says in a cheery tone. "It's all tunnels from here."

I take the seat beside her, bundling my blanket tighter around myself.

"You were injured?" I ask.

"Oh, just a bit." She rubs her thigh. "All better now. At least, I am."

My eyes narrow. "Calden said he healed you. Is that a type of ward?"

Alani averts her gaze. "Yes, and it's a complicated one at that."

"Is it something only Warden Masters can use?"

She lets out a long, shaky hum. "No, actually. All have access to it, but, well, let's just say that not everyone can heal just anyone. It's a Conditional Ward, meaning there are certain stipulations."

"Like what?" I ask, but before she can answer, the sound of shuffling feet draws her attention. I follow her gaze, hoping to find Calden at the end of it, but Elias steps out, bundling a blanket in his arms. He plops the blanket onto my lap as he passes me. I move to push it off but stop, not wanting to seem childish.

"Funny, the things I still remember," he says as he takes a seat across the fire. "You never took to the cold."

Shame sags my posture. How does he remember details like that when it took me two days to recognize him?

"Do you know each other?" Alani asks.

"When we were kids," Elias says.

Alani turns to me like I might offer more detail, but a shrug is my only response.

"Wild. What are the odds of that?" she says, then stands. "I suppose I should get myself cleaned up, now that there's a free room."

My fingers twitch as she disappears. She didn't answer my question, and why do I sense that she didn't want to? Is she ashamed?

"So, Calden can heal Alani, but who can heal Calden?" I ask Elias instead.

His barely suppressed sigh hits me with a slap of guilt. I didn't even thank him for the blanket or remembering about me disliking the cold, and now I'm talking to him about Calden . . . again.

"I can't, if that's what you're getting at," Elias says. "Alani's never had much luck either."

"Why? Alani said there are stipulations to the ward. Are you two not qualified to use it for some reason?"

He flinches, and I bite my lip. Yet my apology stays in my throat.

"Actually, *he's* the problem," Elias says. "Hard to heal people who've wronged you."

"What?" I check my Bind Mark. "What could he have done?"

"Please," he groans. "Don't be so alarmed. Even the Sovereign Prince has his flaws, Nori."

The muscles across my chest tighten, and I burrow deeper into my blanket. Of course, I'm not so dense as to assume Calden is perfect, but didn't Alani almost kill him? Yet he can heal her? What could he have done that was so offensive that neither Alani nor Elias can use the ward on him?

"Could he heal *you*?" I pose.

Elias's brows dip, his attention shifting to the fire. "I don't know. Probably not."

"Well, what happened?"

Elias shakes his head. "Don't worry about it, Nori."

I sit up taller. "Too late for that."

"*Honestly.*"

"Just tell me, *Kieran.*"

The sound of his former name causes his eye to twitch. "I don't go by that anymore."

I almost ask why it offends him before I catch his deflection. "What did Calden do to you that's so bad that you can't heal him?"

He kicks his feet up on the chair beside him, leaning so the chair he's sitting in tips slightly. "Nothing on purpose. So, calm down."

The fire crackles in our pause. Then Elias must be unfairly angry at him. Why? Because Calden's one of the *special* ones?

But what about Alani?

I resist the urge to ask, sensing I won't get anywhere anyway, and return to the original problem. Calden is wounded—again—and no one here can help him.

Actually . . .

I stand, thrusting the blanket Elias gave me at him. He catches it with a raised brow.

"Rude." He wads it onto his lap. "Where are you going?"

"Calden needs stitches, and I doubt he'll be able to stitch his own arm."

A low "oh" is his only response, and I march off, pushing past the self-imposed resistance that met me yesterday when Calden was cut across his face. *Will every day around here involve blood and injuries?*

In the hall, I double-check my Bind Mark for which room Calden went into, but once reaching it, I delay knocking. He's always said I could call on him if I need something, yet what if he wants to be left alone? Though if he accepts my help, then I'll have to go through with the stitching and everything that comes with it—the gore, the proximity, the need to force my hands to still when they are already shaking.

But to leave him unattanded feels cruel. Especially since this is another injury gained while protecting us.

My knuckles tap the door. I pinch the ends of the blanket over my collarbone and wait.

"What's the matter?" Calden calls from inside.

"Nothing," I say, expecting him to send me off, but instead, the door opens wide.

"Wasn't expecting it to be you," he says, pushing back his dried clumps of hair. His sleeves are bunched nearly to his shoulders, a shiny film covering each of the red cuts on his skin. Tary salve, by the tangy smell. That explains why his eyes are red. Easier to cry over the pain from that horrid ointment when there's no one else watching. But it does work wonders for slowing a bleed.

"Do you need something?" Calden asks, lips pinching into a smile as he notices I'm wearing a blanket.

I swallow. "No, you do."

"Oh?"

"Stitches," I say, pulling the wool tighter. "My papa taught me, so I thought I'd offer since I think it's your dominant arm that's hurt."

His brows rise like he means to speak, probably to give a polite dismissal by the nervous look in his eyes.

"Just offering," I add when his reply seems to get stuck in his throat.

"Thank you," he finally says, and I brace myself for the embarrassment of being sent away. "I'm low on thread, have you any?"

My stomach flutters. "I do. Yes. Where should we—?"

"The table in the front room," he says. "I'll be there in a moment."

I nod, returning to snag my first aid pack from the room I claimed. I take it to the table where I wait, trying to soothe my nerves. I haven't stitched anyone in nearly as long as it's been since I practiced with a sword, and all I can hope is that my hands remember what to do, just as they did when that Hunter attacked.

Alani exits the room that Elias must have initially taken, and only then do I realize we don't have enough rooms for all of us. Or beds. I suppose Alani and I will have to share, so Calden and Elias don't kill each other.

Alani pauses at the table, arched brows lifting when she sees my supplies.

"Calden needs stitches," I say, biting back the rest of what I want to say. *Since no one here can heal him.*

Maybe tonight, behind a shut door, I can press Alani for details.

Her shoulders slacken, and her girlish smile from this morning returns to brighten her cheeks. "Oh, I see," she says. "Okay. Well, I'll be down the hall with Elias. He owes me a song, and, uh, I wouldn't want to hover."

She walks off, and I add inquiring about her weird behavior to the list of things to ask when we have privacy. Though, I'd have to be an idiot not to see what she's clearly thinking.

Calden appears with freshly combed hair and an oddly low cast to his gaze. His gait wobbles slightly, favoring his right leg, but he forces it into a normal stride by the time he reaches the table. The ancient chair creaks as his weight settles on it, and he looks over my spread of supplies.

"Did you hurt your leg, too?" I ask.

A corner of his mouth twitches down. "No, that's from healing Alani. The ward transfers the pain from the injured person to the healer, but luckily, not the injury."

I press my lips closed, not wanting to hassle him straightaway with my questions. "I wish I could help with your pain somehow, but I'm afraid I'm only going to make it worse."

"Nothing could be worse than tary salve." His bright expression returns, only to douse a second later, like an ember sparking before it dies. He sets his arm on the table, the brilliance of the ceiling crystals providing an excellent light source—almost *too* excellent. My stomach churns at the thick gashes.

I suck in a breath, assuring myself they aren't that bad. Red is only a color. And it's only skin, like what covers me. I take my pre-threaded needle in hand and try to remember Papa's instructions.

Step one, get the person talking before you poke them.

"Can you tell me about the ward you used to heal Alani?" I ask.

"The Healing Ward?" he says, and at the next sound he makes, I sink the needle into his skin. He barely stirs. "It's a more complex ward than some of the others I've told you about. It's considered a Conditional Ward but also a Consequential one."

I do my best to listen as I continue working the thread through his flesh and gently tugging it back together.

"Consequential Wards have repercussions for the person who uses them. Really, all wards have some consequence, since they all require energy, but these have something more. Such as what I mentioned a moment ago. The healer bears the pain of the person they are healing." He glances at my hands that I've managed to steady, then at his wound with a small grimace before staring into space. "It being Conditional means there are certain requirements that must be met in order for a person to use it. Healing is considered one of the most powerful forms of magic, and therefore, it requires the most powerful form of energy."

The needle grows slick, and I wipe his blood from my hands, then nod to show him I'm still following.

"There are two conditions for using a Healing Ward. First, one must genuinely care for the person they are healing. Because of the consequence, our will to heal may be hindered if we don't care enough for that person to bear their pain."

Well, that explains Elias.

"And the second is that we cannot be actively holding any unforgiveness toward them. Healing must flow from a pure heart toward that person, otherwise the ward will not activate."

My hands slow. *What did he do to Alani?*

"Barring these stipulations, even if one *does* activate the Healing Ward, how effective it is also depends on how deeply that person cares for the other. So, a minor injury could be healed by a well-meaning acquaintance, but say someone was dying. They'd need someone who loved them with their very life. Because in such an extreme case, the healer risks the possibility of overextending themselves and dying in the process."

I tie off the first round of stitches in the trio of gashes. "That is much more complicated than the others."

"Few are like that. Don't worry." He rotates his arm to see my stitching and gives an approving nod.

"Two more rounds," I say, rethreading my needle. I ready my next comment and fire it as I prick him again. "You must care a lot for Alani."

"Of course," he says, and I fight to keep my expression stoic. "I've known her about a year now and we've spent a good deal of time together since." He takes a moment to ponder something before adding, "You could say Alani is more like a sister to me than my true one. At least, she likes me better than Odessa does."

I tug the needle, almost too harshly, and I have to steady my pace. "Then, if I may ask, why can't she heal you?"

He sighs, and I wish I could suck the question back into my mouth. I should have waited to ask Alani herself, not pestered Calden with it while I'm stitching him, as if he's not uncomfortable enough.

"I will tell you," he finally says, after a silence as wide as the ocean. "But I'm not sure now is the best time."

"Is it something she holds against you?"

"Yes, though not for lack of effort to forgive me."

My mouth suddenly feels dry. "I'm open to hearing it, even over stitches."

"I think you might find yourself too stunned to continue."

I lower the needle. "It can't be that bad, can it?"

He almost pulls his arm away from me, but my hand is quick to snatch it back.

"Truly, Norielle, I'd rather discuss this another time."

Something turns over in my stomach. "Well, now I'm afraid."

"And you'll be even more so if I share it."

My grip on his arm loosens. "That doesn't help."

His eyes close, a deep sigh rolling like a hot wind across the table and tickling my skin. "I suppose there's no avoiding it now, is there?"

I take advantage of his pause to brace myself.

"There is something wrong with me," he starts, quieter than before, "and I haven't wanted to share because I feared it might prevent you from coming to the citadel and becoming who El-Alam wants you to be. But now that the others are also here . . ." His words trail away with his gaze, and a chill races up my back.

"What is it?" I press.

Three loud thumps of my heart fill the seconds he takes to answer.

"Norielle, I'm cursed."

Just as he predicted, my hands cease to move, feeling detached from my arms.

"No one really understands it, but I've had it all my life. I suspect it's why my birth parents left me. Either they knew of it or witnessed what happens and became afraid."

"And what happens?" My voice is barely audible, even to myself.

"It's like I get trapped in someone else's mind." He speaks louder now, but his voice trembles. "Simultaneously, I lose control of my power and somehow gain greater access to it. I can use *any* ward without drawing it, not just my Talent. It's incredibly dangerous for anyone near me, because something in this—this other mind—it wants me to hurt anyone who comes near. It deems everyone a threat. And I can't see anything but a world of madness in my head. Outside voices disappear and all I know is terror and grief that I can't begin to comprehend. And worst of all, there seems to be no way to stop an episode once it starts, except to wait it out."

My breath quickens, but I'm speechless. What can I say to that? Cursed? How? Why? All questions he already said he doesn't have the answers to.

"It happened when Alani and I were first traveling together, when I went to inform her she was a member of the Bind." The sorrow that fills his voice seems to sap the energy from my body. "I lost control, and she thought I needed help because I was crying out as if injured. Then I blasted her with energy, throwing her against a rock wall. The impact broke her ribs and pierced one of her lungs. I barely came back to myself in time to heal her, but because I barely knew her then, the healing was incomplete. She suffered all the way to the citadel until the Elders could help her."

I look down, unsure if the needle is even in my hands anymore. His second laceration is only half sewn, and the trembling I did so well to ease has returned sevenfold, shuddering all the way into my spine.

"I promise I've taken every precaution to make sure nothing happens to you. That's why you may have seen me sleeping with a Snare Ward on my wrist those nights in the Rimrook Mountains, but I"—his shoulders curl inward, and his tone falls again—"I would understand if upon hearing this, you wished to keep your distance."

My mouth hangs open, and I'm too stunned to tell how I feel about any of this besides alarmed and confused. But before I think of anything worth saying, another voice cuts into our conversation.

"Not that I was eavesdropping, but glad you finally spilled, Cal. Thought I was gonna have to warn her." Elias's gaze flicks to me. "Not that you'd have believed it coming from me."

I expect Calden to muster one of his usual witty replies, but instead he just stares at Elias as if he'd said nothing at all.

Elias shrugs it off, grabbing a couple of ceramic mugs. "Making tea."

I can't tell if he means to ask if we want any or if he's just announcing what brought him into the middle of our conversation. But, like Calden, I get trapped in the haze in my mind.

Calden is cursed. His power erupts. Alani almost died—

"Stitches look good, Nori," Elias comments as he turns toward the tunnel. "Should've let her fix your face, too, Cal."

He pauses to give me the most apologetic look he seems capable of, then he's gone again. It takes me another twenty seconds to return to Calden's eyes, and the pallid wash of his complexion makes my lip tremble.

"I'm so sorry, Calden," I say.

"I understand. It would be for the best, anyway." He looks at his wounded arm, frowning. "I can finish this. You don't need to—"

"No. That's not what I meant." I fidget with the needle. "I'm saying that I'm sorry about your curse. It sounds absolutely horrible. I can't even imagine what you're describing or how that must feel when you come back and see . . ."

"The damage," he finishes for me.

I nod. "Is there no cure? No way to break the curse?"

"Nothing has been found in over twenty years of searching, and by the brightest minds in the kingdom. I have learned through experience, at least, what triggers it and how best to avoid it, but sometimes it's simply not possible to predict its appearance."

His arm shifts, reminding me of what I'm supposed to be doing. I hold his arm in one hand as I steady the needle for the next stitch. "What are the triggers?"

His fingers flex as I poke into his skin again for the first time in several minutes. I force my hands to work more quickly as he shares.

"Generally, intense feelings of fear or sorrow. Exhaustion. Overexertion." He lets out a sullen chuckle. "This is why sleep is both dangerous and necessary. Nightmares can trigger it, but if I don't sleep, I'm less able to resist having my mind overtaken should something stir it."

I glance at the crystal ceiling.

"Yes," he says. "These have been known to provoke an episode. But I'm taking care."

I think back to how he looked this morning, half-dead. Is that what he calls "taking care"?

"But Norielle"—his fingers suddenly wrap around my forearm, and my heart rate doubles—"you must promise me something."

The tingles inspired by his grip confront me with another reason these fledgling feelings for him are ill-advised. He's dangerous. Even if it's not his fault.

"If you ever see me like that, you must get far away from me," he says. "I don't want to hurt you."

"I'll stay back," I promise.

"Thank you."

His grip loosens, and I return to the stitches, tying off the second row before starting the third. Silence falls until I've finished the sutures and have wrapped his arm in a linen bandage. He inspects the whitish wrap while I stow the supplies and buckle my first aid pack closed.

"I appreciate this," he says, rising. "Hopefully, I won't need any more after this for a while."

I stand also, cradling my first aid pack. "Maybe by the time you do, I'll be able to use that ward instead," I say, not considering the implications of my statement until it's too late.

But to my surprise, he doesn't withdraw. Instead, his smile widens. "I'll try not to upset you in the meantime."

"I don't think you'll have to try very hard."

He holds my gaze for a moment and warmth seems to radiate between us, but as if fear itself came to whisper in his ear, his expression suddenly shifts, and he pivots away. A flash of what happened to Alani plays in my imagination as if plucked from his memory, but I quickly repel it. It's not him. It's something else.

Something I hope to never witness.

"Thank you again," he says, his tone turning impersonal. "I'm going to check on the others."

My arms sag as he walks away, and I feel the distance between us like the two walls of the ravine. With a curse like that, he'd never let anyone too close. Even if they were willing to risk the danger. He's too selfless. Too sacrificing.

And I'm too much of a coward.

NORIELLE

Music from Elias's lyre drifts through the dim tunnels as we begin our first day of traveling inside the Wardens' passages. Calden leads the group, but despite the friendly smiles he gives us any time he finds a reason to turn around, he's been subdued all morning. And I don't miss that his gaze favors the other two members of the party, like he's afraid of seeing judgment in my eyes now that I've had time to process what he told me about his curse.

Alani walks beside me, poorly humming along to Elias's tune. I didn't ask her anything last night since Calden had already told me what I most wanted to know. And I wouldn't have had a chance anyway, since Calden gave us three the rooms and took the couch instead.

The crystals overhead grow in patches, projecting splotches of light and shadow onto a long and winding path. The dirt ground is pressed from the traversing of many feet, with barely a rock to be found besides those trampled deep into the earth. My fingertips trail a lode in the layered stone wall, and I wonder how these tunnels were made. Is this the work of another golem like Rimrir? Or nature? Or of the Wardens themselves? The walls are smooth enough to be sanded wood.

"Faring all right?" Calden asks, and I recall that I mentioned my legs felt wobbly this morning from our long trek yesterday.

I consider the wavering of my knees every few steps before claiming, "I'm fine."

Calden checks his Omen Mark for the dozenth time this morning. "We'll stop at the next haven to rest."

"How considerate," Elias says with a sarcastic edge. "It's only ten miles away, Nori. Not far at all."

"Ten?" Calden echoes, slowing to look at him. "Is it that far?"

"At least."

"That's fine," I say. "As long as we're not running."

Calden unfurls a map, holding it toward the gleaming crystals.

Elias puffs behind us, plucking a new set of notes with a hint of aggression. "It's not like I've been through here a thousand times or anything."

"Twelve," Calden says, rolling up the map. "It's twelve miles."

"I said *at least*."

"Isn't it so fun traveling with them?" Alani pipes in with a gentle nudge to my shoulder.

"Do they ever get along?"

She giggles. "This *is* them getting along."

"Have you three traveled much together, then?" I ask of anyone who will answer.

"I've only been graced with both of their presences once before, but it was an adventure filled with just as much bickering." Alani grins at each of them. "Luckily, growing up with six brothers prepared me for this."

"*Six* brothers?" My exclamation nearly harmonizes with Elias's tune as it vibrates along the walls. "I only have one."

Alani beams. "I was the only girl *and* the youngest. Mum and Pa were determined to have a girl. Only took seven tries. Poor Mum. She's out there at sea somewhere, probably nursing a headache as her grown boys wrestle across the deck." Her smile wilts. "I do feel sorry for her. She finally had her girl, only for that girl to get called away. Mum was proud, of course, and I get to visit now and again. But I know she misses having her girl around."

"So, they're all Wardens?" I ask.

"Every one of them. They're part of the naval sector of Wardens, the ones who guard against the Accursed in the deep and tame the vortexes."

"The vortexes the ships get sucked into?"

"Aye, those," she says. "I can't say we've always done well at getting to them quickly. There are not many Warden ships out there, even with some of my brothers captaining their own ships."

"Can you sail?" I ask.

"Better than any of her brothers," Calden interjects. "Or so I've heard."

"The sea's a wild thing," Alani says. "No different than a brother."

I smile, trying not to miss my own. Though, for every trace of wildness in Milo, there is sweetness. Just like Papa. If he was a sea, he'd be one with soft shores and harmlessly mischievous waves.

"Whatever purpose our Bind is for, I assume we must need a skilled sailor for it," Calden says. "Or else El-Alam just didn't want me to miss the perfect captain for my ship."

A hard *twang* comes from Elias's lyre, and I look back to see him shaking his head at Calden. He pantomimes putting on a crown and rolls his eyes.

I half-scowl, half-smile at him before returning my attention to Calden. "You have a ship?"

"That I've never been on," Calden says. "There are Wardens in the other kingdoms, though not as many as are here in Alémor. Still, my mother must visit them time and again. I'll have to start doing so eventually myself."

"And you think our mission might involve sea travel?"

"Just a theory. Usually Bind members are each chosen for a specific task or skill set." He gestures toward Alani. "Her skill is rather specialized, which makes for an easy suggestion as to why she'd be part of our Bind."

Finally, he's sharing his theories.

"That makes sense," I say, and I wait a few steps before letting my curiosity leap out. "Any theories about me yet?"

Calden gives a low, pensive hum, and Alani turns her face away, though not quickly enough for me to miss her raised brows and thinned lips. I twist to see Elias's expression, but all he offers is a flat stare before he returns his focus to his harp. If not for his playing, the tunnel would be silent.

But Calden must have *some* theories. He can't be just as lost as I am about this—

"Sovereign Prince Calden!" a new voice calls from down the tunnel, and my shoulders tense.

I lean sideways to see around Calden's cloaked shoulder and find a man with a silvery shine to his hair, bowing so low I can't see his face. Behind him is a long rolling cart filled with blankets. A supplier, I realize.

What a disappointment it must be to get *that* assignment.

Elias's song abruptly switches to a new tune with bold, ascending chords that I recognize as an anthem for royal parades. My brows dip, and when I glance at him, Elias is poorly hiding a fiendish smirk.

Calden greets the supplier, yet the man remains bowed until we pass. My cheeks flush, this display of honor reminding me of who Calden really is. A prince—the future ruler of this hidden society. And I'm tagging along at his heels wondering why I matter in his life.

I'm probably supposed to be his servant.

"Elias, really," Calden chides after we're clear of the supplier.

Elias sniggers, letting the parade melody dissipate to a mere echo.

"It's a good thing you aren't in the Bind, lest I worry El-Alam chose you to be my embarrassment of a minstrel." Calden runs his hand through his hair. "Ridiculous."

A small squeak escapes from Alani, and I look to see her face is red from holding back a laugh. I shake my head at Elias, but my smile fails to deliver any reprimand, and his grin only grows more impish. And there I see him, little Kieran—much like Milo, with too good of a heart to really do anything truly *wrong* but always teetering on the edge of what's really *right*.

Elias returns to his former melody, which times perfectly with our footfalls, and once more, our conversation dwindles behind his song. Only now, my mind is swirling anew with thoughts of my destiny, like leaves picked up by a whirlwind. What skills do I offer that might indicate why I'm here? I can barely wield this sword at my hip. I don't know anything about sailing, nor do I possess any other unique and useful talents that come to mind—not for this. Mum always said I learn well and teach better, but what use is that when I'm the new one? They couldn't want me as any form of teacher and certainly not for Calden, who has been *my* teacher all this way.

Elias knew me once. He must have a theory or two.

I glance at him again, alarmed to find his eyes already on me, and yet there's something solemn in them despite the levity of his song. I bite back my question. If he wanted to share his theories in front of the others, he'd have spoken up when I asked. Either that, or his need to obey the rules regarding such discussions kept him silent.

I'll get it out of him later, next time we're alone—should we ever be.

"What do you think your sister's role is?" I ask Calden.

"Odessa?" He delays his response with a long drink from his flask. "To chastise me and keep me in check."

Alani scrunches her nose in what I take to be agreement. How unpleasant is this Odessa, who my destiny is also tied to?

"No," Calden continues more seriously. "Most teams need a second-in-command of sorts. I'd expect that to be her."

My gaze falls to the moss-lined intersection between the wall and ground. Everyone in the Bind seems so important, and I can't help but raise the question again of why El-Alam would want to bring *me* from the outside into such significant company. If it was only to be a servant, why wouldn't he call one of those suppliers? Or someone else who's already acclimated to the Wardens? What could possibly make me matter in this context?

By the end of the twelve miles, my feet feel bruised, and my muscles burn from overuse. We land in another unoccupied haven, which Elias warns should be one of the last without company. It looks just like the others besides a few minor differences, as if whoever constructed these wanted it to feel like we were just walking from hall to hall in one big house, and it always led back to the same place. But the sight of four bedroom doors instead of three prompts a hearty sigh of relief. Guilt for taking a bedroom while Calden slept on the couch nipped at me last night, and I'd only feel it worse now after being reminded he's the next Sovereign.

Why didn't he make one of us sleep out there? Or just leave Alani and I to room together?

We share a quiet meal around the fire in a chamber whose ceiling opens just enough for the smoke to slither out. Through its small crack, I catch a glimpse of one flickering star, and I wonder when I'll see the full sky again or breathe in a fresh breeze that doesn't smell of earth and stone.

When we all have finished eating, I settle into my wobbly chair, hoping to outlast Calden and Alani so I can badger Elias about his theories. But, to my disappointment, Elias is the first to excuse himself, even without an evening tea. I resist the urge to go after him as he disappears around the curve of the tunnel, and a moment later, I hear the *click* of his door locking.

"Did you know they knew each other?" Alani asks Calden.

He stirs from a meditative trance on the licking flames to look at me, rather than Alani. "No," he says, but his eyes request an explanation.

"In Behria," I say, rubbing the hem of the latest blanket I've claimed. "We grew up together there. But he moved away when he was twelve." I reserve the reasoning why, realizing Elias has probably kept a tight seal on his past based on how he seems to despise it. "I feel awful. I hardly recognized him with that beard, not to mention that he changed his name."

Calden's forehead creases, but he withholds any comment besides a quiet, "How strange."

"He's not really how I remember," I murmur, hoping Elias hasn't crept from his room, somehow sensing he's finally the central topic of our conversation.

"Could he always play?" Alani asks.

A hollow pit forms in my core. "From a fairly young age, yes. My papa taught him."

Calden's gaze jerks toward the wall, his irises glinting in the light of a cluster of teal crystals. Still, he holds his tongue. Is he offended Elias didn't mention this? Or just confused at what this means, if anything?

"Oh, your papa is a bard?" Alani asks, resting her chin on a hand like she expects me to tell a long and lovely story.

"He was," I say, and her hand slowly drops into her lap as I continue. "He played around the kingdom when he was younger, but eventually, he traded his lyre for a sword and joined the soldiers during the first war in Raevre. He never stopped playing though, and Kier—" I catch myself and try again, hoping they don't ask for his real name. "*Elias* asked Papa to teach him how to play. That's how I got to know him, from him hanging around my father."

"You two must have been close friends, then?" Alani says, stealing a glance at Calden, who looks pale and stiff enough to be a statue.

For my own sake, I withhold sharing the first thought that comes to mind. *My papa wanted us to marry.*

"We were, but it's been a long time," I say.

"To one of you," Calden says, his voice as flat as his expression, but as if the sound of himself talking reminds him he exists, he perks up. "I'm glad you find yourself in some familiar company. I'm sure that is a relief to you."

My hands curl. *Is it?*

"I think I'll get to sleep myself," Calden says, standing. He barely meets my gaze before he and Alani share a meaningful glance. He turns away, wishing us both good-night, and I sink beneath the shelter of my blanket.

"Is he okay?" I whisper to Alani once I've heard his door close.

Alani smiles. "Sure he is. Just exhausted. It's a hard business, watching over us all."

"He seemed uncomfortable with me and Elias knowing each other."

Alani bites the tip of her finger, thinking far too long about her response. "I think he's bothered that Elias kept this a secret. They've been friends since Elias joined the Wardens."

I almost snort. "Friends?"

She chuckles. "Maybe not the best of them, but deep down I think they appreciate each other's company. It's just that neither wants the other one to know that."

"Clearly."

We both laugh, but hers ends with a solemn expression, and a crease forms between her brows. "What was he like when he was younger? Elias."

I check the tunnel to be sure we're still alone before responding. "Quieter, a little nicer, and a lot less confident."

"And you . . . you said you were very close?"

My hands wring each other in my lap, and I avert my gaze from her curious eyes. *Can I tell her?*

Should I?

"He was my best friend," I say finally, fixing my attention on the wiggling flames. The memories of my childhood with Kieran—*Elias*—are so faint now, as if everything that happened before my father's passing is clouded by the black smoke of death. But through it, I can still vaguely feel the warmth of Kieran's tight hugs and the pinching feeling in my abdomen from laughing far too hard at something he said or did.

Have I laughed like that since he's been gone? Or is such laughter simply a thing of youth that I shouldn't credit him alone for?

"Where I'm from, a girl's father is in charge of her future," I continue without any real reason as to why, besides that my heart is aching and it needs someone to hear its inner cries. "My papa wanted me to marry Elias when we grew up. But things didn't really go as Papa planned. We never expected him to have to leave town."

Alani leans toward me, as if hanging off my every word, and I wonder whether she lives for gossip or if there's something more to her intrigue.

"What happened?" she asks.

"I don't think he'd like it if I shared." I incline my head against the backrest to stare at the crystal-flecked ceiling. "Some terrible things happened to him and his family, and he was forced to leave town. That was the end of my papa's dream for my future."

I sense rather than see Alani's eyes narrowing at me. "And yours? Was it the end of your dream?"

My jaw locks. How many nights did I lie awake as a young girl, reimagining scenes of my mum and papa but as Elias and me? How many mornings did I watch for the sunlight to hit my window so I could go meet him by the lake? How many tears did I cry after he left, haunted by his absence and the memories of his horrific last days in Behria?

But that was when he was Kieran.

"I guess." The words come out in a groan. "But it doesn't matter now. Neither of us are the same anymore. And now—"

"There's Calden."

Her brazen statement reels my gaze back to her now grinning face.

"No," I deny despite the surge of pink to my cheeks. "Now there's no longer the future my papa wanted. Now it's the future El-Alam wants, and all I want to know is what that is."

Alani considers me for a long moment, her smile slowly shrinking. "When you're ready to know it, you will. That's what my mum always said."

My lips twitch, and I want to ask her what she thinks I'm here for, but her attention suddenly shifts upward.

"You know, sometimes I like to sleep out here in these chambers, since the nightmare crystals aren't in here," she says. "I think I'll stay in here tonight. You're welcome to join me, if you like."

I check my Omen Mark. "Is it safe?"

"Sure it is." She stands, pointing as she speaks. "I'll put a few Snare Wards in the entrance here, and I'll be right here, should any Blood Warden dare approach. It's not like a locked door is much security, anyway."

I tap my knuckle, debating. "I guess I could use a night without terrors."

She beams and spins toward the tunnel. "Come along then, let's get our things and set up."

A few minutes later, I find myself sitting cross-legged on the ground with a warm cup of tea resting in my palms and a fire flickering between me and my red-haired companion.

Alani sets her tea aside to lay out her throwing knives on the ground. The fire's orange glow reflects on the lethal steel blades as she nudges them into an even row. She plucks one from the end and sets a grindstone against it.

I sip the mullenberry tea as I watch, and Alani flashes a gleeful smile, pleased to have won me over to her choice of tea that, apparently, Calden calls the vilest of all teas. She trades her knife for another and, as the stone scrapes across it, something occurs to me.

"So, which of those knives is responsible for almost killing the prince?" I ask, hoping my bait works to win me the long-awaited story.

Amusement lights her eyes as she looks across the spread. "Hard to say. They all look guilty, don't they?"

"Did you not realize it was him?" I ask.

She lowers the grindstone and knife to her lap. "I thought he was a Hunter. If Mum and Pa did one thing well, it was raise me to be paranoid about Hunters while on land. It didn't help that he approached me in the middle of the night while I was alone on the beach." She chuckles at the memory. "Wise he may be, but he wasn't that time."

"What happened after you threw the knife?"

"He dodged the second one better and told me to stop by order of the Sovereign Prince."

She giggles and I join her, imagining it myself.

"I'd never seen him before, but it was easy to recognize him after what I'd heard of him. Rumor has it the sea itself is jealous of the pure blue of his eyes." She returns to her sharpening, filling the atrium with the quiet scratching of stone against steel. "I'm sure you've noticed."

I sip my tea rather than acknowledge her comment. "So, you recognized him, and then?"

"I nearly hurled from the embarrassment." She laughs, wiping an eye with the back of her hand. "Oh, it was an awful start."

I look down at the blue flames in the fire, almost feeling humiliated on her behalf. Not that my introduction to Calden was much better—he got to meet me at the bottom of the lake, nearly dead because of my own impulsiveness.

"He handled it with such grace, of course," Alani says, holding up her knife to inspect the blade. "Even complimented my accuracy."

Sounds about right. Someone would almost kill him, and he'd compliment the way they did it.

I turn to hide the way the thought makes me smile, until the recollection of his curse steals it away. Why should such a kind person have to suffer in such a way? It hardly seems fair.

The life of a Warden is often unfair, he once said. Now I wonder if his curse is part of why he said it.

I finish my tea and set the cup aside. "Thanks for letting me stay out here with you," I say as I shift to lie down. "I think I'm ready for some dreamless sleep."

"You and me both," she says, her knives clinking together as she gathers them and tucks them away.

NORIELLE

A yell startles me from my sleep, and I twist to find Alani's bedding empty on the other side of the depleted firepit. Breath shudders into my lungs, and I sit up, a burst of cold slapping me as I toss my blanket aside. My fingers just brush the chilled metal hilt of my sword when a confused mumble comes from around the tunnel bend.

I retract my hand when I recognize the voice. It's only Elias—not a Blood Warden—and he's probably stuck in one of Alani's Snare Wards.

How pitiful.

"Alani!" he hollers just before I move in his direction and then step into his view.

I cover my mouth, trying—unsuccessfully—to hide my laugh at the sight of him caught like an animal with his foot in a buzzing coil of energy.

"Where is she?" he asks, craning to see around the tunnel's bend.

"I don't know." I snicker. "She's not here."

"Great."

"Should have watched where you were stepping."

"Why are these even here?"

I lower my hand from my mouth. "Alani and I stayed in here last night so we wouldn't have nightmares."

He grimaces at his ensnared foot and gives it another useless tug. His dark hair flips over his eyes as he gives me an expectant look. But when all I do is laugh, he groans. "You're gonna leave me like this, aren't you?"

I rub my chin, pretending to consider it. "I think the humiliation might be good for you."

He lifts a brow. "Could be worse. I could've been you, caught by surprise in your frilly nightgown."

"Maybe I *should* go find Alani." I eye the slim path I'd have to creep through to avoid the other wards.

"Maybe you should."

My lips quirk to the right. *Sure, I'll go "find Alani."*

I press my back against the smooth tunnel wall and shimmy sideways to avoid the wards. But right as I am preparing to squeeze past Elias, he yanks me toward him, and I stumble into one of the traps. A warm sensation wraps around my foot. I jerk on my leg, to no avail, then shoot Elias a scathing glower, which loses its edge the moment I meet his gaze so close to mine.

"There. Now we are equally humiliated." He smiles, still holding onto my arms. "The nightgown incident doesn't count."

I want to brush his hands away, yet something in me resists the urge.

"What part of that wasn't humiliating?"

He chuckles. "The part where you looked pretty in it."

I gape at him, unsure if he means it or if he's just trying to embarrass me more. I dismiss the comment with a huff. "Well, good job. Who's going to get Alani now?"

He lets go of my arms. "Didn't think that through."

"Alani!" I holler. "Alani, come release these stupid wards!"

"Don't sound so distressed. It's only me you're stuck with," Elias says after my voice finishes echoing through the tunnel.

"Does that somehow make this better?"

"It should. Or are we not friends anymore?"

My gaze stills on his, and I feel my face turning shades. The more I look at him, the more I see Kieran. But more than that, I see a longing swirling like smoke in his dark eyes—one that has been there since we met again at Ila's, except then, I couldn't place what it was.

Does he still wish things had gone the way my papa wanted? *Do I?*

I shake myself and yell Alani's name again, with no result.

"Maybe you should cry for Calden instead," Elias says. "He'll come running."

My mouth falls ajar. *The nerve of this man.*

"Calden can't undo Alani's wards," I remind him.

"No, but he can find her."

I sigh toward the crystal-flecked ceiling. *He's right.* And what if Alani isn't answering because *she's* in some kind of danger?

I suck in the cool, damp air until my lungs feel stretched thin, then I shriek like my life is at stake. "Calden! Help!"

Elias winces at the volume. "Good, that should do it."

An unwanted laugh escapes me, earning a wider grin from him. I twist my lips into a frown and start counting down from ten before I'll yell for Calden again.

At four, a doorknob twists, followed by a sharp squeak from the hinges. Footsteps pound toward us, only to slam to a stop when Calden sees us. His expression contorts as he takes in the scene—Elias and me practically in each other's arms with Snare Wards on our feet.

Something unpleasant coats my tongue.

"I'm sorry," I say, fighting a nervous tremble in my voice. "Alani and I stayed in here last night. She drew these wards to keep out Blood Wardens, but then Elias got stuck. I was trying to go find Alani—"

"I thought you were in actual danger," Calden interjects.

"Well . . . I don't know where Alani is."

Before Calden has a chance to react, a sharp gasp spins him and Elias around. I lean to see Alani racing from the other passage.

"I'm sorry! I'm so sorry!" she says, but she's cackling.

The energy releases, and all the wards disappear. I retreat three full steps from Elias.

"I heard someone down the way and wanted to say hello." She turns toward Calden with a wince at his flat expression. "I left those up to protect Norielle, but I didn't think about anyone else getting snared!"

Calden runs his hand across his face like we are the three most exhausting people in the world. Then he trudges back to his room and shuts himself away. Alani shrugs, then tosses Elias and me another dozen apologies before slipping behind me to gather the bedding.

I pivot, intending to go help her, but then I freeze, less than a quarter-turn from Elias. There is something I want to ask him. Something he didn't seem interested in saying in front of the others . . .

"For how desperate you seemed to get away from me a moment ago, I'm surprised you're still standing there," Elias says before I can work up the nerve to speak.

My bare toes curl in the dirt, but my delay is so long, Elias turns away with a small laugh.

"Actually"—the word reels him back around—"I need to talk to you. Um . . . alone."

His brows lift, and behind me, Alani stops shaking out one of the blankets. My heart stutters, and I realize how odd this must seem. But I can't explain without risking my chance to get answers being deterred.

Elias runs a finger across his growing smile. "You want to go for a walk?"

As if we aren't doing enough walking already, I'm tempted to say, but then I realize the only other privacy available to us is behind a shut bedroom door. And that would look even worse.

"Sure," I agree instead.

"Okay, then." He glances at my feet. "Put your shoes on, Nori, and I'll take you for a stroll."

A few minutes later, Elias and I saunter into a dim passage, dappled with teal light that dulls the warmth of Elias's tan skin and makes his deep brown hair seem black. We managed to arm up and leave before Calden came out again, but Alani's pale look when we told her what we were doing still lingers in my mind as we follow the snakelike curves of the tunnel.

What does she care if I spend time with Elias? Or is she just afraid of what this could mean for her "brother," and what she seems to think is happening between Calden and me?

Should she be?

"You're not going to get us lost, are you?" I half-joke, half-worry aloud before my previous thought can gain too much ground.

"I practically live in these tunnels, Nori." Elias grins. "I know my way around. That's one benefit of being a scout."

A chilly draft causes my shoulders to shudder, and I tug my sleeves over my wrists. "Do you like being a scout?"

"Not exactly a dream come true, but better than what some people get. 'Least I get to go into towns."

"And play." I gesture toward the lyre he thought to bring along. But then again, I haven't seen him go anywhere without it, besides those few minutes he spent trimming Ila's bushes.

"Yeah, get to do that, too."

"Do you wish that's all you had to do?"

"Sometimes, but mostly I get bored of it. I like it better when Cal comes around to ask me to do something unusual."

I scratch my bottom lip. "So, you *don't* hate him."

Air puffs from his nose. "He's all right. For a prince."

I smile, thinking back to what Alani said. *Deep down I think they appreciate each other's company. It's just that neither wants the other to know that.*

Yet, I wonder what Calden would say if I asked him.

"How could you get bored of being a bard?" I ask after an extended pause. "You get to travel all over, see everything . . ."

"More like go to the same places. See the same people. Play the same songs." His fingers rake through his dark hair. "You know, no one *ever* wants to hear something new."

I laugh. Papa did mention that once.

"But the worst thing is the pretending. I actually have to act like I *like* people. You should know how hard that is for me."

A warmth fills my chest. Yes, I remember that. Little Kieran always had a strong distaste for being around other people. That was part of why I felt so special to be let close.

Has he let any other girls close since?

"My little brother, Milo, was born soon after you moved," I say to dispel the jealous thought. "He wanted to learn to play, but now Papa isn't around to teach him."

Elias turns us down a new passage where a crack runs along the path, a damp smell drifting in from below. "You want me to teach him?"

The image of Elias showing my little brother how to play the lyre in Papa's place triggers a fleeting burn in my eyes.

It's like he was brought back to me. On purpose.

As if our destinies were entwined, not mine and Calden's.

I blink the sentiment away. "If you'd dare go back into town. Why haven't you before?"

"Kinda risky. People might know who I am and ask questions." He looks over at me, his grin fading. "Or maybe not, since even you didn't recognize me."

"In my defense, you're much different now."

He checks his Omen Mark, reminding me I should be aware of mine also. The center arrow is as black as Elias's tunic.

"Good different?" he asks.

I loop a strand of hair around my finger, giving my eyes something to focus on besides his anticipatory gaze. "Physically."

"Why does that both insult and compliment at once?"

"Well, it's been difficult to see who you actually are behind all your pretenses." *Or what I hope are pretenses.*

He watches me a moment before breaking the silence with a small laugh. "So, is that what you wanted? To draw me away and find out if I'm still Kieran?"

My chin lowers as I apprehend how much more selfish my motives are. "I thought you don't use that name?"

"I don't. Doesn't mean I'm not still him at the center." He bumps my shoulder like he did when we were younger. Only this time, it catches me by surprise, and I almost knock into the wall if not for him snatching me to pull me back.

"You're a bit stronger than you used to be," I venture—an understatement.

"No one stays weak in the Wardens," he says, still holding my arm. "Even you might double in size if you stick around."

I laugh at what I think is supposed to be a joke and tug my arm free. As the tunnel falls quiet again, I recognize my opportunity to ask my question. We should be far enough away now, and I better get to it before it's too late.

"Speaking of that," I say in the most casual tone I can muster. "That's really what I wanted to ask you about. You know me . . . or you did. Do you have any theories about why I'm in the Bind, or what role I'm to have in the Wardens?"

His posture droops. "So, that's what this is really about."

"You do have a theory, don't you?" I ask as if I didn't notice the way my change of topic sapped his vitality.

He leaves me squirming in a long silence before giving his lousy reply. "Yeah."

"Well, what is it?" I ask.

"You're too smart to need me to tell you."

I cross my arms. "Apparently, I'm not. Because I have no idea."

He slows, and his attention moves to the walls. "We're not supposed to discuss it, Nori. I'm not about to get myself in trouble with the Lady Sovereign just because you are too impatient to wait like the rest of us had to."

My fingers dig into my arms. "She's not going to know."

"Not nice to ask me to break the rules." He side-eyes me with a smile. "I have a good reputation with her. I'd like to keep it. It's the only thing I have."

I unwind my arms. "What if you gave me a hint, and I figured it out. Would you tell me if I was right?"

"No. I'd tell you to stop pestering me." He gives me a look that reminds me he's as immovable as a mountain. "Go bug Cal about it. I'm sure you batting your pretty little eyes at him long enough will get him to spill his theories. Let him get in trouble for it."

I twist so my hair covers my flushed face. "Why do you have to keep doing that?"

"What? Calling out the obvious?" He stops, turning to face me as if to prevent my attempt to hide. "That's what I'm supposed to do, isn't it? You know, as your buddy. Old friend. Here to let you know what you're thinking when you're being too stubborn to see it."

My brows furrow. "And yet if you sounded any more bitter, I would taste it."

"Maybe it just seems a little unfair. You're the only piece of home that's ever returned to me, and Cal's got you like a fish on a hook, reeling you in to some important destiny at his side. Meanwhile, I'm just here to do a job and get kicked out the moment I've fulfilled it." He takes one step before seeming to think better of approaching me. "Just hard to have you come back all so I can watch you go again. You know, we were friends, Nori. The best of them. Maybe I miss that. Maybe I've missed it for a long time."

I twist another strand of my hair, watching it like the threads are holding the very world together. "I'm sorry," I mutter. "I didn't think of it like that."

"It's fine. I get it." His tone softens. "Being summoned to join the Wardens is a big deal, especially when the Sovereign Prince is the one who comes to get you. If I'm being honest, Nori, I'm scared of what will happen to you once you get to the citadel."

"What do you mean?"

With his sigh, he seems to blow away the pieces of his arrogant mask, leaving behind the true face of my friend. "The world is dying, Nori, and Calden is the next person responsible for preventing that. If your destiny is tied to him, then that means you've been called to bear that responsibility also."

"Then that's your theory. I'm supposed to help Calden find a way to stop the curse from destroying the world."

"That's what's *obvious*," he corrects. "Binds are for missions, and that's the biggest one there is."

"But what's my role?" I look around as if the explanation might be written on the tunnel's walls, illuminated by the crystals. "What am I supposed to do to help? Calden said all the Wardens can really do is damage control until El-Alam sends another Empyreal Guardian."

"If he even does." Elias turns, the teal light rearranging the shadows on his face. "I think Cal knows as well as any of us that's not going to happen."

Goosebumps prickle my skin. "Why do you say that?"

"It's been over two decades. If El-Alam wanted us to have another Guardian, he'd have sent one by now. Why wait?"

My gaze wanders to the smooth dirt ground, gravity seeming to double its pull on me. I'd considered the same when Calden and I discussed it, yet to hear someone else say it . . .

"We're not helpless though, Nori." The fleck of optimism in his voice lifts my chin. "The Wardens are powerful. We have to believe that we're the reason El-Alam hasn't seen fit to send another Guardian. He knows we have the power to fix this. It's just . . . how? And why do *you* have to be so close to it?"

He takes a step toward me, and for once, I don't feel the need to recoil. Instead, my eyes linger on his, and I find myself drifting into their deep chasms.

"I just want to get to know you again, Nori, but I'm scared I'm never going to get the chance to. Once you get to the citadel"—he gestures between us—"this is over.

You're not going to have time anymore. You'll be . . . too important."

I frown. "But you and Calden are friends, aren't you? Can't he relieve you from your scout duties so you can come along with the Bind? He's done it before . . ."

"Sure, he could, but I get the feeling he won't want to."

"Why not?"

He chews the inside of his cheek, stewing on his response for so long I notice my heartbeat throbbing in my ears. "I think he's going to want to keep you to himself. I might seem like a threat."

"A threat?" I echo.

He flicks a slight smile at me, but it lacks its usual flair. "Don't play dumb. You know exactly what I mean."

I suddenly realize how much closer he's gotten and take a step back. "He's the Sovereign Prince and my Bind leader. He's not interested in me, nor should he be."

Yet even as I say it, I realize how stupid it sounds, especially after my conversation with Calden last night. It's not that he's not interested. It's that he's scared.

"A bit late for that," Elias says. "Think it's been a bit late since the Seer dropped that vision of you drowning in his head. And it's not like he's one to follow the rules."

"What does it matter to you?" I ask, though that also sounds stupid. He's the man my father wanted me to marry. And even when he acted like he was against it, I could tell he wasn't. Papa even blamed his interest in learning the lyre on an interest in *me* instead.

"He's dangerous, Nori," he says.

"He's not—"

"He's *cursed*." His tone settles. "I know it's not his fault, but that doesn't change the fact. And even if he wasn't, getting close to him means getting closer to the problem and all the danger that goes with it. And as *your friend*, that bothers me a good deal."

"Then what are you suggesting?"

"Nothing, besides that you think really hard about this. About all of it. I just want you to be careful, because—" He shakes his head.

"Because what?"

"Because I miss what we had." He paces away from me. "Every time my route took me near Behria, I had to fight with myself not to go see you. I didn't want to put you in danger if anyone figured out what I was. And now, look. You're here. In more danger than you've ever been. And still, I have hardly a chance to find out who you are now or what we could have."

What *could* we have?

All my old dreams seem to flutter like butterflies through my rib cage. His words—that gaze—

I drift closer to him, just one step.

"Kieran, I—" I don't mean to use his old name, but before I get a chance to correct myself, a staticky whir blooms in my ears.

"Nori!" Elias shouts, gripping me with both hands to push me away.

I stumble and crash into the wall as a semitranslucent orange sphere collides with his breastplate, knocking him to his back.

Breathless, I look down the passage for the assailant. Nothing. But now I feel it, the tingle of my Omen Mark. A quick glance shows its brilliant red arrow, pointing in the direction the sphere came from. I draw my sword, cursing myself for getting so distracted.

Elias recovers, taking up his own sword. He scours the dimness until another sphere launches after him, its warm radiance engulfing the smooth tunnel in a flash. Elias dodges it, and it hits the curved wall behind him with force enough to crack the stone.

At his command, I step behind Elias's protective stance. Then a figure emerges from the other bend, followed by two others. Their hoods deepen the shadows across their painted faces, shrouding their features. I conclude the one at the center is female based on her comparatively smaller frame. Red stains her lips between the black paint lining her pallid cheeks.

She glides ahead of the others, sizing up Elias with a sweeping gaze.

"Hand over the girl, scout," she says. "And we may consider letting you go on your way."

I gasp, suddenly recalling the vision the Seer sent with Elias. *I'm to fall into Blood Wardens' hands. While away from Calden.*

And now I've made it so easy.

"Walk away, and I may consider allowing you to live," Elias says, a splayed hand extended toward them.

She reads the ward on his palm, her stoic expression unaffected. "Big talk for a scout."

A bluish sphere launches from Elias's hand, but the woman deflects it with a wave of warm energy. The sphere rebounds, decimating a chunk of the wall.

"Last chance," she says, the flick of her finger raising her companions' hands toward us.

"You realize who she is, don't you?" Elias asks.

The woman smiles, bending the drawn lines on her face. "She belongs to the Sovereign Prince, yes. We are quite aware."

"You take her, he'll come for you."

I swallow, his switch in tactics alerting me that he is not prepared for this battle.

The woman steps closer, pushing her hood from her onyx hair. The crystals illuminate her face, revealing its youthful curves. "Let him."

"Corene?" Elias says, and my grip on my sword tightens.

He knows her? This isn't Calden's lost friend, is it?

"He wouldn't hurt *me*," she says with a snide grin.

Elias's sword twitches. "Doesn't mean I won't."

Her laugh is cut short by a flurry of energy from Elias's swung sword. She lunges, the sphere nipping the shoulder of her cloak. Her hand lifts, but before I see her attack, a sheet of darkness falls over my face from behind. I scream, only for my voice to get smothered in fabric. A hard knot ties against the back of my head, yanking strands of my hair, and a pair of powerful hands jerk me backward. I raise my sword, only for a boot to kick my hand. My thumb cracks, a sharp pain shooting up into my arm, and my sword clangs against the ground by my feet.

In seconds, my wrists are bound behind my back, and strong hands are lifting me off the ground. My assailant hoists me over a wide, masculine shoulder, his strength unyielding despite my desperate kicks and writhes. My strangled screams are lost in a chorus of shouts and grunts from the fight I can't see as my captor carries me away.

The last distinct sound I hear is Elias's pained cry before the fight fades into a murmur though the walls.

CALDEN

A pinch on my wrist as I'm wrapping fresh linen across my stitched arm catches my attention.

The Omen Mark is red, if only faintly.

I wince, quickly finishing the bandaging and adding my armguard before running from my room to find the others. But I'm met by Alani's wide eyes before I can exit the hall.

"Where is she?" I ask before her rattling lips form a full sound.

"She and Elias went for a walk—"

"A walk?" I exclaim, holding up my Bind Mark to see the arrow pointed away from our haven. Anger blazes across my entire body. *Elias.*

I give Alani a once-over to be sure she's dressed for a fight and, finding her body shielded by armor, I bolt for the passage the arrow points to.

"I'm sorry, Cal. I'm so sorry," Alani says, chasing after me. "I should have advised against it, or at least told you."

Yes, you should have, I think, but I spare her the chastisement to focus on running as fast as my legs can carry me through a winding shaft.

The buzz of energy finds my ears first, followed by the taunting remarks of a male. But the lack of commotion otherwise shallows my breaths. Whatever struggle occurred, it's already over. Or close to it.

The whir gets louder as I round another curve in the channel, and at last, figures come into view up ahead.

"Lias!" My voice roars down the tunnel, dissolving an attack just as energy sparks from a woman's palm.

Elias is curled on the ground beneath a shield of energy, one I sense by its flickering has been up for too long and is soon to collapse. Two men flank him, daggers ready to penetrate his flesh the moment the shield fails. But the woman, standing with her back to me, lowers her hands. Her frizzed dark curls cause my chest to tighten with dread. *But it couldn't be,* I assure myself.

"Let him up," I order as Alani reaches my side, hands raised. "Or today your souls will see the pits of Gehenna."

No one moves, and I use the pause to search the vagueness ahead for Norielle. There's no sign of her.

The woman's head tilts to the side, and slowly, she turns. "Don't be so harsh, love. It's only a scout."

My chest hollows as I recognize her face behind its painted stripes and dots.

Corene.

After all these years—

"They took Norielle," Elias growls, the edges of his shield peeling back.

His words wash over me without recognition, the sight of Corene robbing me of my senses. Elias shouts it again, and the name hits me like a backhand against my face.

Norielle.

Corene smiles, a sight that once entranced me, but now seems to twist my heart into a knot.

"Oh, don't worry about her," Corene says. "You'll just get another."

My fingers twitch.

"*Cal?*" Alani whispers. Her hands shake in my peripheral vision, awaiting my command to attack, but I can't muster a sound.

Corene steps away from her allies with not even a knife to defend herself, as if she already knows my weakness.

"Dispel your wards, and I'll let your scout go," she says.

I force my mouth to awaken. "Where is Norielle?"

"The little girl?"

I scowl at the way the darkness has tainted even the beauty of her voice, turning it from a flowing stream to stagnant water, poised to kill.

"She's off to meet her new family, assuming she will be compliant," she says, coming even closer. She jerks a hand toward Elias's fading shield. "Better hurry, love, or you'll be the reason another of your friends died."

"*Calden,*" Alani hisses again, her hand flinching as if she's resisting the urge to fight without my permission.

"Oh, but what does he matter?" Corene says, twirling one of her disheveled curls. "It's the girl you want. Now, why does that feel so familiar?"

My teeth grind together, her words pulling long-banished memories to the surface. She and her brother, Corwin, and I were sent on a small mission together so I could practice leading a team. But Blood Wardens attacked us, capturing them both. The defectors divided into two parties, and I had to choose between them who I'd rescue. I chose Corene, thus forsaking her brother. But even after I had her safe, I knew I couldn't handle the mission to rescue Corwin without returning home to get help, and by then, locating him would be nearly impossible. I took us back to the citadel, and Mother forbade the quest to find Corwin, deeming it too dangerous.

Corene defected within a week of Mother's decision.

Only then did I go against my mother's wishes to chase after them. I found Corwin two years too late, and when I handed him over for rehabilitation, Mother determined him a lost cause and killed him herself.

"By all means, take your time," Corene says. "I'd hate to pressure you."

"Shut up, wretch," Elias snaps, his shield fizzling out—intentionally, I realize by the speed of it. His sword thwarts the immediate plunge of his nearest enemy's dagger, but the other defector grabs Elias by the hair and slides a blade against his throat.

Corene raises her thin brows and turns back to me with a twisted smile. "Well, there. Wasn't that helpful? Now you can take all the time you need to surrender, and meanwhile, your dear girl will just get farther and farther from your reach."

"Let him go," I order.

"Or what? You'll take me to your mother so she can kill me, too, since you aren't man enough to do it yourself?"

Energy buzzes in my hands, but still, I can't will my Vitality Ward to attack her, even when my every thought bends toward doing so.

"That's what I thought," she says, turning toward her accomplice. "Ralek—"

But a flash of silver shoots between us, a small knife sinking into the hand of Elias's captor. The man yowls, his dagger dropping into Elias's lap. Elias snatches the weapon, but before he can twist around to bring down the wounded man, Corene raises a hand toward Elias, ready to cast the ward I distracted her from using before.

Finally, my ward ignites, and a translucent ball launches from my palm, crashing into Corene. The energy throws her into the wall. Stunned, she freezes, blood trickling from her nose.

I summon my swordstaff, marching toward her with my mind centered on one thought, and one thought alone: she has stolen Norielle, and I will not allow her—or anyone—to damn a member of my Bind to this same depraved fate.

Her eyes widen the closer I get, yet she makes no effort to attack, by blade or magic, even as I swivel the tip of my swordstaff toward her throat.

At my back, Elias's blades collide with his opponents', and Alani swishes her rope dart, as if to do what I won't, should I fail to act.

A bead of red dots the edge of my blade, but my arms go stiff.

"Will you kill her, too? Once she becomes one of us?" Corene asks, voice like the shed skin of a snake—frail for something that once held such bite. And yet, she sounds so much more like the woman I once loved. The gentle woman who once looked past my curse—the first and last I'll ever allow so close.

A sudden wave of dizziness steals my focus, the ground seeming to shift beneath me like a ship over waves. My eyes flutter, only for images to invade my mind—images of dust. Walls of it, surrounding me as if I'm in a storm. It billows around me so thick, I taste it on my tongue as if it were real.

I blink, hard, and see Corene again, an even more horrified look on her face than before.

"Mercy, Calden," she pleads. "Mercy."

The dust sweeps over my vision again until I see nothing else, no matter how much I blink. A clang of metal resounds, followed by fast-moving footsteps, then an array of shouts—Alani and Elias calling my name.

I stumble back, hands suddenly emptied of my weapon, yet pulsing with energy eager to escape.

No. Not now—

"Get away!" I manage before a scream tears from my throat.

A ferocious roar of wind in my mind overtakes their replies. I clench my fists, using what little remains of my consciousness to hold my power inside, but it's like trying to stop a squall. A hand coils around my wrist, and I jerk away from it, suddenly unaware of who it is besides that it's an enemy.

I twist from their hold, another scream bellowing out, and energy bursts from my hands. But I see nothing of what I've done. No attacker. Only the dust.

I scramble to my feet, only for something to catch my arm. A rope? It yanks me with force enough to push me against the ground. The dust swells around me, stifling my shout with a harsh cough.

Where did this dust come from?

Something warm envelops my hand, holding it to the ground as I'm trying to rise. I attempt to tug my limb free, only to nearly dislocate my shoulder.

The enemy shoves me further to the ground, and I swing my loose fist in her direction. More energy launches from my hand, but a different enemy with a stronger grip grabs my wrist and wrestles it down. Another warm trap seizes my once-free arm.

I scream again, but as it's fading, I hear the female enemy's voice.

"Come back, Calden," she says. "You need to come back."

Calden? I don't recognize the name. Is she not talking to me?

"Norielle needs you," she says, then her voice is taken by the wind.

My body goes limp, but everything is trembling. I don't know who Norielle is either. All I know is that the dust is thick, and it never ceases. It was I who made it, wasn't it?

What have I destroyed to make so much? A forest? A village? A mountain? I cry out to ask but no one answers. Not even the enemies. I'm alone. I can sense that now, though it makes no sense.

There's no one for miles who will hear me.

NORIELLE

The brute flings me to the ground after what felt like hours of being crammed against his large shoulder. I struggled until I ran out of strength, and yet his powerful hold never once faltered. His heavy footsteps move behind me, then his merciless grip encircles my arms again, surely bruising me as he jerks my body upright against something cold and hard. The ropes around my hands tighten, burning into my skin and turning my fingertips hot as he secures me to whatever is behind me—a pole?

With a grunt, he walks away, knuckles cracking. I wriggle and whine, wishing he'd at least remove the blindfold to free me from the darkness. Instead, I hear the loud *thump* of his large form sitting somewhere, followed by a bearish gulping as he replenishes himself.

Then everything goes quiet and seemingly still.

My exhausted body has no strength to cry or tremble, but my mind whirls with questions and fears that repeat over and over as if I'm trapped in a cyclone. Did Elias survive? Does Calden know what's happened? Will anyone come for me? Will I die here? Why did that woman want *me* specifically?

I writhe in the mystery, scorched by the uncertainty until finally, a rattling sound comes from farther down the shaft. The thuds of rushed footsteps—*two pairs? Maybe three?*—grow louder until they stop close to me in what I assume is an atrium by the slight scent of evergreens on the breeze. But the fresh aroma is tainted by something rotten—something dead.

"Mistress," says a burly voice, which I can only assume belongs to the brute who carried me here. He says nothing else, leaving me to wonder again.

Someone's steps near me, and I hear the whine of their leather armor as they crouch close by. Nails scratch my face as they jerk my blindfold up, leaving it to dangle in the threads of hair the brute tied into it.

I meet a woman's deep-set eyes, framed by tousled curls and black designs.

Corene.

My throat clenches as I notice the two men behind her—the two who helped her ambush us. *Then Elias must be dead.*

A wail is smothered by the fabric still covering my mouth.

"You need not be afraid, girl." Corene straightens a garnet pendant over her bloodstained collarbone, the red gem glimmering in the candlelight of this otherwise black space. "The hard part is over, so long as you cooperate."

My eyes plead for an explanation.

"You have information," she says. "Information we'd very much like to gather without causing too much of a fuss, but of course, how this goes is up to you."

I glance at the men hovering at her back. One's hand is covered in blood. The other has a welt under his eye. Behind them, I notice the cause of the stench, lying near the brute's battered boots—a fellion with navy blood pooling across the dirt around it.

My face goes numb.

"You see, dear," Corene taps the gem on her necklace with a nail, "this was given to me by someone you know."

Calden, I register.

"He loved me once. In fact, my brother and I were both good friends of his." Her red-lipped smile matches the blood and garnet almost fashionably. "But he betrayed us, even going so far as to deliver my brother to his death when it was *his* fault that my brother defected in the first place."

I scratch at the ropes as if somehow my nails could tear through them and give me a slim chance of escape.

"I suppose you could say, he's not exactly the man you think he is. Which is why, dear, I felt the need to rescue you from him, and offer you an alternative." She pushes a strand of my hair away from my eyes. "I'd like for you to join us, have access to our unlimited power, and a place to *truly* belong."

I suck in a breath, air whistling through the fabric.

"But in exchange, I need information from you." She reaches behind my head, freeing my mouth with a harsh yank. "What do you say?"

"I'd rather die," I say, my voice stronger than I expect despite its hoarseness, but the tear slipping down my cheek ruins the effect.

"You don't even know what information I want," she says, an amused lilt in her tone.

"It doesn't matter. I don't want to join you."

"Well, it was worth a try." She shrugs as if she'd expected my answer. "No need to worry. I will get my answers, one way or another. Though, I did hope you would tell me first, so I could spare you my . . . methods."

My soul shivers, an array of horrors already rising to my imagination.

"What makes you think I have this information?" I ask. "I've not even been inducted yet."

"Because I know your Bind leader, and the man can't keep secrets to himself. Especially considering that little bit we overheard of your conversation with the scout." She rubs the garnet. "You know, I almost felt sorry listening to him. Poor man. Overshadowed by the false glory of a cursed prince."

"Where is he? The scout?"

She chuckles at my foolish question. "I'll tell you, if you tell me what I want to know."

"Is he dead?" I press.

"You first, sweetheart."

My jaw clenches, my gaze lowering to her pendant. In its smooth face, I glimpse a vague reflection of my pathetic form, but the thought that the face it once reflected was Calden's nauseates me even more. She's the one he's been running from all this time.

He'll never come for me, not if it means facing her.

"What do you want to know?" I ask.

"Ah, that's better," she says, sitting beside me as if to settle in for a long, productive conversation. "I need you to tell me what you know about Toaph Elbara's whereabouts."

My head jerks back at the sound of our original Empyreal Guardian's name. "His whereabouts? He's dead. Ta'Nathel killed him."

She shakes a slender finger at me. "Now, don't do that. Honesty, dear, or no answers for you."

My heart sparks with an energy that mingles with my fear. *Is Toaph Elbara still alive? Is that why El-Alam hasn't sent another Guardian? But why hasn't Toaph stopped Ta'Nathel yet?*

And why didn't Calden tell me? Does he not know?

"Come on. Speak up." Corene rests her hands on one knee, stretching her other leg out in such a casual posture I want to spit on her. "Calden has surely seen *something* helpful by now. Something you can tell me."

"Seen it how?"

She scowls toward her accomplices in a silent complaint. "Through the visions. His curse. Stop acting so ignorant. I won't be played for a fool."

My boots skid against the dirt as I curl into myself even more. "I have no idea what he sees. He never said anything about Toaph Elbara or visions. Just—"

I stop myself, recalling the way he described it. *It's like being trapped in someone else's mind.*

"Just?"

"He just told me about how frightening it is. How he feels overwhelming fear and grief. That's all I know."

"Why do I still not believe you?" Corene says, shifting so she can rest her elbows on her knees.

My lips curl. If only she knew me—knew how incapable I am of telling a lie, then maybe she would.

"I really don't know anything. Calden himself told me Toaph Elbara was dead. I—I don't even think *he* knows he's alive. If he is."

"Fine, then." Corene stands. "I suppose this means you don't want to know if your scout friend is alive."

"I told you what I know. That's all. Honestly."

She leans down to meet my gaze again, studying me like a wolf looking for the best place to bite. "He's dead," she says, straightening. "So, I wouldn't get too hopeful, darling. No one is coming for you. You either comply or we make you. There is no other option."

Even the throbbing pain of my broken thumb seems to numb at her confirmation. She killed him. Elias is dead.

Kieran is dead.

And it's all my fault. Had I never lured him away to interrogate him about my destiny, this never would have happened. Why couldn't I have just waited? Not been so selfish?

My tousled hair pours across my face, catching on my wet cheeks. Corene backs away with a bitter laugh as weeping wracks my body. She watches with satisfaction before suddenly twisting toward the man with the bruised face.

"Go get it," she orders.

I glance up between tangles of brown. *Get what?*

The man nods, casting me a menacing look, then he turns into the shadows.

CALDEN

A taste like bitter iron rises in my throat as bright drops of blood spurt from my mouth and sink into the dust. I swallow more blood and try to cry out again, but the only sound I have left to make is choking. I shut my eyes, cries turning inward.

I failed. I failed.

It's all I can think as my body melts into the ground, depleted of all energy.

Tears lace the sides of my face. This is what I deserve. To be ignored. To be left here to suffocate in the dust of all I destroyed in my failure to save this world from Ta'Nathel's clutches.

I fled. *I failed.*

I don't deserve mercy, not when I've abandoned my world to destruction.

A voice shouts—a woman, young and afraid. "You can't fight the coven by yourself! You'll die."

I don't recognize her, yet I recall hearing her before.

A man responds in a low, grating voice. "And Norielle will die if I don't try. He's taking too long."

"Just wait, please. He'll be back any minute . . ." Weeping overtakes her words, but I haven't the strength to turn my head to look for her. Yet something about that name the man used—Norielle—rings in my ears. I think the woman said it before, but now, I can almost imagine a face. A lovely, freckled face with long hair gently framing it like a bride's veil.

Norielle, I repeat to myself as if this name is the key to free me from this prison.

Suddenly, a mighty wind blasts from the north. Another howls from the south. Then the east and west. The wind sweeps the dust off the ground and into the sky, carrying it so far it turns into clouds in my vision. A drop of strength returns to my spirit, and I turn my head to see my arms still bound to the dust-coated earth by the strange magical confines.

Snare Wards, I suddenly remember.

"Calden?" the woman says again. Her voice turns away. "Elias! Come back! He's waking."

My eyes open—though I thought they already were—and the sky is gone. Above me is a curved ceiling speckled with glowing teal crystals. Under their cool light, a woman stands at a distance, but my glazed eyes can hardly discern her. I blink until I see her red-splotched, tear-drenched face.

"Alani," I rasp. Just saying her name burns my raw throat.

She rushes to my side. "I'm here."

"Hurt?"

"No."

The Snare Wards release, but I lie stiffly, struggling to remember what my mind last saw. I feel the sweat and tears saturating my face and hair, and the heavy pulsing of my heart. But all I can remember seeing is dust.

Yet why do I feel like I've just done something horrid? Something . . . unforgiveable?

Who did I hurt?

Alani offers me a hand to help me up, though she eyes me like I'm a wounded animal who might turn on her if she gets too close. I accept her aid, every muscle aching as I sit. She withdraws, hand shaking, as Elias jogs into view. I squint at his troubled expression, then scan the surroundings, finding chunks of stone missing from the tunnel walls.

And no one else with us.

"Where is Norielle?" I whisper for lack of a voice.

Alani clutches her arms, turning to Elias.

"The Blood Wardens," Elias says. "They took her."

My hands ball into fists. Vaguely, the memory returns of Alani and I charging to rescue Elias and Norielle, only to find Norielle gone, and—

Corene.

My body curls inward, another bellow worsening the rawness of my throat. "No!"

This curse. This wretched curse.

In how many ways must it destroy me?

"How long?" I ask, my eyes burning. "How long have they been gone?"

"Twenty minutes, maybe," Alani says.

My fist smacks the wall behind me, shooting pain into my elbow. I crumble toward my lap again. *Corene has Norielle and twenty minutes on us.*

For what vile purpose did she take her? Revenge?

I push myself up, staggering in the direction my Bind Mark points.

"Cal." Alani chases after me. "Are you sure you're ready—?"

"We're already too far behind." I check my Bind Mark. It doubles in my blurry vision, but Norielle's arrow is still present and dark as ever—they haven't killed her yet. "It points southwest."

Elias's gaze narrows. "The pits."

"Take the lead," I tell him, but he's already turning.

I stumble after him, the ground seeming to wobble underfoot. Alani comes to my side to support me. I hold the wall with the other side and urge my depleted body forward on willpower alone.

NORIELLE

The man with the bruised face returns, clutching a small black box. Fear douses my cries to a whimper. *What could they possibly threaten me with that could fit in there?*

He passes the box to Corene, biting back a smile beneath his moustache. A spark lights Corene's dark eyes as she lifts the box, like she's presenting me with a gift.

As she crouches before me, something scratches on the inside—something *alive*.

"I don't suppose you'd recognize this," Corene says as she slides the wood top off just enough for me to peer inside.

My eyes bulge at the phantom blue body of the creature. Its eight legs skitter across the base of the box, pincers clicking as it tries to escape. A gold stinger shines from the tip of its upward-curved tail—the distinct mark of a crypt crawler scorpion.

Just like the one that killed Elias's mother after putting her through the worst pain known in all of Alémor.

Corene closes the lid. "I take it you do."

I seal my lips, sweat beading on my nape.

"Let's try this again," Corene says. "You can tell me where Toaph Elbara is, or I can let my crypt crawler begin the countdown to your death."

"I already told you," I say through gritted teeth. "I don't know anything. *Calden* doesn't know anything."

"My Oracle would disagree." She taps the box, inducing an angry scuttle inside. "He's sensed communication between Calden and Toaph Elbara."

"If that's true, Calden didn't tell me. I swear to you, I don't know anything."

Her eyes narrow, and finally, I see the disbelief fade from her gaze. She wets her ruby lip, seeming lost for a moment, before malice contorts her expression again.

"Then you're worthless to me." Her chest expands, as if readying to scream. But as her breath hisses out, her composure returns. "Or are you?"

She shakes the box as she raises it to eye level, her sudden cackle turning my blood cold.

"Perhaps I can still find some use for you and my little friend here." She slides the lid off, and with a pinch below the crypt crawler's tail, she lifts it from the box. The blue scorpion wiggles as she holds it between us. "Once your pathetic life starts to drain, your arrow on his Bind Mark will fade. He'll know you're dying, and he'll come racing."

Will he?

"Then I'll have myself a perfect trade. His secret for your life."

"It won't work," I say, hoping despite my terror that I'm right. If Toaph Elbara is alive and Calden knows where he is, then Blood Wardens gaining access to that location can only mean trouble—worse trouble than we're already in.

"Oh, don't underestimate the rashness of infatuation," she says. "Believe me, I've seen for myself how much of a fool he can be."

My mouth opens to contradict her, to tell her Calden won't be manipulated so easily—not for my sake.

But she brings the scorpion to my neck, holding it so close, I feel the scrape of its pointed legs.

"Last chance to confess your knowledge, should you possess it," she says.

My eyes squeeze shut as memories resurge, of Elias's mother flailing and crying under this venom's affliction. Two hours. That was all she lasted once it struck. That's all Calden will have to find me . . . if he even tries.

And yet, I hope he doesn't. For his sake. For Toaph Elbara's.

Corene drops the crypt crawler, and it skitters along my neck like it's been trained to know exactly where to strike for maximum impact. I have just enough time to steal one last breath before the sharp tip pierces my skin. The venom enters my body in a burn so intense, I can't hold in my scream.

Corene snatches back the scorpion, crushing it before she drops its carcass beside me, then she gathers her candle and walks across the atrium. The pain prevents me from hearing what she says to the men, but their eyes fix on me, watching the tears and sweat beading on my face with such boredom, I now understand what it means to have your soul be corrupted. It's a complete loss of humanity.

The incinerating sensation spreads from my neck to my torso and all the way to the base of my feet. Within minutes, my lungs are straining to do more than wheeze. Do I even have two hours?

My thoughts break into fragments of prayer and distress. Is this what I deserve for abandoning Papa? Death in its most painful form? Will Calden come for me? What will Corene do to him? Won't I still die regardless of whatever deal she attempts to strike?

But loudest of all, my mind cries for Toaph Elbara to be alive. Even if I must die here, if he still lives, there is hope for this world. There is still hope for Milo and Cas to see their old age, their grandchildren—to live a life in an unbroken world.

A world I will never know.

CALDEN

I've finally regained enough strength to jog on my own when a strange tingle on my wrist slows me. I raise my Bind Mark toward the purple crystals overhead and find that one of my three arrows has faded from black to gray.

Norielle's arrow.

"We're losing her," I say, sprinting ahead.

Elias curses, accelerating.

Our feet beat against the solid ground, the sharp sound of our breaths echoing through the tunnel as we reach a divide. Elias takes the westward path, and after a stretch, he makes a sharp turn down a staircase nearly hidden by a protrusion of the wall. He runs two steps down and leaps over the last four, entering a decrepit passage with hardly a crystal to light it. I follow behind, carefully minding my steps in consideration of my frayed state, and Alani trails after us, watching over me like a mother. The three of us light our lanterns in near unison.

"Still pointing southwest?" Elias asks, waving his lantern between two different paths. A rat wriggles into a crack in the lower wall.

I check the Bind Mark with a flutter of nerves. Is it even lighter or is that only my fear?

"Yes," I answer.

"This way." Elias charges into a shaft with jagged walls.

The tortuous decline aggravates my clinging light-headedness, but I jog onward. I did not pull Norielle from those waters for her to die among the Blood Wardens, or worse, be converted into one.

Like Corene.

I curse Corene with my innermost being, then I curse myself. I should have done all I could to help her brother after rescuing her. Then perhaps Corene wouldn't have turned against me and the Wardens—and against El-Alam himself.

It's my fault the woman's soul has been damned, isn't it?

Hers and Corwin's both.

Elias suddenly halts up ahead, his lantern light filling a wide space at the end of the channel. Paths riddle the bumpy walls from every side with ancient stairs leading both up and down. I stop beside Elias in the center of the silent atrium, studying it. Carved images of the Accursed watch us from the stone arches of each path—fellions, redarian snakes, wildernwolves. Below our feet, a circle with intricate weaving embellishes the stone floor.

"What is this place?" Alani asks.

"Warden crypts," Elias says before I can recognize it. "Defectors use them as routes."

His nostrils flare as his attention pivots between three, then two, of the channels. I hold the Bind Mark up in his view, but the arrow points indistinctly between them, even when I pivot to test its direction.

"She's too far away to indicate," I say. "What's your call, Lias?"

His fingers rake through his hair. "I don't know. I don't exactly spend time down here. Could be one just as well as the other."

The temptation to separate rises and falls with my breath. I start toward one tunnel on no more than a hopeful guess. Our lanterns dazzle the jagged walls, glinting on the sharp edges of teethlike black stones. The air grows staler the deeper we venture into the crypt, and soon caskets line the narrow walkway on each side. Their disrupted lids and the bones littering the corners suggest the Blood Wardens have done more than offend the dead by using their passages. They have also defiled their remains for their ritual purposes.

Better than using the living, I suppose.

But the thought only returns me to Norielle, quickening my steps. There's no telling what Corene has done to her that would cause her to fade so slowly. I dare not imagine the possibilities, lest my curse find root to overtake me a second time.

I follow the crypt for what feels like a century before a figure ahead pulls me up short. I still, Alani and Elias halting behind me, but quickly I register what I'm seeing is not a person, only a statue in the distance. I slow as we approach it, studying the intricately carved stone wings extending from the man's back. The eyes of someone who I realize is Toaph Elbara stare almost directly at me as he seems to guard a crossroad behind him, clutching a swordstaff not terribly different from my own. My hand draws toward the edge of one of the stone blades, and I run a finger across its dull edge.

"*Cal,*" Elias barks.

I blink, suddenly realizing I've stopped altogether. I twist toward him, the crypt seeming to spin for several seconds after I've stilled.

The taste of dust salts my tongue.

"Which way?" Elias asks.

I swallow the taste away and lift the Bind Mark again. Norielle's arrow is even paler than before, almost lost against my light skin.

I veer left, not bothering to give any other answer, but only get a few paces before a voice raises goosebumps across my arms.

"*I fled. I failed.*"

I turn, expecting to see someone behind us.

Yet all I find are Elias and Alani's confused faces.

Why does that sound so familiar?

"What is it?" Alani asks.

I walk between Elias and Alani without answering, returning to the crypt to inspect it, but find it empty.

"Hello?" My voice reverberates through the dry crypt.

"Cal, come on," Elias urges from the crossroads.

"You didn't hear that?" I ask.

Elias scoffs and carries on without me, but Alani takes a step nearer.

"Hear what?" she asks.

I look around the crypt, gaze stopping on the statue. The urge to return to it tugs at me, as if somehow, Toaph Elbara spoke from the statue himself—or the ghost of him did.

Nonsense.

It's surely some Blood Warden trickery. I snap my attention back to Norielle's fading arrow.

"Nothing. Never mind," I answer Alani.

I chase after Elias, but before I can find him around the tunnel's tight bend, his shout freezes me yet again.

"Dead end," he says, and there's a loud *thump* like he kicked something. "Wrong crypt. The other path goes east."

I form a fist, nails digging into my palm.

We'll never make it, I think as I bolt back the way we came.

NORIELLE

An untamable shiver works through my body as a fever sends a chill across my skin. Inside, I feel the crypt crawler's venom like lava seeping through layers of soil, incinerating everything along the way. My teeth chatter, my mouth left uncovered, as if the defectors desire to hear me scream and wail until the end.

But I give them no such pleasure.

I suppress my agony as if Cas and Milo were here, and I didn't want them to know how bad it is. Thank the Empyrean they aren't. They are so far.

So far.

And somehow, Calden—my only chance of survival—feels farther away.

With my hands still bound behind me, I can't see my Bind Mark and the tingling across every inch of my skin makes it impossible to feel any sensations from the mark. But even if I could see it, I probably still wouldn't be able to tell if he's coming or not.

I hope he's not. I hope he and Alani are rushing back to the Seer right now to discover my replacement, and that my replacement is someone who deserves to be among them—deserves to help them with whatever it is that Toaph Elbara must want.

That's what the Bind is for, I've realized in this hour of torture. Toaph Elbara is alive, and he needs Calden and the Bind for something.

He must be trapped or wounded. *Something* is preventing him from bringing Ta'Nathel down alone, and he needs someone like Calden to aid him.

It makes so much sense. The state of the world, the length of Calden's "curse." It equates too perfectly for Corene to have lied. Toaph Elbara *has* been trying to reach Calden all his life. The curse isn't a curse at all—it's a mortal man's reaction to being contacted by such a high being.

But I won't get to tell him. I won't get to tell him there's hope.

Flecks of light sparkle in my eyes, like foam on black waves that sweep over my vision. The darkness clings, and my body wilts against the pole I'm tied to, going still besides the spontaneous convulsions. My thoughts scatter, images of all that I've treasured in this life flashing through my mind and sustaining my slowing heartbeat. Papa playing his lyre while Mum rocked baby Milo to sleep. Opening my drawer to find a drawing from Cas and hugging her so tightly until she griped for me to let go. Racing with a boy I once called Kieran, knowing I'd never beat him besides when he let me. Then hearing him sing Papa's song in the haven, and now realizing he was singing it about me. *I* was the girl in the song, torn by distance only to return to him—with my heart already set on another.

Now Elias is dead because of me. Just like Papa.

The agony of that reality pierces deeper than the venom, almost winning the Blood Wardens the cry they are likely salivating for. I shove it down, desperate for comfort and not more pain in what I sense are my final moments. El-Alam can judge me for my actions when my heart finally stops—but it's too much to bear right now. Too much to die with.

Another memory sweeps in to rescue me—Calden handing me a soulcast flower, and it turning purple and gold against my palm. It replays slower than life, and I cling to his smile—one of the most genuine ones he ever wore, like for that one moment, he was actually happy. I can't remember what he said the colors meant, besides that the gold had something to do with being refined by fire.

Yet I'm in the fire now, and I don't sense I'll live to see the refining. Even if he came now, I'm certain my internal organs are damaged beyond repair. But maybe then I could shout to him—if I even have the voice—and tell him what his curse is. Tell him our world isn't as doomed as we think.

Maybe then I'd have done something worth being called for.

"Wardens."

The sound of the defector's voice shocks my consciousness back to awareness. I bat my eyes, seeing dimly the Blood Wardens rising to assume their stances before the blackness clouds my vision again.

Calden.

"About time," Corene says. "I was beginning to worry I'd have to heal the girl. *Places.*"

I lower my head so my tangled hair covers my face, hoping it keeps them from noticing they left my mouth free. Their feet shuffle, murmured exchanges passing between them as they ready for an attack. I bite the inside of my cheek, praying Calden and Alani are prepared for what they are walking into, and that I have enough strength left to deliver my message before the darkness consumes me.

My ears ring in the stillness, wheezing breaths growing more labored with every inhale.

Just hold on, Norielle. Just a few moments longer.

Those few moments pass like a decade before a sound like sizzling lightning launches into the space. The brute grunts, but in alarm, not pain, and a hiss of metal announces what I fear will be a battle to the death. I force my eyes open, but the flares of light and darkness in my vision impair my sight, preventing me from distinguishing anything.

My mouth trembles open, and I pray Calden will hear me through the immediate uproar of whirring magic, shouts, and clanging blades. But when I try to yell, my voice is nothing but air. I swallow hard and try again, only for Calden's voice to slice through my attempt.

"Lias, tend to Norielle."

Lias? He's not dead—?

Boots pound toward me, then another heavier pair follows. I fear it's the brute until Calden speaks again, closer.

"Get her out of here."

His voice doesn't sound right, I realize. It's strained nearly as badly as my own.

But I forget it the moment I feel rough fingertips brushing my face. "I got you, Nori," Elias says.

I blink rapidly, straining to see him. My vision remains glossy, but I can just discern the dark outline of his hair and beard. If I smile, I can't feel it anywhere except inside.

"You're alive," I whisper, or maybe I only think it. Even the noise of the battle is fading as death crawls over me.

Elias frees my arms, speaking to me, but I can only hear every few words. His hot grip surrounds my wrist and something cold slides across my skin, like when Calden drew the Bind Mark on me.

And suddenly, I remember what I was supposed to be shouting.

"Toaph," I say, this time feeling the slight vibration in my throat. Elias stills, signaling that he heard me. "He's alive."

"What?" Elias asks.

"Toaph's alive. Calden's curse . . ." The blackness rolls over me, then draws back like a curtain. "It's not a curse."

Elias remains motionless another second before finishing the ward on me. "Just hold on, Nori. Tell me later."

Will there be a later?

His palm presses against the finished ward, and I finally understand he's trying to heal me. My heart pulses, thrumming as I wait for life to return to me and the pain to dissipate. All around us, stone cracks and blades sing between angry voices and cries of pain.

A woman yelps, but I can't tell if it's Alani or Corene. Then steel clashes so close to us, I feel the breath of the blades, followed by a dusting from a disintegrated sword. Through a flutter of my eyelids, I vaguely catch Calden blocking the brute's attack on Elias. He forces the fight away from us. Yet, with every orange orb launched at him from Corene, he never returns one attack. Her wicked voice taunts him, laughing. He says nothing in reply.

I return my focus to Elias's indistinct form in front of me. The pain seems to be amplifying, not decreasing, and the pull to surrender to my end feels as strong as it was at the bottom of Lake Daleia.

Elias releases my arm with a distressed moan. His head turns in different directions as he curses to himself, and I realize he's failed.

He can't heal me.

I've offended him too much for it to work.

"Just—just hold on," he says, voice breaking. "Hold on."

The cry I restrained before finally breaks free as I curl toward my hands.

"Cal!" The misery in Elias's shout takes me back to his mother's bedside, when she lay dying from the same venom. Except then, he was calling for his father—his *dead* father, as if the loss of his mother would bring his father back to protect him from the pain. "Calden!"

He rises, and through my splintered vision, I see him leap between Calden and Corene, thwarting the woman's attack with an energy field before stealing the one-sided fight for himself. He hollers my name at Calden, who doesn't peel his gaze from Corene until Elias knocks her to the dirt with a blue orb.

But when Calden turns, his swordstaff drops from his hold, dissolving in midair before ever touching the ground. He runs toward me, darkness swarming his blurred figure.

When he grabs my arm, I can't feel it, not even the warmth of his touch. Instead, the heat from within seems to spill over my skin, scathing like a steam burn. I try to yelp, but my suppressed lungs make less than a squeak in my throat.

"It's not a curse," I whisper, fearing Elias may not live to pass the message on.

His pen glides over my skin, not pausing at my words. *Did he not hear me?*

My eyes shut, too weak to stay open any longer.

"Toaph's alive," I wheeze.

The pen rolls against the ground, and the faintest sensation of being pulled closer dizzies me, even beneath closed eyes. Then everything goes silent and dark.

NORIELLE

The searing heat in my body subsides to something gentle, like the warmth of a campfire after being caught in the late Alatûm rain. Air drifts into my lungs, evening my heart rate with every steady inhale. My trembling slows, muscles and joints loosening as a sensation of safety caresses my soul.

All the pain that had overwhelmed me dissolves into a distant memory, and in its place something swells in the hollow of my heart. A feeling like the overwhelming devotion that stirs when I think of my family, and yet, there's something different to it—a yearning. One I can only identify as the kind I've suppressed for much of my journey with Calden.

The emotion seems to wash over me as if it were mine, yet I feel it from the outside coming in. It floods every vein, every breath, every part of me the venom touched—and makes it new. Alive. I sink into its embrace until I'm at such peace, I can't remember what hurt me at all.

But then I hear a sound—a pained moan—and my eyes open.

First, all I see is a tipped lantern in the distance, a flame flickering to its end as the oil bleeds over the wick. Then the blue hem of a cloak registers right beneath my gaze. The internal sensation slips, awakening my body's feeling, and I become aware of Calden's hand holding my wrist against his steel breastplate and his arm around my back, supporting my curled body against his.

I pull back as much as his tight hold will allow and see his flushed and strained face. The reality of what he's done strikes me with a punch to my stomach—he's absorbed my pain into himself. Now the agony that almost killed me is swarming through his body, while I lie here, sheltered and nearly pain-free.

His eyes squint open, and somehow, he manages to bring a smile to his lips.

"Norielle," he says, pressing my wrist closer to his heart.

And in just the way he says my name, I realize what that overwhelming sensation was. It was what it took for him to heal me—how he feels toward me. The care. The affection.

I lean my weary head against his chest, wishing I could take the pain back. But even after my healing, I still feel too weak to respond. Exhaustion slips back over me like a wet wool blanket and before I notice I'm fading again, I'm asleep.

CALDEN

With unsteady hands, I wipe my face with the edge of my cloak, clearing both tears and sweat. The silence at my back tells me the fight is over. We've won, and yet the relief that should bring me doesn't come.

Corene is dead.

I feel it even before I twist to find her body lying limp on the ground, face covered. Yet the ruby pendant I gave her protrudes from beneath the cloth, matching the blood pooling from underneath her. The three men are sprawled around her, also covered and leaking red. Acid crawls up my throat, and I turn back to Norielle cradled in my lap.

Her soft features look so tranquil—so oblivious—and for that, I am grateful. She need not see the blood spilt for her.

The pain I absorbed from healing her comes in waves, like a fire-breathing dragon is curled in my core, rising to release its blaze every time I think it will end. How Norielle outlasted this boggles me. The pain alone is enough to trigger a mental shutdown, if not constantly resisted.

She fought well. She deserves this rest.

I dig my arms beneath her to lift her, but my wobbling elbows and fatigued muscles can't bear the weight.

"Lias," I croak, the word aggravating my sore throat.

His grave trance dissolves, and he turns from gazing at the slain.

"Take her."

He grimaces at the dead one last time before rushing to pull Norielle from my lap. He lifts her between his blood-laced arms, and presses his slick forehead against hers, murmuring an apology.

Alani rushes to my side, a singed section of shirt at her shoulder exposing her skin. Half her tied hair has fallen loose. She reaches for me, taking my hand in both of hers, and pulls me to my feet. My balance falters, but she reinforces my right side with a hand around my back.

"Let's get out of here," I say, but my gaze returns to Corene's corpse, and I forget to step.

Alani grabs my right arm, squeezing it reassuringly. "It's not her, Calden. Corene's been dead for years."

I know, I think, but fail to say so.

We leave her body with the others for their allies to gather and start the long journey to a safer part of the underground.

Elias lays Norielle's unconscious body against a ragged couch in the closest trustworthy haven we could find. I flop into a kitchen chair, nearly toppling out of it, even with Alani's aid. She stays beside me with her fingertips on my arm, ready to catch me, but when I prove myself independent, she pulls over a chair for herself and sits.

Elias, surely as worn as me by now, remains with Norielle, choosing to kneel beside the couch rather than sit with us. He brushes Norielle's hair from her face, and I try not to grit my teeth. She's his far more than she'd ever be mine. And I owe him his moment. After all, he spared me from having to take Corene's life.

Not that I ever could have.

Alani pillows her head in her arms against the table. Her shoulder wound cries out to be healed. Elias could use tending also, but I know I haven't the strength to help either of them right now.

Elias presses his fingers to Norielle's wrist, feeling for her pulse.

"Cal, how's her arrow?" he asks.

I twist it into view, not having thought to check it yet myself. "Dark."

"Her pulse is racing."

"She's still sick," I say, dropping my gaze. "I couldn't take it all. Not at once. I'll try again after some rest if her body hasn't fought off the venom by then."

Elias nods, his face more somber than I've ever seen it. He clasps her hand and lowers his head as if in prayer. I almost implore him to try healing her again, unless that's what he's doing now. But I need him strong since I'm not. An inexperienced healer could endure three times the damage that I've taken.

I glance at Alani, considering asking her to try since she hasn't offered. But the thought of making her suffer stills my tongue. Though I can't help but wonder why she hasn't tried. Does she not care enough for the newest member of our Bind? Or does she simply fear the pain too much?

I dismiss the thoughts. Norielle is alive. That is what matters, and the sooner I give in to rest, the sooner I can recover to heal her fully and get her home.

I push myself up and take a shaky step away. "Come get me if she worsens."

Elias looks up, and I swear there are tears trembling in the corners of his dark eyes. He stares at me without responding until I turn all the way to face him.

"Wait," he says. "Nori told me something earlier."

My brows scrunch. Faintly, I recall her speaking to me also, now that he's mentioned it. Something about Toaph, was it?

"She said Toaph Elbara is alive," he says.

Alani shoots up straight at the table, and my body seems to solidify in place.

Is that what Norielle said to me?

"She mentioned something about your curse, too."

I step toward him, rekindling my dizziness. "What about it?"

"Just that it's not a curse. I don't know what she meant. She didn't say anything else." His thumb runs across Norielle's hairline. "But if Toaph lives . . ."

"Then there's still hope," Alani says.

But how does she know? I wonder, though the real question should be, *how do* they *know?* Norielle clearly learned this from Corene and the others, but can the information be trusted, coming from such an untrustworthy source?

And what does my curse have to do with it? With Toaph Elbara?

I turn toward the rooms, too weak to keep standing and desperate to ponder this information in privacy, but as I'm clutching the cold keyring to my door, something echoes in my memory.

"I fled. I failed."

The voice I heard in the crypt—

I *know* it. I've heard it in my mind.

No. *In the other mind.*

The key thumps to the ground. Flashes of the nightmarish dust world fan through my mind yet again, but my consciousness remains, letting me recall the voice as clearly as if it speaks into my ears.

It's him, isn't it?

Toaph Elbara.

Is that what Norielle was trying to tell me?

Was it not when I approached Toaph's statue in the crypt that the visions stirred again, and his words replayed in my head? Could it be that all this time, he's been alive and calling out to me? Seeking me?

For what?

What does he need me to do? Where is he?

I catch myself on the wall, knees buckling beneath me.

My heart aches to believe it, and yet, doubts cloud my thoughts like a late Soltûm storm. It doesn't make sense. Why me? Why from my very youth? Why would his reaching out cause my power to erupt in such dangerous ways?

No. It's a lie. All of it—a trick or distraction of some kind. Toaph is dead. He's been dead for a quarter of a century, and I am cursed, surely by Ta'Nathel himself.

I cover my face with a palm, dizziness making the tunnel around me wobble.

"Oh, El-Alam," I whisper, but I find no other words to pray before my strength slithers from my body, and I topple to the ground.

NORIELLE

A melody eases me awake. I turn my face away from the mildewy back cushion of the lumpy couch and find Elias in a chair beside me, gently plucking his lyre. His fingers still the moment I notice the song—the same one he played the day I realized who he was. *Papa's song.*

The one Elias sang about me.

The resonance of the strings fades into the silence of the haven as I sift through my memories to recall what got me to this couch, and why I feel stiff enough to have laid here for two days.

"Morning, Nori," Elias says, resting his lyre in his lap.

His gaze waits for my answer like a child watching for the first flake of snow to fall in Veratûm.

I rub my eyes, muscles tingly but returned to strength. As I push myself upright, I scan the haven for the others, but seeing no one else, I turn back to Elias. He looks like he's been awake all the time that I've been asleep. Bandages wrap his arms and half his fingers, and what looks like a burn has singed the side of his face and part of his hair.

"Feeling okay?" he asks.

I take inventory of my body, wiggling my once-broken thumb and taking in a full breath. Nothing aches from the long sleep besides my bones. "Yeah," I say, my voice parched. "How did we get here?"

"Carried you here myself." He winks, grabbing my flask from a chair-turned-end table. He pulls off the cap and passes it to me. I gulp the water; the cool sensation soothes my internal drought.

"We're hoping to leave today if you've got the strength to walk," Elias says. "The citadel is just a couple of days away. We want to get you there."

"That close?" I ask.

"Your detour led us near an underground river. It'll cut some days off the journey, now that we're near enough to bother with it."

I sigh at the thought of riding in a boat the rest of the way. Pity the entire underground isn't made up of rivers. "Where are Calden and Alani?"

Elias leans back in his chair, tucking his lyre into its satchel. "Alani's a late sleeper. Cal's up but going slow. He's still recovering."

"From healing me."

Elias shrugs. "From everything. He had an episode after you were taken. That was what waylaid us. Then healing you and dealing with Corene . . . Been a lot."

My hands fold in my lap, my mind fixated on the mention of Calden's episode. Vaguely, I recall a moment here on this couch. I woke to find Calden with me—healing me again. I told him what his episodes are, I believe, but I fell unconscious again before I could see his reaction.

What did he make of it?

"Hey Nori, I . . ." Elias starts, a timidness in his tone that reels me back to him. "I'm sorry I couldn't do it."

It takes me a moment to figure out what he means. *He couldn't heal me.*

"It's okay," I say, reaching for his hand. He sets his into mine, and a sense of long-lost familiarity steadies my heart. "I understand."

"If he weren't there . . ." he mutters, turning away from me.

"We have a lot to work through," I say, squeezing his hand. "*I* have a lot to work through."

He gives a half-hearted smile that bears not even a hint of his usual pride. "I think you've got bigger things to worry about right now," he says, and as if summoned by the turn of conversation, a door opens down the short shaft. Elias withdraws his hand.

Calden steps into view with his armor cinched tight, and his hair combed like he knew I'd be up today. Even the stitched wound across his cheek looks lighter, like it's finally started to heal, and his eyes are bright.

It's only now that I realize this haven doesn't have the nightmare-inducing ceilings but is lit by warm golden sconces and auburn crystals. He must have slept for once himself.

Calden steps away from the wall but stands at a distance from us. "Norielle," he says, voice still rough but fuller than when I heard it last. "Good to see you awake."

Just looking into his eyes, I feel a hint of the sensation that filled my entire being when he held me. But only now, when I'm fully conscious, can I think of the right word to describe it.

Belonging.

"Are you okay?" I ask.

He smiles, and the glow in the room seems to intensify. "Yes, I am now."

I reserve the rest of what I'd like to say for a time when we're alone so I can spare Elias the awkwardness. "We're headed for a river?"

He pivots toward the floating shelf along the wall, retrieving a sack of dried berries and nuts. "Yes," he says, taking a handful of the mix for himself before bringing it over to me. "It'll be a quick journey from there, so be prepared. You'll be meeting my mother before long. Not to mention my sister . . ."

"I hope they'll forgive me for what I've put you through." I glance at Elias. "All of you."

Calden gives a soft chuckle. "There's nothing to forgive."

I dig out a sun-dried blueberry from the bag. The tart taste almost sickens me after so long without food, but I force myself to keep eating.

"Lias," Calden shifts his focus to him. "Will you be accompanying us the rest of the way?"

Elias holds himself stiffly, staring at the ground. "That's up to you and Nori."

Calden's eyes swivel to me.

"Please," I say.

Calden nods, even if part of the light in his eyes seems to dim. "Good," he says. "Mother will want to honor him for his valor back there."

I expect my answer or at least Calden's to puff Elias up, but he remains partially slouched and only the slightest smile indicates he's grateful for our decision.

"I'd like to leave soon, if you think you can handle the walk," Calden says, and when I nod, he turns toward the rooms. "I'm going to wake Alani, then."

"Calden," I say before he can walk away. "About Toaph Elbara and your curse . . ."

He spins back, oddly calm for such an important mention. "Yes. I want you to tell everything you heard to the Seer. He will interpret what is truth and what is deception from the Blood Wardens. I'd like to not get too hopeful until then."

My mouth shuts, but I accept his answer with a nod. Then he turns away.

After two light days of travel, I finally hear the rush of water from yet another long and winding channel. We quicken our pace toward the river until I see it glistening below the rounded, crystal-lined walls. Alani hoots, running ahead to claim one of the large canoes tucked just shy of the water's edge.

"Are you ready for this?" Calden asks.

For an instant, I think he means riding in a boat again after my last experience in one, but when I see the sparkle in his gaze, I realize he means what lies beyond the river.

I ready a cheap response—*Is anyone?*—but a surge of anxiety tightens my chest, squashing my reply. I turn my back to the river.

"Actually, no."

Calden falls quiet, as if waiting for my explanation, but my teeth clench. All this way, all that we've been through, and I *still* haven't confessed to him what really happened with Papa.

Something sharp stings my eyes, and moisture rises, blurring my vision. I can't go to the citadel without telling him. He'll find out eventually, and how angry might he be then, learning I kept this secret from him?

I wipe my eyes before looking back at him.

"There's something I never told you, and I—" I squeeze the collar of my cloak. "I don't feel right going there without saying it—without giving you a chance to . . ." My voice trails off before I can say, *"dismiss me."*

"A chance to what?" Calden asks.

I ignore the question and thoughtlessly grab his arm, pulling him away from the others.

His concerned gaze reaches into mine as we stop behind a bend in the tunnel. "What's the matter?"

I blink more tears from my eyes, quickly swatting them away.

"Calden, before you allow me to officially join your Bind, there's something you should know . . ." My fingers thread through my hair. "The first time Lake Daleia came alive, I was there on the water with my papa. It went after him first, but I . . . I . . ."

"Swam to safety?"

I shake my head. "I abandoned him."

And with that, the dam breaks and my subtle crying escalates to gushing tears. I cover my face with a hand, twisting to hide from him.

"Norielle . . ." His words are slow to form, seeming to confirm the worst of my fears—that he'll realize the coward I am and not want me bound to him in the important fate we surely share, should the Seer deem my information truthful.

He takes a small step closer, drawing me back into the blue depths of his irises. "Any loving father would rather you live than die trying to save him. I think his heart would have broken, even in the Empyrean, to see you follow him there so very young and with so much left to offer this world."

I sniff, turning to hide my tears as more pour out. I know I'd say the same to someone else. Anyone else. Yet, his words seem to collide against a stone wall encasing my heart. "I was a coward. I *am* a coward. I didn't even try, Calden. Why should I be let into your Bind? What place could I have with . . . *you?*"

I hope he understands my meaning, because weeping cripples my ability to clarify. *You*, the Sovereign Prince of the Wardens.

He glances toward the wall behind us, as if to be sure we're out of Elias and Alani's sight. "You risked your life to test that lake after you watched your father die in it. You left home, leaving family and security to follow me into a life where you'd be hunted. You fought for two hours against the most lethal venom in Alémor just to deliver me a message, probably assuming you'd die the moment you spoke it." He grabs my hands, folding them gently into his own. "If you aren't both brave and worthy, my friend, I don't know who is."

I look down at our hands, perplexed by every word of his statement. But he doesn't allow me the chance to linger on it.

"Joining the Bind is ultimately your decision. But if it were mine, I'd have you."

He lets go of my hands, his cheeks pinking faintly as he awaits my answer.

My heart thrums as his words enter it, filling it with new life, much like the way he healed my body.

"Please, don't let a lie steal your destiny," he says when I still fail to answer. "El-Alam summoned you knowing every action you'd ever take or fail to. And I need not remind you, He's not one to make mistakes."

Another tear cools my cheek, glimmering in plain sight. His gaze tracks it until it slips beneath the curve of my jaw to roll down my neck. As it sinks beneath my cloak, his meaning fully seeps into my soul. Questioning my right to be here is questioning El-Alam's perfect judgment.

I have no right to do so. I didn't form the skies or the land I walk on. Who am I to challenge what El-Alam says is to be or not? And is it possible that even the Creator looks upon my perceived failure with the same grace and understanding Calden possesses?

"Tell me, what do you want to do, Norielle?" Calden asks. "Do you wish to join us? Or shall I make other arrangements for you when we arrive?"

My lungs expand and, at last, I speak. "I want to be in the Bind . . . if you're sure you want me in it."

He smiles. "I've never had one doubt."

Gratitude and relief loosen my muscles, and, without thinking, I throw my arms around him. It's the only "thank you" I can muster before I'm fighting a—for once—happy cry. A small laugh blows from his nose, tickling the back of my hair as he returns my abrupt embrace.

He allows it a few seconds before patting my back and pulling away to give me an almost shy smile.

"Come then, Norielle," he says, motioning toward the river. "You've yet to see Alani's Master Talent."

NORIELLE

The canoe, guided down the river solely by Alani's hands and heart, cuts through a glittery cloud that billows in from the mouth of the tunnel. A steady roar rumbles through the stony walls, growing louder as we reach the end where sunlight is tossing rainbows through the glowing vapor. Elias, who shares my seat, nudges me, and without a word, I know what he means. *This is it. We're here.*

The brilliant sky is almost blinding as the boat slides from the tunnel and onto calm water. My eyes flutter as I desperately seek out the citadel that I've traveled so far to find. But all I see are waterfalls. *Everywhere.* Some are thin streams, like water being poured from a jar, but others are as thick as rivers dumping themselves into the massive lake we're on. I crane my neck, trying to follow one that tumbles over a moss-covered cliff, but the top is lost in the shimmering fog.

I whirl around toward Calden, who beams at me, dewdrops glistening on his damp hair and face. I want to ask where in Alémor we are, but the thunderous waterfalls are too loud to speak over.

Alani's arms move in dancelike motions, conducting a current around the water that pulls the boat further into the sprawling lake. *Her Master Talent.* Through the fog, enormous cliffs poke into view. They enclose the entire lake, sheltering the hidden citadel from the rest of the world. The canoe glides deeper into the glimmering haze, and as we circumvent a large bluff, I spot something like a pillar of glass shimmering up ahead.

More of them come into view, but as I squint, the glass darkens, transforming into stone towers. Walls appear between the turrets, with windows adorned by speckled copper sills. Moss dangles from the pointed rooftops, decorating the castle-like building in shades of green and hints of red. My jaw drops as we drift beneath a bridge that suddenly forms overhead. Six others appear, stemming from the building in each direction and connecting with tunnel mouths along the cliffsides.

I finally exhale, and Elias elbows me.

"Welcome home, Nori."

My unrestrained smile shifts from him to Alani then Calden, and something stirs in my stomach. Papa used to say I would never find this place—no one can besides the Wardens themselves.

And here I am. Among them. Seeing their citadel with my own eyes.

I wonder if Papa would actually be proud and not ashamed.

The boat bumps against a dock where Warden guards stand at the ready. Their attention zeroes in on Calden, and they abandon their rigid stances to bow to him. He greets them as Alani hooks the boat to the dock. She hops out first, lending me a hand to step out. My stiff legs wobble on the rigid ground after hours of riding in a boat.

"I feel so lucky," Alani says, grinning like the journey here was no more than a short trek through a flowery field. "I've never gotten to walk a newcomer to the citadel before."

I smile, turning as Calden and Elias join us on land. Both stand apart from me, their expressions like dawn and dusk—Calden's, the dawn, renewed and excited. Elias's, the dusk, still fighting for a bit of light.

I turn away, recalling my conversation with Elias before the Blood Wardens attacked. The start of my new life here is also the end of our time together.

Or so he said.

I focus on Alani, the safest and least emotionally complex of my three companions, and she guides me past the hooded guards and onto a moonstone bridge with copper rails. The polished path shoots across the wide waters and into a cluster of unfamiliar trees. I study their twisted trunks and dangling branches as we pass them to approach a gate about half as high as the ones in Aldrian and painted an inviting white. Guards flank it beside statues of winged creatures that remind me of fellions, only they're more serene. The guards open the gate just in time for us to step through, greeting Calden again with the usual respectful gestures.

My attention is immediately stolen by a vast courtyard filled with flowers. Their unusual shades slowly fade from light to dark as they recede into the distance, as if planted with the same delicacy as an artist would paint. Just beyond this final stretch stands the colossal doors to the citadel where my life will change forever.

My steps begin to drag, even as the guards open the doors for us. I look back for Calden and Elias, only to see that Elias isn't with us anymore. He's turned down a path leading away from the main entrance. He glances at me and waves, a smile pressed onto his lips that says, *Goodbye.* As if this truly is the end of our time together.

I come to a standstill, shoulders lowering as I watch him disappear.

"He'll be around," Calden says, reassuring me with a smile.

I nod my thanks and take a deep breath.

"It's time to meet my mother," Calden says, his voice dropping to a whisper as he adds, "Maybe don't tell her I started your training."

I give a small laugh, and he steps beside me, a hand on my shoulder lightly urging me onward.

We pass through the door, and I vaguely hear the guards greeting us as my boots pad down a lengthy rug coating the moonstone floor. A massive stained glass window casts a mosaic of colors into the foyer, glinting against the copper columns and the railing of a wide staircase. I gawk at the artistry, a depiction of a winged

Toaph Elbara kneeling before a brilliant light, which I presume is meant to symbolize El-Alam.

Our Empyreal Guardian and our God.

And *me*—standing in what might as well be a holy temple.

A door opens before Calden can usher me in any direction, and a woman in a pearlescent gown with slit sleeves that nearly drag across the ground steps out. Her smiles shines against her deep brown skin—a shade that tells me she isn't from Alémor, but Schillon, the island kingdom south of our own.

"Calden?" she calls, her voice as rich as soil. Three people shuffle in behind her, all dressed in matching stone-colored robes. They give Calden a synchronized bow, then they smile at me and Alani with their lips tightly sealed.

Is this—?

"Mother," Calden says with such warmth, I'd never have believed he once complained about her.

Alani curtsies, and I quickly mimic her pose as Calden and his mother embrace. I rise after Alani does, and the Lady Sovereign releases her son, moving her adoring gaze to me.

"Welcome, Norielle," she says, her faint Schillon accent gently embellishing my name. The cadence reminds me of how Calden says it, though I'd never connected him to Schillon before with his lighter skin. "We've all been greatly anticipating your arrival. I do hope my son made your journey . . ." She looks over his bandages and stitched face, seeming to recalibrate her sentence. "Tolerable."

Words elude me, and a silence drags until my palms heat.

"Mother, there's something rather urgent," Calden cuts in, sparing me the pressure of responding. "We need to take Norielle to the Seer immediately."

The Lady Sovereign raises her brows. "The girl has just arrived—"

"It can't wait," he says. "Trust me."

Her eyes narrow, but she nods, stirring the copper ringlets decorating her hair. "To the Seer, then."

I'm led in haste through a number of halls and up a spiral staircase before we reach what is announced to be the Seer's sanctum. The double doors are propped open, leading into a room that seems half-library and half-garden with a wall of water pouring from ceiling to floor at the back. In front of the trickling wall, an ornate chair crouches at the center like a miniature throne, and in it, a man sits as if awaiting us.

He leaps to his feet as we file in behind the Lady Sovereign, his cheerful gaze passing over both her and Calden to find me. A smile lifts his dark mustache, and he rushes forward, his fingers fluttering under the sweeping sleeves of his gold robes.

"Ah, there she is!" His midnight eyes remain locked on mine. "The girl from the bottom of the lake."

Everyone takes a step away from me, giving space for the Seer to approach. I feel the distance like a thousand miles, as if only the Seer and me were present.

"You've made the world very angry," the Seer says, but he sounds more amused than judgmental. "I think that's a good sign."

I glance toward Calden, who gives me an encouraging nod.

"Seer," I say, my voice small. "I was captured by the Blood Wardens, and they shared something with me. Calden said you'd be able to discern if it's true or false."

The Seer's fingers bounce against each other, delight and curiosity flashing in his eyes. "Do tell."

I swallow, strengthening my voice as if my little siblings were here watching me. "They said Toaph Elbara is still alive, and that what seemed like a curse on Calden is really Toaph trying to communicate with him."

The Seer's fingers still, every breath in the room seeming to cease besides that of the water pouring along the back wall.

"I think that must be the purpose of the Bind," I say, rushing my words as if someone will interject or silence me before I have the chance to speak. "We're supposed to find Toaph Elbara . . . because he needs our help."

The Seer stares back at me, the silence continuing for an age before he abruptly turns with a hand curled against his forehead. He strides away, robes undulating around his heels. I look to the other faces for some show of approval for what I've said, someone to confirm there is hope for our world after all.

But every face is turned toward the Seer, looking as anxious as my own.

The Seer walks midway to his chair before stilling again. Then, suddenly, he drops to his knees, weeping aloud.

My hands ball, confusion swarming my mind until the Seer's hands lift upward with a declaration of praise to El-Alam.

And that's all it takes to know it's the truth. Toaph Elbara lives. Our world can yet be saved.

But first, we must find him.

TO BE CONTINUED...

WARD GLOSSARY

About Wards:

Wards are what Wardens use to wield their magic. The symbols are derived from the Empyreal language which is written in glyphs rather than letters. To use wards, one must first be endowed with power from El-Alam, the Creator God. Wards are broken up into various categories, such as Standard, Master, Conditional, and Consequential Wards. How much a Warden can use a ward before it "expires" (meaning, it fades and must be redrawn) is dependent on that Warden's skill level with that ward. All Wardens can access Standard Wards, but only those who have excelled to a Master Warden status can use Master Wards.

The following is a list of every ward that appears in *These Hallowed Binds*. More wards will be revealed throughout the saga as they become important.

Wards in *These Hallowed Binds:*

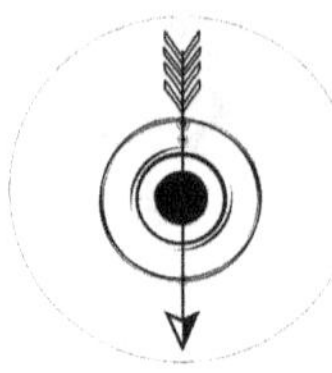

BIND MARK (MEMBER'S)

Sustained, Conditional

A Bind Mark may only be drawn by a Bind leader onto a member of their Bind. The arrow moves on its own accord, always tracking the Bind leader. The Bind Mark will vanish if the Bind leader dies. It cannot be controlled by anyone once drawn, not even the Bind leader.

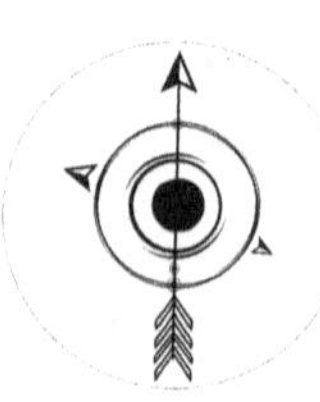

BIND MARK (LEADER'S)

Sustained, Conditional

A leader's Bind Mark is a divinely imparted mark, placed on the wrist of El-Alam's chosen Bind leader. As members of the Bind are selected by El-Alam, arrows will appear on the leader's Bind Mark. The arrows point to each Bind member independently. However, a Bind leader can choose one member to track with precision. This appears as the largest arrow. If a Bind member dies, their arrow will disappear.

CONJURATION WARD

Master

The Conjuration Ward allows a Master Warden to conjure the weapon of their choosing into their hand. This includes conjuring arrows for use with a conjured bow. No one else can wield the weapon. If dropped or claimed by someone besides the Master Warden who conjured it, the weapon will dissolve.

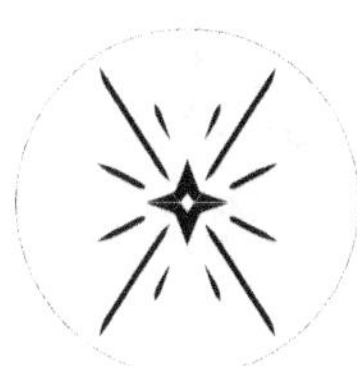

GLORY WARD

Standard

A Glory Ward is used to generate light which is drawn from the glory of El-Alam. This is most often used to power lanterns but can be wielded directly from one's hand. This ward is off-limits to defectors (because El-Alam is the direct source of the light).

HEALING WARD

Standard, Conditional, Consequential

Allows a Warden to heal someone who is injured or sick, but they must bear the afflicted's pain. The Warden must care for the afflicted and hold no bitterness or unforgiveness against them. This ward cannot resurrect.

KEY WARD

Standard

A Key Ward is used to seal or unlock the Warden's hidden doors or passages. This ward requires minimal energy. It cannot be used to create new passages or doors.

OMEN MARK

Standard, Sustained

Omen Marks are permanent wards that turn red when an enemy is nearby. It also points to an enemy's general location. A Shroud Ward can negate the effectiveness of this ward if wielded by a Master Warden.

PEACE WARD

Standard

The Peace Ward is used to calm forces of nature, including, but not limited to, storm crystals, raging seas, and fires. To work, this ward must come into direct contact with the force needing to be quelled or its source.

PURIFICATION WARD

Standard

The Purification Ward is used to cleanse water of impurities and make it safe for drinking. Water treated with this ward is blessed with purifying properties allowing it to be used for ridding infections, cleansing wounds, and even hygienic uses.

SNARE WARD

Standard

A Snare Ward creates tendrils of energy which will hold any one or thing captive until the user releases the ward (or dies). Snare Wards cannot be released by anyone but the person who drew the ward.

SHROUD WARD

Master

A Shroud Ward can be applied to a small area to help prevent detection by enemies. This ward keeps the Accursed from sensing a Warden's use of magic in the marked location and blocks defectors from detecting them with their Omen Marks. This ward must be applied directly to a major surface in the area the Master Warden wishes to shroud and cannot be worn for use while traveling. The effects last for a limited time (dependent on the skill level of the Master Warden who wields it).

VITALITY WARD

Standard

The Vitality Ward allows a Warden to pull from their own life-force (vitality) to create and manipulate raw energy. This ward can be used to create shields, explosive balls of energy, and more.

MEET THE CHARACTERS

NORIELLE

BIRTHPLACE: Behria, Kingdom of Alémor
AGE: 18
STRENGTHS: bravery, resilience, compassion
WEAKNESSES: impulsiveness, critical of others
GREATEST FEAR: suffering regret
GREATEST DESIRE: to find her place of belonging and contribute to it in a meaningful way

Norielle is from a sheltered town that believes they are immune to the curse over the world, but after seeing the lake come alive and kill her father, she knows they aren't safe. When no one believes her, she is forced to choose between going silent and leaving town (and everyone she loves behind her).

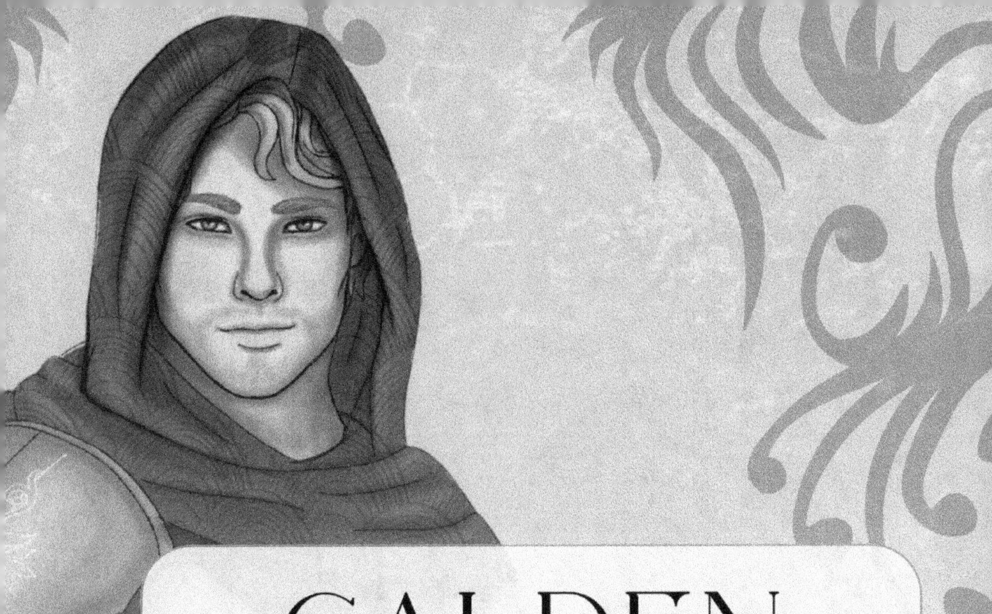

CALDEN

BIRTHPLACE: Unknown
AGE: 25
STRENGTHS: leadership, selflessness, courage
WEAKNESSES: lacks vulnerability, stubborn
GREATEST FEAR: hurting others w/ his curse
GREATEST DESIRE: to be free from the weight of his responsibilites and his curse

Calden is the Sovereign Prince of the Wardens by adoption and the leader of the Bind charged with stopping the world's destruction. He is known for bucking against traditions and his self-sacrificing nature. Calden is determined to save his people no matter what the cost. But his resolve is soon compromised by his growing feelings for his latest Bind member. . .

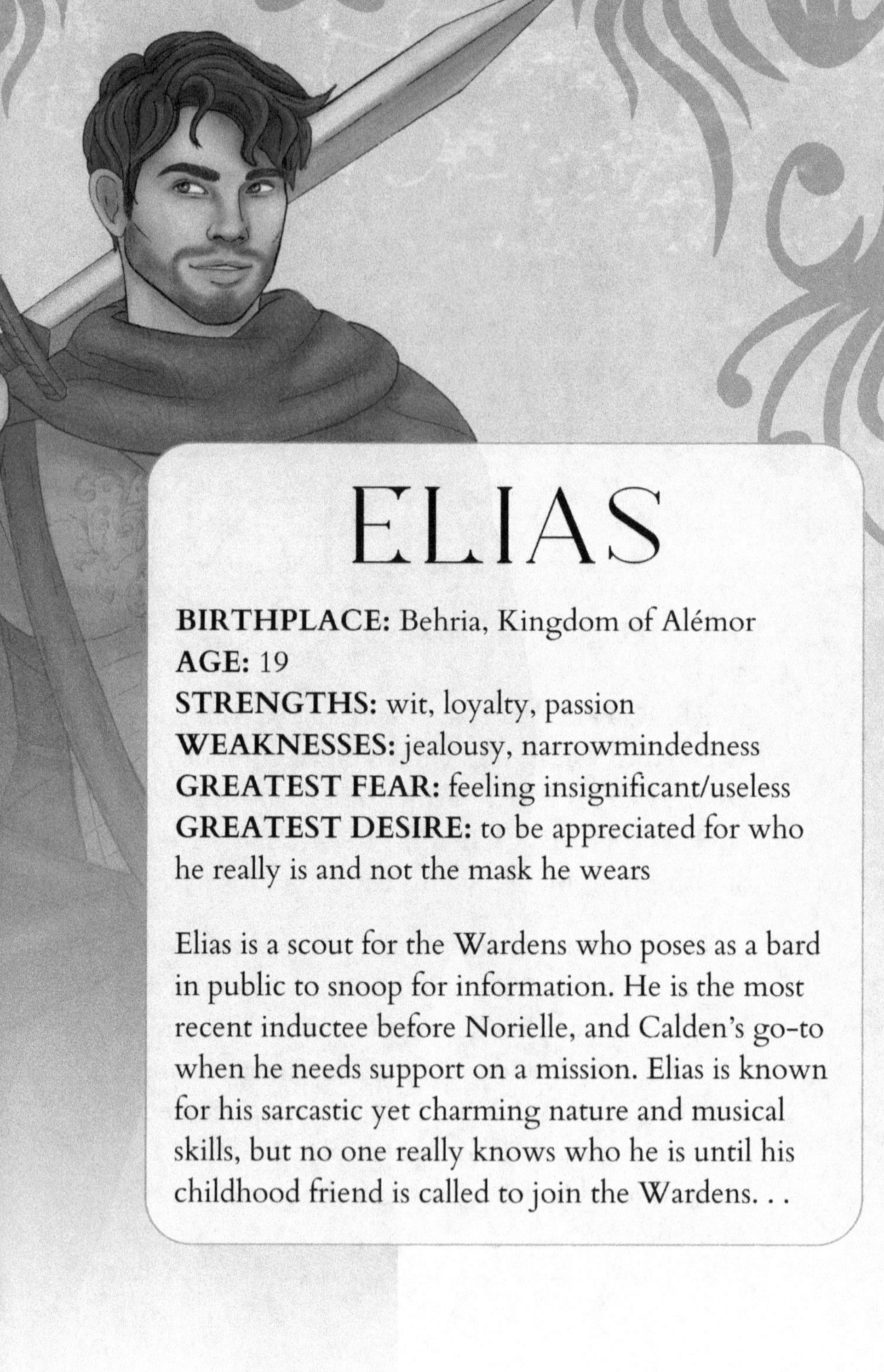

ELIAS

BIRTHPLACE: Behria, Kingdom of Alémor
AGE: 19
STRENGTHS: wit, loyalty, passion
WEAKNESSES: jealousy, narrowmindedness
GREATEST FEAR: feeling insignificant/useless
GREATEST DESIRE: to be appreciated for who he really is and not the mask he wears

Elias is a scout for the Wardens who poses as a bard in public to snoop for information. He is the most recent inductee before Norielle, and Calden's go-to when he needs support on a mission. Elias is known for his sarcastic yet charming nature and musical skills, but no one really knows who he is until his childhood friend is called to join the Wardens. . .

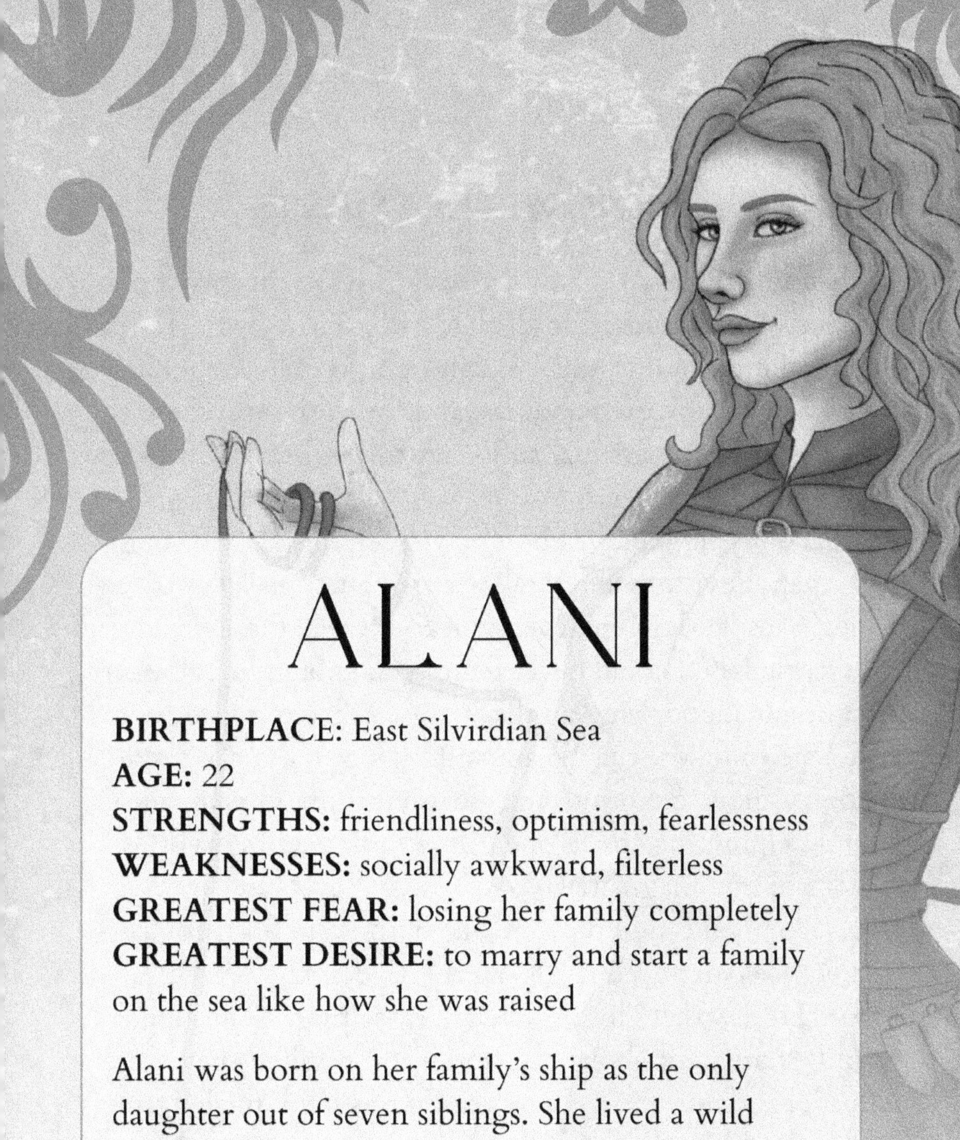

ALANI

BIRTHPLACE: East Silvirdian Sea
AGE: 22
STRENGTHS: friendliness, optimism, fearlessness
WEAKNESSES: socially awkward, filterless
GREATEST FEAR: losing her family completely
GREATEST DESIRE: to marry and start a family on the sea like how she was raised

Alani was born on her family's ship as the only daughter out of seven siblings. She lived a wild childhood wrestling with her older brothers and fending off vortices and beasts on the sea. However, she always longed to go ashore to meet someone and start a life. She got her wish--partially--when Calden retrieved her as a member of his Bind.

ACKNOWLEDGEMENTS

First and always, I thank my Savior, Jesus Christ, who is my creative source for all that I do. Thank you, Lord, for calling me into this beautiful purpose, for equipping me beyond my own abilities, and for all the ways you've redeemed my personal suffering through my stories to speak to others' hearts.

To my husband, Rob—you've seen this story through so many revisions and total rewrites, and *somehow* you've never lost faith in me (even when you read those dreadful early drafts!). I could never thank you enough for all your constant support and all that you sacrifice to make room for me to follow this dream and calling. I also can't write this without crediting you for giving me *so many* ideas and helping me create one of the most exciting worlds I have in my imagination.

To my mom—you were one of the very first people to meet Calden and Elias (formerly, Caden and Micah) before I threw them into a full-fantasy setting. Your support and excitement about my stories, even when they were just chaotic ideas, is a huge reason this book finally came together. Thank you for believing in my writing dreams and for fostering them from the very beginning.

To my editor, Jasmine—your care, attention, and passion for this story have filled my heart. It was an absolute joy to work alongside you with this story (and by "work" I mean "fangirl" haha!). Thank you for all the love you showed my characters, especially, and for the added time you've invested in helping me get this series where it needs to be.

To all the rest of my incredible family, friends, and early readers—you have no idea how much your collective support has helped me overcome my own doubts in myself and encouraged me to keep writing, even when I feared no one would ever care about my stories. I am genuinely floored by the enthusiasm I received when I announced this book. You all are the sunlight that keeps my stories growing.

And lastly, a huge thank you to everyone who contributed to my Kickstarter. Your financial investment made this book possible. I am so grateful for all your support—large and small—in bringing this book to life!

Kickstarter supporters:

Abigail Hathaway, Addie Grace Putnam, Amena Jamali, Annarose Willhite, Annette Scheible, Annie, AslansCompass, Bailey, Bella Easterbrook, Benita J. Thompson, Breana Johnson, Brigitte, Chloë Mali, Christina Thomas Gonzales, D. E. Carlson, David DeHaan, Elyse C. (Elias's #1 fan), Emma Bahnmiller, Eric Mancia, Eric P., Gabriella, Gabriella Tejada, Giselle, Grace Hoffman, Gracie Niehaus, Hannah Gaudette, Holly Morgan, Isabel K., Jenni Satnic, K Hendrick, Kaori Keiroz, Katherine Malloy, Kathryn Jordan, Katie S., Kelsey Chapman, Kiersten Lillis, Kristee Preudhomme, Laurel Burgess, Lilly T., Maria Gilbert, Marlene Renteria, Meghan Endahl, Melissa Ring, Melody Faith, Michalia, Natalie Colburn, Rachael

Ritchey, Rachel Lowe, Rachel Rohde, S.L. Klein, Samantha Newberry, Sarah Everest, Stacy Lincoln, Stephanie Crachiolo, Susan Laspe, Susan Rackley, Tama Gray, Tania Ibrahim, Tiffany Goldman, Tommie Michele, Vannah Leblank, Wendie Esqueda.

ABOUT THE AUTHOR

A. M. Daylin is a wife, mother of two young girls, and follower of Jesus Christ from Phoenix, AZ. She has a deep passion for connecting with others' hearts through the power of stories, and hopes that her words will help others experience healing as they go on thought-provoking, imaginative adventures. When not writing (or daydreaming about writing), you can find her drawing past her bedtime, hanging out with her family and Jesus, going for long drives whilst blasting cinematic music (that's normal, right?), obsessing over social media aesthetics (hey, it's part of her job!), and occasionally writing a song or two. Connect with her on Instagram (@a.m.daylin) or at amdaylin.com.

If you enjoyed this book, please consider leaving a review on Amazon and/or Goodreads.